VIDALIA
IN PARIS

SASHA WATSON

Viking

AUTHOR'S NOTE

Many of the settings in this novel are actual places. Readers can and should visit the Jardin du Luxembourg, Shakespeare & Company, and la Sainte-Chapelle the next time they find themselves in Paris. Others are fictional. If anyone goes looking for the Musée Apollinaire, for instance, they will not find it; it is an entirely imagined museum. The painting that Vidalia copies there, *La jeune fille à la licorne*, also exists only within these pages.

Viking

Published by Penguin Group

Penguin Group (USA) Inc., 345 Hudson Street, New York, New York 10014, U.S.A.
Penguin Group (Canada), 90 Eglinton Avenue East, Suite 700, Toronto, Ontario, Canada M4P 2Y3
(a division of Pearson Penguin Canada Inc.)

Penguin Books Ltd, Registered Offices: 80 Strand, London WC2R 0RL, England

First published in 2008 by Viking, a member of Penguin Group (USA) Inc.

1   3   5   7   9   10   8   6   4   2

LIBRARY OF CONGRESS CATALOGING-IN-PUBLICATION DATA
Watson, Sasha.
Vidalia in Paris / by Sasha Watson.—1st ed.
p. cm.
Summary: Teenage Vidalia's summer in Paris studying art settles into a stimulating and
enjoyable routine until she becomes romantically involved with a mysterious
young man who seems to have ties to an art-theft ring.
ISBN 978-0-670-01094-3 (hardcover)
[1. Artists—Fiction. 2. Interpersonal relations—Fiction. 3. Art thefts—Fiction.
4. Conduct of life—Fiction. 5. Paris (France)—Fiction. 6. France—Fiction.] I. Title.
PZ7.W3292Vi 2008
[Fic]—dc22   2008008381

Printed in U.S.A.
Set in Fairfield
Book design by Nancy Brennan

For my mother, who started it all

CHAPTER 1

"UM, THAT'S MY SEAT."

Vidalia stood in the airplane's narrow aisle looking down at the spot she'd left empty moments before—and at the girl sitting in it.

"Oh, *sorry*," said Heather, widening her blue eyes with fake regret.

Vidalia raised a skeptical eyebrow. Heather had barely spoken to her on the two-hour drive from East Hampton to JFK and now she was *sorry*? Yeah, right.

She considered her options. Heather was occupying 26E, the middle seat between an older woman next to the window and Becky, the other girl from East Hampton High, who sat on the aisle. Throwing a hissy-fit about a stolen seat seemed a little fifth-grade, but handing it over was just as ridiculous. Heather might have the entire football team on a short leash, but as far as Vidalia was concerned, that didn't mean she could just steal her seat. So Vidalia crossed her arms, met Heather's eyes, and waited.

Heather looked back, her expression getting even more ex-aggeratedly apologetic.

"I just *really* have to talk to Becky about something," she said. Becky, obviously confused by the showdown taking place over her, turned to Heather questioningly.

"Uh-huh." Vidalia tapped one combat boot on the airplane floor as she waited, her hip cocked in a stretchy black mini-skirt.

"At this time we'd like to ask all passengers on Flight 011 to Paris–Charles de Gaulle to take their seats as we prepare for takeoff."

And then again, in French.

"Le décollage étant à présent imminent, nous prions tous les passagers du Vol 011 à destination de Paris–Charles de Gaulle de bien vouloir regagner leur place."

The first of these announcements had come over the loud-speaker while Vidalia washed her hands in the tiny airplane bathroom. It was getting more urgent with repetition.

"Vidalia, please sit down."

That was Madame Geen, the administrator from the American Institute in Paris, where Vidalia, Heather, Becky, and a dozen or so other kids from the New York Area would be spending the next six weeks on what the brochure called "a summer study-abroad program for talented high-school students." Vidalia saw a hint of triumph creep into Heather's smile.

"But that's my seat." Vidalia tried to sound clear, not whiny, as she pointed to Heather.

A male flight attendant in black pants and a gray Air France vest appeared in the aisle next to her.

"Just take that one." The man was rushed. He slammed an overhead compartment shut and pointed to seat 27F on the aisle behind Becky—Heather's seat. "You can switch later."

"Yeah," agreed Heather in her too-sweet voice. "We'll switch later."

"Fine," said Vidalia with an exasperated sigh. "Just pass me my bag then."

Heather pulled Vidalia's black messenger bag from under the seat and passed it over, whispering to Becky while she did. Now that she'd won her little battle, she was done speaking to Vidalia. Becky looked up with a genuine mixture of regret and confusion. She shrugged helplessly and mouthed, "Sorry," to Vidalia.

Vidalia waved her hand in a "don't worry" gesture and sat down hard in the seat behind Becky. A balding guy was already snoring in the seat next to her. As she buckled her seat belt, the cabin lights went dim and the airplane began to move. Heather's and Becky's voices drifted back to her. Vidalia looked through the space between their seats at Heather's profile. She always appeared to have stepped out of some teen movie with her ski-jump nose and shiny girly style. When they were kids, playing together in one of their bedrooms or back-yards, Vidalia had wished she could trade her thick dark hair for Heather's honey blonde waves, her boring brown eyes for Heather's blue ones. But all that was way in the past. Vidalia turned to look out the window, but there was nothing to see. It was nine o'clock at night, and the sky was dark. She closed her eyes and felt the deep rumble of the engines.

Vidalia wished Ellie was here with her. They'd laugh at the music playing in the plane, a soft-rock version of "My Favorite Things," and sing with fake sincerity into imaginary microphones. All of a sudden she missed Ellie sharply, and it hit her that they wouldn't be able to do things like that anymore. They'd become good friends this past year when they were both working in the art room all the time, getting ready for the spring art show, and they'd even formed a kind of crew with a few other art-room kids. But it was already over. Ellie and the others had been seniors this year, and they were off to college in the fall. Vidalia had said good-bye to Ellie the day before.

"Paris is yours, babe," Ellie had said. "You'll come back a better *artiste* than any of us." She'd hugged her. "I'm really proud of you."

Vidalia was proud of herself, too, or maybe just surprised that she'd won a full scholarship to study studio art in Paris this summer. The scholarship committee had agreed that her art would make her "a valuable member of the intellectual community at the institute" based on the slides she'd sent and on the strong recommendations of both her art teacher, Mrs. Greenberg, and her French teacher, Madame Macarthy.

"I just wish you were coming with me," Vidalia had told Ellie.

"Me, too."

Vidalia wasn't looking forward to senior year and being a loner all over again.

The plane lifted into the air and she felt herself pulled back into her seat, her head pressed to the headrest as they rose from the runway. All at once, the ropes holding Vidalia to the ground seemed to have been cut loose. This was freedom.

Screw Heather. She was on her way to Paris.

CHAPTER

2

MADAME GEEN HURRIED THROUGH the gleaming white corridors of Charles de Gaulle Airport while the dozen or so kids in their group followed sleepily behind. Vidalia, who had packed light, saw that Heather was struggling with her big suitcase.

They never had switched seats—Vidalia didn't feel like continuing the argument, and Heather certainly didn't offer—and Vidalia had spent the seven hours of the flight alternately sketching and trying unsuccessfully to sleep. Heather had conked out early on, but Becky had been awake, too, and she'd leaned back to talk to Vidalia.

"I think we're the only ones not sleeping here," she'd said.

Vidalia looked up the dimly lit aisle and saw feet and elbows sticking out at various awkward angles.

"Yeah," she agreed. "I wish I could. I know I'll be exhausted tomorrow."

"I'm too excited, though." Becky laughed.

"So I know I've seen you around school," said Vidalia. "Were you a freshman this year?"

She'd seen Becky in the halls with groups of girlfriends and various jock guys. Becky was probably more like Heather than she was like Vidalia, but she seemed pretty nice. Maybe she was just too young to have been corrupted yet. Although, Heather had shown her true colors in the first week of high school.

"Sophomore," Becky said. Then she looked up like she was making a discovery, and said, "Vidalia . . . Sloane, right? Didn't you do those house things? With the rabbits?"

"Oh, yeah," Vidalia said, flattered. She'd spent most of the past year in the art room with a hot wire and an X-Acto knife, cutting Styrofoam and cardboard into walls and rooftops.

"Wow," Becky went on. "Those were awesome. I loved how they were decorated. How did you get all the detail into those tiny little rooms?"

"I painted the walls and did the wallpaper and furniture and everything before I put them together," Vidalia explained. A lot of people had asked her that same question. She'd labored over the tiny candelabras, family portraits, and band posters that decorated the walls of her miniature houses.

"Aha," Becky said. "I loved dollhouses when I was a kid. The rabbits were awesome, too, with their clothes and all the different things they were doing."

"Thanks." Vidalia smiled. She considered going into her shtick about the houses—these weren't just dollhouses, they were distilled lives, each one like archeological evidence of a unique world, all held within the walls of a house, the lives of the tiny rabbit-people who lived there—but decided against it.

"Very cool!" said Becky. "God, those were my favorite things at the art show. You won first prize for them, right?"

"Yeah," Vidalia said. She'd been the first junior to win the prize in years. It usually went to a senior.

"Wow, that's awesome," said Becky, her eyes wide.

Maybe it was just the flattery, but Vidalia liked this girl.

Now Becky was keeping Heather company at the back of the group. It was just like Heather to overpack. Not only was she a fashion victim, but she was also incredibly disorganized. Even as a little girl she'd been like that. Her pink-carpeted room, filled with American Girl dolls and a constantly renewed supply of toys and clothes, had only been neat on the days their cleaning lady came.

"Now, ladies and gentleman." Madame Geen had stopped in a small lounge area, and the students were gathering around her, dropping their bags onto the floor with relief. "Those of you taking French language for your major course—that's almost all of you—will meet at the institute at nine A.M. tomorrow morning. Vidalia, your studio-art class will meet at the École des beaux-arts. Your host family will drop you off there and then you'll come to the institute for your afternoon class."

One of the reasons Vidalia was recommended for the program had been her language skills. Her mother, who loved all things French, had started teaching her before she went to kindergarten. Raised on French children's books and movies, Vidalia had passed out of the required classes freshman year and since then had been taking upper-level French literature and film classes with seniors.

"*Oh, Monsieur et Madame Ostier!*" Madame Geen cried.

She raised her arms in greeting as a pleasant-looking couple approached them.

"Voici Heather!" She pulled Heather forward and introduced her to her host parents. "Heather, the Ostiers have hosted several of our students. You will have a wonderful stay with them!"

Vidalia glanced over at Heather, who looked grumpy and tired even as she forced a smile for her host parents.

"Monsieur Dubois!" Madame Geen called joyfully.

Vidalia recognized her host family's last name from the information packet she'd received at the orientation meeting. She'd spent a lot of time trying to picture the two parents and their nine-year-old daughter. Maybe it would be like she had a regular family for six weeks, and the girl would be the little sister Vidalia had never had.

"Voici Vidalia!" Madame Geen said, and Vidalia stepped toward the short, bald man in khaki pants and a blue oxford, who was smiling jovially at her.

"Ah, voilà," he said in a satisfied way, taking Vidalia's hand and pulling her toward him, surprising her with the press of each of his warm, cushiony cheeks to hers.

"Bonjour," Vidalia said.

"I am Roger Dubois," he said, "and this is my daughter, Clara."

The little girl wore a red raincoat, and her chestnut hair was cut in bangs across her forehead. She stood perfectly straight, her hands behind her back.

"Bonjour," said Vidalia, smiling at her in what she hoped was a big-sisterly way.

"Hello." Clara spoke English with a strong British accent and stared up at Vidalia without smiling. It took Vidalia a second to realize that Clara was waiting to be kissed. She leaned down and pecked each of the girl's cheeks. Clara accepted the greeting and then turned and ran to the exit, weaving through legs and luggage as she went.

"Eh! Clara!" Monsieur Dubois called.

Vidalia followed him through the crowd after Clara.

"Good-bye, Vidalia!" called Madame Geen. "We will see you tomorrow afternoon!"

"Your flight was good?" asked Monsieur Dubois once they were in a car that, from the outside, Vidalia had thought was too small for all three of them. He pulled out of the airport parking lot. The road and the fields were wet from an early-morning rain, and everything shone in the bright sun. The day felt fresh and clear, nothing like the muggy heat at home.

"Oh, it was great," Vidalia said. "Very, uh, smooth." She didn't have much experience assessing flights.

"And have you been to France before?" he asked.

"No," Vidalia said, trying to read a billboard with a picture of a scruffy guy in striped pajamas. "This is my first time."

"We will have to show you a very nice holiday, then, isn't that right, Clara?"

Clara didn't answer. Instead she leaned forward between the seats and gave Vidalia a critical up-and-down appraisal.

"Why do you wear these shoes?" Clara asked, gesturing to Vidalia's combat boots.

"I like them," Vidalia said, smiling. Maybe now was when they started their big sister–little sister mentor thing.

"They are like a man's," Clara said disapprovingly. "Not very *chic*."

Or maybe not, thought Vidalia. Clara slid back in her seat.

"Clara!" barked Monsieur Dubois.

Vidalia glanced back to see the little girl gazing calmly out the window, apparently unperturbed by her father's scolding voice.

Soon, they were driving into the city. Vidalia looked out the window at the damp cobblestone streets and the people walking along the sidewalks. There were old ladies pushing wire baskets full of vegetables and paper packages, and people carrying loaves of bread wrapped in pink and white paper as they walked beneath the tall trees.

Along the way, Monsieur Dubois pointed out monuments and buildings, telling her about the different characters of the *arrondissements*, which was what the neighborhoods were called. It all went by in a blur. Vidalia was too caught up in looking at the little cars flying by them and the bright colors of the city to retain much of what he said.

"We live in the seventh *arrondissement*. Most people living here are boring like me, working in business and finance," he told her as they pulled up to the curb of a narrow street. "It is a very old part of the city and a little, how do you say, snob?" He gave her a twinkly, conspiratorial smile as he said this.

Vidalia looked up at the gray buildings with their tall windows. Clara leapt out and dashed across the street to a big wrought-iron door.

Monsieur Dubois jumped like he wanted to stop her, but she was already gone.

"She is very fast," he said in a rueful voice, shaking his head as he took Vidalia's backpack from the trunk.

Vidalia followed him across the street and into a cool marble foyer. As she stepped onto the dark red carpet inside, she heard Clara's quick footsteps fading on the spiral staircase overhead.

"Maman!" Clara yelled as a door swung open somewhere up above. *"Elle est là!"*

She's here, Vidalia translated to herself.

Upstairs, Vidalia followed Monsieur Dubois into a big apartment filled with rich cooking smells. They walked down the hall toward the sound of clattering pans and Clara's voice, which stopped abruptly as they arrived in the doorway. Clara was standing on a chair by the stove, her red raincoat folded neatly over its back, wearing a plaid skirt and a white short-sleeved collared shirt, almost like a school uniform. Next to her stood a small woman in a belted brown dress.

"Hello, Vidalia," said the woman crisply, "I am Catherine Dubois." Like Clara, she spoke English with a British accent. In French she told Clara to stir the pot on the stove before she gave Vidalia a dry kiss on each cheek. "Clara told me there were no problems with your flight?" She spoke in a business-like tone that had none of the warmth Vidalia had been hoping for from her host mother.

"Oh, no." Vidalia felt flustered. "Everything was fine."

"Good, we will have lunch in just a moment, and then we will talk. Clara!" she cried, slapping Clara's hand away from the pan where she'd just grabbed a green bean. Clara, who obviously had no problem with being yelled at, climbed onto a chair and took a stack of plates from a cabinet.

"Put these on the table," the little girl said, handing the plates to Vidalia.

"Clara!" her mother scolded again and, in French, she told her to be polite.

"It's okay," Vidalia said. "I can help."

"You see?" said Clara scornfully to her mother, and she jumped down, two glasses in each hand. Vidalia followed her into the dining room with the plates.

On the wall above the dining-room table hung a painting of a green cat with a human face sitting on the sill of a tall window, looking out at a brightly colored Paris. A man with a parachute floated from the sky toward the Eiffel Tower.

At the table, Madame Dubois quickly passed a meat dish with onions and sauce.

"The *boeuf bourguignon* is left over from last night, when we had Roger's business associates for dinner," she said. "I don't usually cook such elaborate meals—I'm too busy with my teaching—but one must keep up appearances."

"What do you teach?" asked Vidalia.

"I teach English at a school for students of business," said Madame Dubois.

"No wonder you speak so well," said Vidalia. She'd been surprised to find the entire family spoke English to her.

Madame Dubois gave a dry laugh. "Yes, and now we hope Clara's English will improve as well. Isn't that right, Clara? You will speak English with Vidalia?"

Clara scowled at Vidalia.

"So you will study at the Beaux-Arts this summer," Madame Dubois said to Vidalia as she spooned green beans onto her plate.

"Yes," agreed Vidalia.

"This is very impressive," her host mother said, but somehow Vidalia got the feeling that she wasn't complimenting her so much as warning her that she might be in over her head. "The École des beaux-arts is one of the great artistic institutions of France," she said sternly.

"Oh," Vidalia said, a little uncomfortably. "Yeah, well, I'm really excited about the class. We'll be working mostly at the Musée Apollinaire."

"Le Musée Apollinaire," said Madame Dubois. "Roger, do you know it?"

"Ah, yes," he said. "It is a little museum in the south of Paris, housed in what was once a church."

He smiled his twinkly smile at Vidalia.

"And what kind of work will you be doing?" asked Madame Dubois.

"I'm not sure," said Vidalia. "All I really know is that we'll be copying paintings from the museum."

She'd gotten a big packet of information at the orientation meeting, which listed her major course as Studio Art—Painting at the museum, hosted by the École nationale supérieure des beaux-arts and taught by someone named Laurent Benoît. She'd imagined a wise French master teaching her the age-old traditions, encouraging her as she learned, passing his secrets down to her. Her minor course would be art history, which she'd take at the institute in the afternoons.

Then Madame Dubois surprised her.

"And your mother works in the art business?" she asked. All three of the Dubois turned toward Vidalia, who almost choked on a mouthful of bread.

"Oh, right." She swallowed. "Yes, she does."

Vidalia had almost forgotten about the form she'd filled out in Madame Macarthy's French class at the beginning of June. It had been easy to write a firm "N/A" after the blanks for father's name and occupation, but she'd chewed on her pencil as she'd tried to come up with an occupation for her mother. *Delusional dancer?* she'd wondered, picturing her mother "taking a turn" in the living room as she often did. *Hysterical hausfrau?* Or maybe *crazed cook?* Nothing made the greatest first impression. Almost without thinking, she'd printed the words "Art dealer" in the blank space on the form. Her mother loved art and she liked to tell Vidalia about how she'd been an assistant in a gallery in New York when she was young.

"What exactly is her work?" asked Monsieur Dubois.

It was too late to change her story, so Vidalia forged ahead.

"She has a gallery," she said. "She deals mostly in sculpture, environmental art."

That sounded good, and she could picture the sculptures scattered around the lawn of an East Hampton gallery. "Big stuff," she said, and she glanced up at the picture of the green cat over the table. "Some painting, too," she added.

She took a forkful of green beans and faced the Dubois, all of whom were staring at her again. Not knowing what else to do, Vidalia smiled. That broke the spell. Madame Dubois went back to cutting Clara's food, Clara crossed her arms and sulked, and Monsieur Dubois shifted his gaze off into space. Business as usual, it seemed.

After lunch, Madame Dubois told Clara to show Vidalia to her bedroom. Sighing, Clara led her up a set of stairs in the dining room and past a bedroom that Vidalia thought must be the Dubois'. Then the little girl unlocked a bolted door and stepped out of the apartment into a dusty hallway.

"My room's out there?" Vidalia asked, dubious.

"Yes, hurry," Clara said. "I have to get back down for my television program."

Vidalia followed her past narrow doors until Clara stopped in front of one.

"This is our *chambre de bonne*," she said as she slid a skeleton key into the lock. "You know what is *bonne*?"

"Doesn't it mean 'good'?" Vidalia answered.

"*Non,*" Clara said, turning the key. "It is like a worker. Like someone who live in the house and cook for you, or clean."

"Oh," Vidalia said, "like a maid."

"Yes," said Clara, and opened the plywood door. "This is where the maid used to live, a long time ago." The room was just big enough to hold a bed and a small desk and chair. There was one window on the slanted ceiling, framing a patch of blue sky.

Vidalia stepped inside and dropped her overstuffed backpack next to the bed.

"Does anyone else live up here?" she asked, thinking of the doors in the hall.

"No," said Clara. "The others, they just put furniture and things in their maid room."

"Oh," Vidalia said. She sat down on the bed and sank into squeaky springs.

"There is a staircase," said Clara. "Down the hall. You can take that to the outside if you want, and then you don't have to go through our apartment."

"Okay," Vidalia said.

"Here are the keys." Clara handed Vidalia a ring. "This one is for your room," she said, indicating a big skeleton key. "This is to our apartment down the hall, and this one is to the entrance door downstairs." Then she turned and ran down the hall. Vidalia heard the apartment door slam behind her. Well, the Dubois weren't quite as warm and welcoming as she'd imagined them. She'd just gotten here, though. Things would probably get better.

Vidalia lay down on the bed and closed her eyes. Suddenly, she was exhausted.

CHAPTER

3

"VIDALIA!"

She buried her face in her pillow. Whoever was yelling at her would probably stop if she ignored them. But who was it? For a moment, she couldn't remember where she was.

"Vidalia, you must come now!"

Oh, right. Paris. Clara.

"Okay," Vidalia said weakly, trying to remember how great it was going to be to have a little sister for the summer. There was a pounding on the door. "Okay," she said, more loudly this time.

Silence.

"Vidalia!" Clara yelled.

"What?"

Vidalia realized too late that she'd answered in the voice she would have used with her mother; that is, highly irritated. She winced with regret and threw her hand over her eyes. What time was it anyway? How long had she slept?

"My mother says you have your class at the Beaux-Arts very soon, and you'll be late if you don't come now." There was another pause and then, in shocked disapproval, "You slept since yesterday afternoon!"

No wonder she felt so out of it.

"Okay." Vidalia removed her arm from her face and opened her eyes to see the blue sky framed in the window above her. She cleared her throat. "I'll be right down," she said.

A second later she heard Clara's footsteps head off down the hall. She sat up, suddenly taking in what Clara had said. She needed to shower, brush her teeth. She could feel the grime of the trip and the long night of sleep as she rose.

Once she'd gone downstairs, showered, and dressed in a black skirt and Strokes T-shirt, she wandered out to the kitchen to find Clara waiting impatiently for her.

"There is toast for you there. Hurry! I'm late for my dance class," the little girl said. "My mother will meet us on the street."

Vidalia picked up the toasted baguette, which had been buttered and spread with jam, and followed Clara out into the hallway. She pressed the button for the elevator. When they'd squeezed into the tiny octagon-shaped elevator, Clara reached into her bag and pulled out a cell phone, which she handed to Vidalia.

"*Tiens,*" Clara said. "My mother said to give it to you. It's an extra portable phone."

"Thanks," said Vidalia, taking it from her. "How do I know what the number is?"

"It's there," said Clara. "On tape on the back. It used to be mine, but I got a new one that is much nicer. It can take photographs." The little girl looked disdainfully up at Vidalia.

Madame Dubois met them in the car at the curb, and as soon as they got in, she took off, whipping around corners and gunning the engine whenever they approached a traffic light. She also talked a mile a minute all the way to the studio, telling Vidalia how to use the Métro and the public phones and how she shouldn't go home with strange men. Vidalia considered feeling insulted about that last one but decided it wasn't worth the energy. Her mind was on her art class. For the past year, she'd been yearning for somebody to challenge her and show her how to do new things. Mrs. Greenberg was encouraging, but Vidalia felt like she'd learned as much as she could from her. Laurent Benoît might teach her something that Mrs. Greenberg couldn't.

Madame Dubois pulled up in front of an old stone building right by the river Seine.

"Here you are, Vidalia," she said, handing her a small zippered purse. "There is a phone card there. You can follow the instructions on it to make international calls either from a pay phone or from our home. Clara gave you the cellular telephone?"

Vidalia nodded.

"You can make international calls on the phone if you need to, but it's much cheaper to use the card at a *cabine*, a pay phone. There are also some euros for you in the purse as well as a map of the Métro. You remember how to get to the institute from here?"

"Take line four from Saint-Michel to Montparnasse." Vidalia repeated the instructions Madame Dubois had rattled off minutes earlier.

"Yes, and call me if you get lost or need anything at all," Madame Dubois said sternly. "Now we must go or Clara will be late for her class. Oh, and I have a private student as well." Madame Dubois looked even more stressed as she turned back to the steering wheel.

Vidalia thanked her and waved good-bye to Clara, who stared blankly at her from the backseat. Now out of the car and all alone, Vidalia looked up at the imposing stone building.

She walked inside and turned down a quiet, airy hallway. The room numbers climbed as she walked, and her nervousness grew along with them. When she reached room 16, which was the number written in her information packet, she paused in front of the big wooden door, listening for voices. Nothing. She lifted her hand to the knob and slowly turned it.

The room was darker than she'd imagined it, sort of gloomy and dim, but it was big, with a high ceiling, and full of white plaster casts of heads and hands and feet. There were easels stacked against the far wall, and there was a strong oily smell in the air. This was nothing like Mrs. Greenberg's art room, with its watercolors and boxes of pom-poms. This was a real art studio, an *atelier*, as it was called in French.

Across the room, a cluster of eight or so students, all about Vidalia's age, kneeled on the floor, working on something she couldn't quite see. To her left, she noticed an older man in paint-spattered clothes standing by a big sink. That must be Laurent Benoît, the wise old art teacher.

"Excusez-moi," she said when she was just a few feet from him. He looked up, turning off the tap and shaking a handful of wet brushes into the sink. *"Je m'appelle—"*

"You're the American," he said in French, and he stuck the brushes in a glass jar.

"Oui," she said, relieved to be recognized. "I'm—"

But again he cut her off.

"You're late," he said, fixing her with watery blue eyes.

Vidalia's own eyes widened with surprise. This wasn't the welcome she'd expected, and she was only, what, ten minutes late? Laurent Benoît spun around and headed across the room to where the others were crouched on the floor. Vidalia hurried to follow him.

"Here," he said when she reached him. He handed her a pale wooden frame and a piece of canvas that he cut from a big roll. When she looked down at the other people, she saw that they were all stretching canvas onto their own wooden frames.

"Monsieur?" Vidalia asked. But he was already walking away. She'd never done this before. Okay, she guessed she was about to try. She got down on her knees and glanced at the guy next to her as he pulled the canvas over one edge of his frame with a small pair of pliers, then hit the corners with a stapler. Then he flipped the whole thing to the side and did it on another side of the frame. Vidalia pulled the canvas tight the way he had, and picked up his pliers and his stapler once he was done with them. But even though she tried to mimic what he'd done, hers came out crooked. The guy next to her looked down at her canvas and then back at her, one eyebrow raised, his brown hair falling into his eyes.

Vidalia frowned. He didn't have to be smug about it. She pulled at her canvas with the pliers again and stapled, but the stapler slipped and hit the wood at an angle. A pair of paint-spattered leather boots appeared in her line of vision.

She looked up to see Monsieur Benoît and sat back on her heels, hoping for some friendly advice.

"You ask for help when you need it," he said in a not-so-friendly voice. "We don't waste materials here."

He took the rumpled canvas from her.

"You work over here today," he said. He walked to an easel on the other side of the room and dropped a box of charcoal next to it. Then he picked up a big sketch pad from a table nearby and put it on the easel.

"Draw this," he said, pointing at a plaster bust on a pedestal nearby. Some of the other students glanced over at her, including a girl with long blonde dreadlocks, who gave her a sympathetic smile before turning back to her own canvas. Vidalia felt like she'd gotten a time-out on her first day of preschool.

The morning seemed like it would never end. Vidalia worked on her sketch while the other students stretched canvases and then painted a still life together. When it was finally time to clean up, Monsieur Benoît walked by, glanced at her sketch, grunted, and went over to talk to the guy who'd smirked at Vidalia's failed canvas. Some teacher. Vidalia rolled up her sketch and shoved it in her bag.

As the class gathered by the sinks, Monsieur Benoît looked at Vidalia. She felt herself cringe when his eyes landed on her.

"Our colleague, Mademoiselle Sloane," he said in French, "arrived too late for our earlier introductions. She comes to us from the American Institute, and she has already demonstrated that country's well-known lack of economy."

Vidalia stiffened.

"I hope that she will join us in our European efforts to preserve our artistic resources in the future," he finished.

The other students glanced back at her. Vidalia saw the guy who'd raised his eyebrow at her canvas actually snicker. What was everyone's problem? Vidalia felt her face flush.

"As you know," said Monsieur Benoît, "we will be working in the museum this semester. Each of you will choose a painting to copy and you will work on that for the rest of the course. Copying is a fundamental task of the artist," he went on. "Contrary to what many fashionable critics would tell you, there is no great artist who has not studied the old masters. We must pay them our respects and learn from them before we go on to do our own work."

Everyone gazed up at him like he was *le Maître*, the master, Vidalia thought. She wasn't convinced. What kind of teacher started class by humiliating his students?

"This week we will work on various techniques that you will use in your copies. Beginning next Monday, one week from today, we will meet at the Musée Apollinaire promptly at nine o'clock each morning." He looked pointedly at Vidalia, who bit her lip and felt her anger rise again. "I expect each of you to have completed a copy of your painting by the end of the program," he went on, looking around at everyone. "We won't be able to tell it from the original, correct, Bruno?"

A guy with blond hair and blue eyes laughed and said, "Of course not."

Everyone chuckled knowingly. Why did it seem like they all knew each other on the first day of class?

When Monsieur Benoît said they could go, a group of people gathered around him, talking. Vidalia, the blood rushing in her ears, headed for the door. As she pulled it open, the girl with dreadlocks slipped out alongside her.

"T'inquiète pas," she said with a pitying look. *Don't worry.* "He's always like that in the beginning," she said in French.

"Really?" Vidalia said incredulously, as they walked down the long, quiet hallway.

"Yes, he's just picking on you because you're new. The rest of us all took his spring class, so we've known him for some time."

No wonder they all seemed so comfortable, Vidalia thought.

"And he's probably pleased to have an American to tease as well," the girl said, looking up at Vidalia with an impish smile. "I'm Caroline," she added.

"I'm Vidalia," she answered, really looking at the girl for the first time. She was fair, with light freckles crossing the bridge of her nose. Her frame looked almost too small to support the mass of thick dreadlocks that hung down her back.

"You can ask me questions if you need help," Caroline said, pushing open the door to the street. "And don't worry, Laurent will be nicer with you soon!"

She waved and turned to walk down the street away from the boulevard Saint-Michel where Vidalia was going.

Feeling calmer, Vidalia looked across at the Seine and took a deep breath. She was hungry, she realized. She walked up the hill toward the boulevard. The sidewalks were crowded with people holding cameras and speaking different languages. She stopped in front of the first stand she saw that said CRÊPES and ordered one with ham and cheese, taking out the purse and paying with the euros Madame Dubois had given her.

I have to tell Mom how good this is, she thought as she ate, and then remembered that she hadn't called home yet. Her mother had been in a near panic when Heather and her parents, Mr. and Mrs. Warren, had pulled up in front of the gate into Vidalia's yard to get her.

"That's Heather!" her mother said, turning, hurried and breathless, to Vidalia, who was in the front hall, checking for her passport. "Oh, have a wonderful time. You're going to love Paris!"

Her mother, dressed in a blue velour jumpsuit with a red turban wrapped around her head, fluttered between the fogged window next to the door and Vidalia, anxiety rising off her like noxious fumes.

"I will," said Vidalia. "I told Mr. Nichols to stop by every once in a while, so don't freak out if you see his truck." Mr. Nichols had been the groundskeeper when her mother was a kid and the Sloane family was still one of the wealthiest in East Hampton. Now Vidalia called him when they needed a door fixed or a branch cut down, and half the time he wouldn't even take money for it. He also happened to be the only person other than Vidalia that her mother would allow inside the house.

"I know," her mother said. "I'll expect him."

"And Fresh Direct is coming Friday," Vidalia said. That was the online grocery-delivery service that was going to keep her mother from starving while she was gone.

"Yes, of course," her mother agreed, pushing her toward the door.

"And don't forget to put that check for the power company out for the mailman tomorrow," Vidalia said.

"Good-bye, darling," her mother said, and folded Vidalia in a brief hug, her neck moist against Vidalia's cheek in the humid afternoon. "I love you." Her voice was soft and less wild-sounding than it had been a moment before.

"You, too, Mom," Vidalia said, trying not to think about all the things that could go wrong while she was away. "I wish you'd let me call Aunt Pat so she could come over and check on you every once in a while."

"No, you promised!" her mother cried, immediately panicked.

"Okay, okay," Vidalia said. "You're right, I promised."

"Now, go!" her mother said. "You don't want to keep them waiting!"

Vidalia looked at her mother's face, the dark brown, almond-shaped eyes wide with panic, long lashes fluttering. She had been beautiful enough to model when she was younger, but now her face was so marked by anxiety and fear that her prettiness only came through in flashes. Vidalia had inherited her mother's pale skin and dark hair but she was always aware that the beauty had somehow skipped a generation. She was too tall, for one thing, too skinny and flat chested for another. She hugged her mother one last time.

"You should get out of the house, too, Mom," she said. "Go for walks. I don't want you to be alone here the whole time I'm gone."

It hadn't been that long ago that her mother did go out for walks, if only short ones. Vidalia was hoping that during her six weeks away, her mother would start going out again. In a way, this summer was a test to see if she could live on her own. After all, ideally Vidalia would be leaving home for college the year after next.

"Of course," her mother said. "Oh, darling, you should go!" But she was holding on to Vidalia's arm, too, even as she was pushing her away.

"Okay, I'm going," Vidalia said, carefully removing the tightly gripped hand. "I'll call you when I get there."

Vidalia's mom stepped quickly away from the door as her daughter opened it, making sure that no one outside would catch a glimpse of her.

That was her mother—frantic and loving and always at home. She was probably waiting for the phone to ring right now. Once Vidalia had taken the last delicious bite of the crêpe, with its gooey cheese and soft shell, she looked around for a phone booth. Then she stepped inside the glass *cabine* and took the phone card from her bag, remembering Madame Dubois' instructions.

"Hello?" Her mother's voice was high and expectant.

It was about twenty after noon in Paris, which meant it was 6:20 A.M. at home, but Vidalia wasn't surprised to hear her mother wide awake at that hour. Her mother got up early and did most of her gardening and cooking and redecorating in the morning. Afternoons were her lazy—and often depressed—time.

"Hi, Mom," Vidalia said.

"Vidalia!" she cried. "Where are you?"

"Paris," she said, leaning back in the booth and looking out at the busy street. "Where do you think?"

"Tell me everything!" her mother said, ignoring the sarcasm.

Vidalia looked down and scuffed the toe of her boot against the bumpy steel of the floor.

"I started my art class today," she said with a sigh.

"How was it?" her mother asked. "Did they peg you for the next Mary Cassatt?"

Vidalia groaned. "It didn't go that well, actually."

"Oh, never mind," her mother said when Vidalia had described her morning. "He's probably just testing you. The French are like that. But tell me about Paris. Where are you right now?"

"Saint-Michel," Vidalia said, looking at the name on the Métro stop she could see from where she stood. "Right across the river from Notre-Dame."

"Oh, there used to be the most wonderful English-language bookstore." Her mother sighed.

Vidalia's mother had spent time in Paris when she was young, after she'd dropped out of college to model. She'd been telling Vidalia about it her entire life, so this wasn't the first time she'd mentioned the bookstore. "Shakespeare and Company," her mother said. "It's where all the American literary types would meet up. Right across from Notre-Dame on the Saint-Michel side. You've got to go over there."

"I don't know if I'd call myself a literary type," Vidalia said.

"Vidalia, go!" her mother cried. "Do it for me!"

"Okay, okay, I'll see if it's still around." She sighed.

Once she'd described the Dubois, the view from their apartment, and what the people on the street were wearing, Vidalia was ready to get off the phone.

"Mom, I should go. I don't want to use this whole card up at once," she said. "And it's, like, a million degrees in this phone booth, too." She opened and closed the glass door a few times, trying to create a breeze.

"Oh, oh, of course," her mother said.

Vidalia could see her sitting by the hall phone, wrapping the cord around her finger. "Don't forget to call me, darling. I want to hear all about it," she said wistfully.

"I won't forget," said Vidalia. "I'll call again soon. And let me give you the number for this cell phone I'm using, too."

When her mother had written down the number and they'd hung up, Vidalia stepped out into the bright Parisian day outside the phone booth. Art history didn't start until two o'clock, and it wasn't even one now. She decided to walk along the Seine, looking absentmindedly for the bookstore as she went. She found it almost right away, tucked into a corner next to a café across from Notre-Dame. In the courtyard in front of the glass storefront, there were shelves and a table piled with books. Several people stood outside reading and talking beneath a big yellow-and-black sign that read SHAKESPEARE AND COMPANY.

Vidalia crossed the street and went to look at one of the bookshelves. She scanned the spines of beat-up paperbacks—*The Sheltering Sky, Ulysses, Nightwood*—before noticing an olive-skinned arm moving quickly by her feet.

There was a guy crouched on the ground next to her, taking books from a cardboard box and stacking them on a table. He wore faded jeans and a black T-shirt and had a mop of brown curls that gleamed in the sun and fell into his eyes.

He glanced up at her.

"Can I help you find something?" he asked, squinting up into the sun. He had a French accent.

"Non, merci," she said. Wait, he'd spoken English. Why had she answered in French?

"Vous êtes française?" he asked her. *Are you French?*

Vidalia shook her head quickly, not sure which language to answer in now.

"English?" he asked. He sat back on his heels. "No, Swiss!"

This time Vidalia just smiled, playing along with his guessing game.

He leaned back on one hand and really looked at her like he was thinking.

"I know, you come from South Africa," he said, like he was sure he'd gotten it this time.

"I just fell out of the sky," she said, thinking of the painting in the Dubois' dining room. "With my parachute."

She raised her arms and whistled like she was falling.

The guy shook his head and lifted the box of books as he stood. Walking toward the door to the store, he turned back to Vidalia.

"You Americans are so strange," he said, smiling at her as he pulled the door open and went inside.

Vidalia looked after him for a second, surprised and pleased with their little interaction. She'd made a joke with a French person. She turned back to the shelf for a minute before deciding to see what the inside of the store was like.

She stepped into a room filled floor to ceiling with books. The guy was standing in front of a cash register.

"So, I guess you like to read," Vidalia said, looking around at the books piled up on the floor, climbing crooked shelves to the ceiling. She was trying to be funny, but it came out kind of dumb.

"This is your first time at the store?" he asked.

"Yeah," she said. "My mother used to come here, though, a long time ago."

She looked around again. It was hard to picture her mother standing among these shelves, leafing through a book, walking up to the register to pay. Of course, it was hard to picture her mother anywhere except inside their house these days.

"I'll give you a tour if you want." He tilted his head so that his curls fell out of his eyes.

"Sure, okay," she said. "But you have to give it in French. You *are* French, aren't you?"

He laughed and was about to say something, but just then a girl in a long skirt and a purple cloth wrapped around her head came hurtling through the door from the back.

"Julien, love," she said. She sounded Australian. "I can't fit all those children's books up there. There's not enough room." She waved her hand at the ceiling in a fed-up gesture.

He turned to her.

"You have to *make* room," he said. "Henry wants all the travel stuff moved to the front."

"Where?" the girl asked pathetically.

"I'll show you." He sighed. "Can you wait a minute?" he asked Vidalia.

"Oh, actually . . ." She knew she'd feel lame standing around waiting for him, and besides, she had to get to the institute.

He leaned over the register to grab what looked like a postcard.

"Okay," he said. "But you should come back. There's a poetry reading tonight at seven thirty. It's not in French"—he grinned at her—"but he's quite good, right, Margie?" He held the card out to Vidalia, who took it.

The girl in the doorway had her arms crossed·and her eyebrows raised as she waited.

"Andy's pretty good, yeah." She stretched the *yeah* out in a long Australian drawl.

"Cool," Vidalia said. "I'll try to make it."

"My name's Julien," he said, softening the *J* with his French accent. He smiled and put out his hand. It felt warm in Vidalia's.

"I'm Vidalia," she said.

"Really?" He leaned toward her, his eyes sparkling. *"Alors tu es un oignon?"*

Vidalia rolled her eyes.

"Yeah," she said. "As you can see, I'm an onion." It wasn't

the first time she'd heard the joke, but somehow she didn't mind it coming from him.

He pulled his hand back and laughed, his brown eyes sparkling.

"And this is Margie," he said.

"Nice to meet you, Vidalia," Margie said matter-of-factly before turning back to Julien. "Now can you please show me what I'm supposed to do up there? I've got to meet Michel in an hour."

She turned and spun back through the door past a couple of customers who stood perusing the shelves.

"Come to the reading," Julien said, "and we'll speak French." He flashed Vidalia a smile before disappearing into the back of the store.

Vidalia stared for a second at the door that Julien and Margie had gone through. *What do you know?* she thought. Her mother had pointed her in the right direction for once. She looked at the card, and then tucked it into her bag as she headed out the door to the Métro. She was looking forward to tonight already.

CHAPTER

 **4**

THE AMERICAN INSTITUTE WAS halfway down a cobble-stone street off the busy boulevard du Montparnasse. When she pushed open the heavy wooden door and stepped inside, Vidalia found a glass-walled hallway encircling a courtyard filled with trees and people. These were the gifted high-school students from throughout the United States that the institute's brochures had bragged about.

East Hampton High School made a big deal out of its con-nection to the American Institute summer-abroad programs. The programs were academically rigorous; everyone chose a major and a minor course of study, and there was a lot of work required. The guidance counselors always talked about how great it looked to colleges. Vidalia had never expected to go, since she knew her mother didn't have the money, but then Mrs. Greenberg, Vidalia's art teacher, had ganged up with Madame Macarthy, her French teacher, and together they'd convinced her to apply for the scholarship. Vidalia hadn't ex-pected anything to come of it—she was in competition with kids all across the country, after all—but, in the end, she'd gotten it. All she had to come up with was the airfare, which she did by scooping ice cream at Dreesen's in town all spring.

Of course, the first person Vidalia saw in the courtyard was Heather, sitting at a green metal table in the courtyard with Becky. Becky waved, and as Vidalia waved back, Heather glanced up at her and then, when she saw who it was, looked quickly away. Vidalia sighed and walked over.

"What's up, girl?" Becky asked, pulling her smooth auburn hair away from her face.

"Not too much," said Vidalia. "I had my art class this morning."

"How'd it go?" asked Becky. Without waiting for an answer, she added, "It had to have been better than French. I don't think I can handle three hours of grammar with Madame Geen every single day. It is *sooo* boring, isn't it, Heather?"

"Pretty bad," agreed Heather, shuffling through her purse, which was probably some designer label.

"So how's your French family?" Becky asked.

"They're okay," said Vidalia with a shrug. "They seem really busy."

"I've got three little kids in mine," said Becky. "They're adorable, but they make so much noise. They were all jumping on me at seven o'clock this morning." She sighed.

Vidalia tried to imagine Clara jumping into bed with her, but it was impossible.

"You're cutting it close, though," Becky said. It was almost two already. "Where've you been?"

"Been exploring a little," Vidalia said.

"Oh, yeah?" Becky said. She picked a piece of lint from

her tight brown sweater tank top, smoothing it against her side when she was done.

Heather was making a point of not paying attention, Vidalia noticed.

"After my art class this morning, I went to this American bookstore, Shakespeare and Company. There's a reading I might go to tonight. . . ."

Vidalia fished the card Julien had given her out of her bag and handed it to Becky.

"Wow, cultured. How'd you find out about that?" Becky inspected the card and then handed it back.

"I just went in there and the guy working there invited me."

"No way, a little expat action?" Becky said.

"He's French, actually," Vidalia said. "He's really nice."

"Whoa, wait a minute." Becky sat up. "We haven't even been here two days and you've already got a date with a *French* guy?"

Vidalia noticed with pleasure that Heather was waiting for her response, too.

"It's not really a date," Vidalia said modestly.

"Right. Very impressive, Lady Vidalia," Becky said, shaking a finger at her.

"Time for class," Heather said. She turned to Becky. "I have European history and politics. What's your afternoon class again?"

"Art history," said Becky. "What about you, Vidalia?"

"Same," said Vidalia. "Do you know where it is?"

"Totally," said Becky, standing and looking at her watch.

Vidalia followed Becky to the art history class on the other side of the courtyard. When they got inside, Becky grabbed Vidalia's arm and pulled her into a seat.

"Did you see that hot, *hot* skater guy outside?" Becky whispered to Vidalia.

Vidalia smiled and shook her head.

"Oh, wait, he's in this class. Don't look," Becky squealed.

Vidalia looked out of the corner of her eye and saw an Asian guy with a skateboard under his arm walking to the front of the room.

"He's cute," Vidalia agreed. He had a friendly skater-dude expression on his face and a blond streak in his spiky hair.

"I am so talking to him after this," Becky whispered.

"Hello, class," said a woman at the front of the room. "As most of you know, I am Madame Zafar." She looked like she was made out of a stack of triangles, her black-and-gray hair cut into a frizzy pyramid around her face. Beneath that, she wore a brown tunic and a skirt that reached to the floor, both made out of the same heavy brown cloth.

Becky raised her eyebrows at Vidalia, like, *get a load of this,* then whispered, "She came into our French class this morning. She and Madame Geen make quite a team. Like the hobbit and the warlock or something." She giggled as she turned back to the front of the room.

"For those of you who were not here this morning, I am the director of the institute." Her long fingers extended from flared sleeves as she wrote her name on the board.

After handing out the syllabus, Madame Zafar turned the lights out and flipped on a projector to show slides of Gothic cathedrals. Vidalia settled into the dark room and enjoyed it.

If Monsieur Benoît's art class kept going the way it had this morning, Vidalia thought, at least she'd get to come here and look at pictures in the afternoon.

At four o'clock, Vidalia stood with everyone else, papers rustling into folders and notebooks.

"Vidalia." It was Madame Zafar standing right behind her. Vidalia jumped. "You started your course at the Beaux-Arts today?"

"Yes," Vidalia said, gritting her teeth a little as she remembered the embarrassment of the morning.

"Very good," Madame Zafar said. "I am always pleased to have artists in this class. You can bring an interesting perspective."

She peered at Vidalia over small rectangular glasses. "I look forward to seeing what you produce while you're here."

"Oh, well, so do I, actually," said Vidalia with a nervous laugh.

Madame Zafar swept out of the room, and Vidalia followed, wondering if maybe this teacher would take her under her big brown wing and teach her the ways of weirdness in France. She kind of hoped so.

Outside, Becky had already sat down at a table. Vidalia paused next to her.

"See, there he is," Becky said. The skater guy was talking to a group of preppy-looking girls on the other side of the courtyard. "Don't look!" Becky yelped.

Vidalia shook her head at the conflicting instructions.

"Sit, sit!" Becky whispered.

Vidalia sat down on the opposite side of Becky from Heather, who was wearing dark sunglasses.

"So Vidalia, Heather and I are going on the trip to Avignon this weekend," said Becky. "Are you coming?"

"Oh, no," Vidalia said vaguely. "I think I'll stay here and go to some museums."

The weekend trips that the institute ran cost extra, and Vidalia wasn't planning to go on any of them. At home, this hadn't seemed like much of a sacrifice—six weeks in Paris was good enough for her—but now she felt a twinge of jealousy.

"So serious." Becky sighed. "Well, maybe you'll come to Brittany with us next weekend?"

"Maybe . . ." Vidalia said uncomfortably.

"I want to do as much traveling inside France as I can during the program, because I have to go straight home after, unlike lucky Heather, who gets to go to the south."

"Oh God," said Heather, rolling her eyes. "Two weeks in a farmhouse with my parents is not the vacation of my dreams. I'd so much rather just go home and hang out on the beach with my friends."

Becky was staring across the courtyard at the skater guy now. "Okay," she said. "I'm making my move. Watch my bag."

And with that, Becky stood up, slung one hand on her hip, tossed her hair over her shoulder, and strode across the courtyard to the skater guy. She planted herself in front of him with a wicked little smile and said something that made him look up with a startled expression and then laugh. The J.Crew girls he'd been talking to dispersed, giving Becky irritated looks as they went. But the guy, Vidalia noticed, was transfixed. He nodded eagerly as Becky talked and twirled a lock of her long hair around one finger, her head bent slightly to the side, her hip cocked.

"Wow," said Vidalia.

"Girl's got skills," agreed Heather in a bored voice.

"Well, I've got to take off," Vidalia said. "See you later."

She wanted to get something to eat before going to the reading. She'd called Madame Dubois after leaving the bookstore and told her she'd be out later than expected, letting her think it had something to do with the institute without actually saying so.

"We'll expect you after dinner then," said Madame Dubois, sounding harried. "Call if you have any trouble with the Métro."

Vidalia had been pleased that getting permission to stay out had been so easy. At home, her mother always wanted detailed descriptions of what she was doing and who she was with. It wasn't so much that she was strict as that she was ravenous for information about the outside world. Sometimes Vidalia wanted to tell her just to go see it for herself, but she never did.

"Later," Heather said, without looking at her.

Vidalia rolled her eyes as she walked away.

As she walked out onto the street and through the crowds of people on Montparnasse, she couldn't help thinking about the last real conversation she and Heather had ever had. They'd been best friends since they were five, and their friendship had ended abruptly at the end of their first week of ninth grade. That was almost three years ago, but the memory still hurt like a fresh burn.

Vidalia had gotten her lunch and then looked for Heather at the table they'd sat at all week. But Heather wasn't there. Finally, Vidalia saw her at a different table, with a big group of girls. Among them she recognized Melody and Maraya, two popular girls whom Heather and Vidalia had laughingly called the M&Ms. Vidalia was surprised, but she went over without thinking too much about it. Maybe Heather had just had class with them.

Melody and Maraya looked her up and down as she walked toward them. She could still remember exactly what she'd been wearing: black-and-white-checked tights and a slightly too-big lacy black dress that she'd bought at a thrift store with Heather just a few weeks before. The two popular girls turned to Heather with their eyebrows raised and their mouths twisted scornfully, and Melody said, "Heather, I think the Wicked Witch of the West would like to speak with you."

Melody and Maraya both started laughing. Vidalia looked at Heather, confused.

"Sorry, Vidalia," Heather mumbled. "No more seats."

She shrugged and then bent in to whisper with her two new friends.

Vidalia stared for a second, her stupid orange tray in her hands, and then she turned and walked to the other side of the cafeteria. When Vidalia called her that night, Heather's voice was cold in a way she had never heard it before.

"What . . ." Vidalia started shakily. She paused and

then said more firmly, "What's up with you and Melody and Maraya?"

"What do you mean?" Heather asked casually.

"I mean, what was that about at lunch today?" Vidalia just wanted Heather to say she was sorry, that she'd messed up, and then they could go back to inhabiting the world that the two of them had been making up together since they were kids.

Heather sighed.

"Vidalia," she said, like she was talking to a five-year-old. "We're in high school now. We can't hang out together forever. I think it's time to grow up, you know?"

Vidalia was silent. She didn't know.

"I need to have other friends, too," Heather said, a little more gently.

"Okay," said Vidalia, still hurt but ready to accept this. "That's normal, I guess."

But then Heather's voice changed again.

"You're just so *weird*, Vidalia." She sounded frustrated, even angry. "I mean, maybe it's time to stop playing make-belive and start having, like, a life."

"I'm not playing anything!" Vidalia said, stung.

"Whatever," sighed Heather.

"Yeah, whatever," Vidalia said, her voice catching in her throat.

And that was it. Eight years of best-friendship, done.

CHAPTER

 **5**

AFTER TAKING THE MÉTRO back to Saint-Michel, Vidalia bought a miniature quiche Lorraine to eat for dinner. She carried it down to the edge of the Seine and watched tourists stroll along in the warm evening with cameras, parents calling out to kids in Japanese and German and Italian. After she'd eaten, she sketched for a while, watching the people, feeling the breeze on her arms, hearing the music of the city.

When she got to Shakespeare and Company a little before seven thirty, the store was full of people. Vidalia made her way to the back, where she found Julien wrestling a mic stand from a closet beneath a narrow set of stairs.

"Hey there," she said.

He turned and pushed his hair out of his eyes to look up at her.

"Vidalia!" he said, leaning back on his heels and planting his palms on his knees. "You came!"

He seemed so surprised that Vidalia felt embarrassed. Maybe he hadn't meant it when he'd invited her? Before she could answer, the stairs above them creaked and someone came rushing down. It was a little old man in a red velvet suit. His white hair rose in a gravity-defying sweep from the crown of his head, and his white goatee pointed straight down. He spun toward Julien.

"Give me that. We should be set up by now. I thought that girl was going to put out the chairs." He was American, and he spoke in a cranky rush.

"Margie did the chairs," said Julien, relinquishing the mic stand.

"There aren't enough. We've got a full house tonight," said the man.

"I'll bring some more up." Julien's voice was soothing.

The old man turned and went up the stairs just as erratically as he'd come down.

"Who was *that*?" Vidalia asked, laughing.

"Henry," Julien said, standing and reaching into the closet, his voice apologetic. "He's really quite an amazing—"

"Who moved that table?" It was Henry's voice from the top of the stairs. "Julien!" Henry pronounced the name the American way, like he was saying "Julie-Anne." The French pronunciation was so much nicer, thought Vidalia. "I can't find the plug for this thing."

"Coming, Henry," called Julien. He pulled a bunch of chairs out of the mess of the closet and tried to lift about six at once.

"I can help you with those if you want," offered Vidalia.

"Thanks," he said, and gave her a grateful smile.

Vidalia took a chair under each arm and followed Julien up the steep, narrow stairs into another cramped room filled with books, where people clustered together, talking. Henry was at the front of the room shaking the mic stand to free it of the cord, and Vidalia saw Julien give him a worried look.

"I'll put the chairs out," she said. "You can go help him."

"Thanks," he said again. "Just line them up here at the back."

He rushed over to Henry and gently took the mic stand from him.

"All right," Henry said into the microphone a few minutes later. "Might as well get going."

It took a minute for Vidalia to realize that Henry was actually speaking to the audience. She sat down in the last chair in the row she'd just made. There were people crowding in the doorway. The room was hot and there was only a slight breeze making its way in through the window behind Henry.

"Andy Willett is going to . . ." Henry announced, then he raised his head and looked around the room. "Where's Andy?" A man in jeans and a flannel shirt with the sleeves cut off at the shoulder stood in front.

"I'm right here, Henry," he said.

"Oh, all right then." Henry drew himself up at the microphone and in a formal voice, said, "I will introduce Andy Willett from . . ." He looked down. "Where are you from again?"

"Oregon," the flannel guy said.

"Right." Henry paused and shuffled some papers in his hands. "His poems are all right, I suppose." He looked around. "Aren't they?"

"They're fantastic!" That was Julien. Vidalia craned her neck and saw him standing off to the side. A couple of people in the audience hooted and clapped.

"Well, good. Here he is. And thank you for coming."

The old man bowed stiffly and wandered to an empty seat.

"Well," said the poet once he'd made it to the microphone. He cleared his throat. "Thanks a lot for coming out. And thanks to Henry for having me."

An incoherent grumble came from where Henry sat. Andy Willett continued.

"This is a long poem that I wrote about growing up in Oregon and about the logging industry."

He cleared his throat and read.

"It was in the woods that a man became
What he would become:
Hard, the bark
Biting from his hands.
Good work, long days of it."

Vidalia tried to listen but she felt her eyes glaze over, and eventually she just gave up and looked out the window behind Andy instead. It was getting darker now and, across the Seine, she could see Notre-Dame lit up against the sky, casting a greenish light onto the water below. Andy finished his long poem and moved on to a series of shorter ones that Vidalia had just as much trouble staying focused on.

She tried to imagine her mother here again, looking out at this same scene. How long ago would that have been? Twenty years? Twenty-five? Her mother had come here when she was nineteen. As far as Vidalia could tell, she had spent the entire time going to parties and modeling. Some of the photographs were still around the house. Had the view been the same from this window when her mother was here? Vidalia looked at the lights of the cathedral, and the boats full of tourists going past underneath. No, she thought. Notre-Dame had been there for hundreds of years, but it had never looked exactly like this before.

She was jerked from her thoughts when the crowd burst into applause. Vidalia looked at her phone. It was 20:35, which translated to 8:35. An hour had gone by. She clapped as Andy blushed and bowed awkwardly in the front of the room.

"What did you think?" Julien asked her. After taking the mic out of the room, he'd come in the door behind her and was already folding up chairs.

"I liked it," she said, standing.

"No you didn't." He laughed. "I saw you staring over there." He waved his arm toward the cathedral. "I don't think you even heard it."

"I did!" Vidalia protested. She tried to remember something about the poetry. A bear and a snake came to mind. "I liked . . . the animal ones."

Julien smiled.

"Me, too," he said. "Can you stay? There's some food."

Vidalia looked up and saw the girl from earlier today, Margie, putting a tray of cheese and crackers on the table at the front of the room.

"Sure," she said. "I can stay for a while."

"Good," said Julien. "I'm just going to clear some of the chairs and I'll be back."

Vidalia got a plate and some cheese and stood by the window. She looked around the room at the people talking and laughing, all seeming happy to speak English to other Americans and Anglophones.

"Michel!" Near her, Margie dropped another tray of cheese roughly onto the table and rushed toward a guy with brown hair wearing a button-down shirt. He looked shyly at Margie from under long lashes. Vidalia watched as Margie enthusiastically kissed him.

Julien walked over to Vidalia with a cup in his hand. They both started talking at once.

"You're in school?" he asked.

"How long have you worked here?" she asked.

He laughed. "You first," he said.

"I'm studying art," she said, "down the street."

"At the Beaux-Arts?" he asked.

She nodded.

"Very impressive."

"You think?" Unlike Madame Dubois, Julien really did look impressed. "I'm actually a student at the American Institute over by Montparnasse," she said. "I just take my art class at the Beaux-Arts. We'll be working at a museum starting next week, though." She shrugged, trying to act like she wasn't incredibly nervous about the class. "So what about you?"

"I've worked here a few years," Julien said. "Full-time in the summer. I start university in the fall, though, so it will be part-time then."

They talked about her art classes and how he wanted to study American literature. His favorite authors were Ernest

Hemingway and F. Scott Fitzgerald. Vidalia was surprised at how easy it was to talk to him.

"What time is it?" she asked after a while, wondering if the Dubois would be worried about her.

"About nine," he said. "Do you have to go?"

"Yeah," she said, a little regretfully. "I'm staying with this family and I told them I wouldn't be back too late."

"I'll walk you to the Métro," he said.

At the entrance to the Métro, they stopped and said good-bye.

"Maybe I'll stop by . . ." she said.

"Are you free on the weekend?" he asked quickly. "We could go to a museum. I think maybe you like paintings better than poems." He swatted her arm teasingly.

"I guess I do," she laughed. "So, yeah."

"I finish work at three o'clock on Saturday," Julien said.

"Okay," Vidalia said, smiling. "I'll see you Saturday."

"Good night, Vidalia," Julien said, and he leaned in to kiss her quickly on each cheek.

Vidalia skipped down the stairs into the Métro station. She'd been here two days and already she had a friend.

It was around nine thirty when Vidalia got to the apartment, and she was a little nervous that the Dubois would think that was too late, even though nobody had given her a curfew. She stepped into the living room and found Monsieur Dubois on one of the couches, his eyes closed, a glass of amber liquid in one hand. She coughed to see if he was awake. He sat up with a start.

"Vidalia!" he said cheerfully. "You are back."

"I'm back," she agreed, relieved that he didn't seem to notice the time, or care.

"Excuse me, Vidalia." Madame Dubois passed her, carrying a tray. "Would you like a coffee? Sit with us." She set the tray on the table.

"Oh, no thanks, I can't do coffee at night," Vidalia said, but she sat anyway. Everything Madame Dubois said sounded like an order.

"Did you have a pleasant evening?" Monsieur Dubois' eyes twinkled at her over his glass. Vidalia noticed that Madame was pouring coffee into three espresso cups. Was one of those cups for her?

"Um, yeah, I did," she said. "I went to a poetry reading."

Just then, there was a creak from the stairs. All three of them turned to look. To Vidalia's surprise, she saw a guy who didn't look all that much older than her descending into the dining room. There were still plates on the table, Vidalia noticed. He must have been here for dinner. Vidalia turned back to the stranger and almost jumped when she found him looking directly at her, his eyes a pale, pale blue.

"Vidalia, this is Marco," said Madame Dubois. "The son of a very dear friend of ours." There was something almost catlike about the way he moved, Vidalia thought, as if he were trying to walk through the room without touching it. "And Marco, this is Vidalia, our American student."

"Nice to meet you," said Vidalia, half standing as Marco came in for the *bise*, the hello–good-bye kiss on each cheek that she hadn't quite gotten the hang of yet. This one ended with an awkward cheekbone-to-nose bump. Vidalia sat down again, embarrassed.

"*Enchanté*," said Marco. "The Dubois have told me you are a talented artist."

"I don't know about that," said Vidalia modestly.

"She is a very cultured little American," said Monsieur Dubois. "She attends the Beaux-Arts, goes to poetry readings, and her mother owns an art gallery in New York."

"Very nice," Marco said, stirring a cube of sugar into his coffee. "I think New York City is the best place in the U.S., no?" He looked up from his cup and gave a condescending smile.

"I'm from East Hampton, actually," said Vidalia.

"Oh?" Marco said. "And there are real artists in East Hampton?"

She'd spent about thirty seconds with this guy and she was already over him.

"A lot of great artists have lived there, actually," she said, a little defensively.

"For example?" Marco asked, raising an eyebrow.

"*For example*, Jackson Pollock," said Vidalia.

She'd been to the Pollock-Krasner house more times than she could count. Looking at his paintings—or even just photographs of them—made her feel like she'd drunk a gallon of coffee.

"He did all of the famous drip paintings at his house there," she added.

Marco nodded, watching her closely.

"And does your mother represent someone like Jackson Pollock?" he asked.

"Oh, well," Vidalia said airily. "She represents mostly sculptors."

It was the second time she'd done her riff on the gallery, and she felt inspired.

"There's this one who works in wood, Richard Hogan." Mr. Hogan was her sixth-grade shop teacher. "And Evelyn Wright"—Home Ec—"does cloth collage."

"Oh?" Marco asked, his blue eyes meeting hers across the coffee table, his mouth curled in a mocking smile. Vidalia had a sickening feeling that he knew she was lying.

She stopped, feeling suddenly, horribly exposed.

"And how is my little friend Clara?" asked Marco as he sipped his coffee.

"Ah!" said Monsieur Dubois enthusiastically. "She is brilliant, no, Catherine?"

Madame Dubois nodded, a little skeptically, Vidalia thought.

"She was first in all of her classes this year," Monsieur Dubois went on.

"Don't exaggerate, Roger," said Madame Dubois. Turning to Marco, she acknowledged, "She is very good in history."

"And English," said Monsieur Dubois. "Am I right, Vidalia?"

"Her English is great," agreed Vidalia.

A while later, Marco and the Dubois had finished their coffee, and Marco stood to leave.

"It's getting late," he said.

"Yes, and I take the train tomorrow," agreed Monsieur Dubois. "It is tiring this life of business travel," he said cheerfully.

"Yes, yes," said Madame Dubois. "And Vidalia, you need your sleep—you have class at the Beaux-Arts and the American Institute tomorrow."

"I know the American Institute," said Marco, meeting her eyes again.

"Oh?" she asked, trying to convey that she didn't really care.

"A friend took English classes there," he said. "It has a very nice courtyard."

"It does," agreed Vidalia coldly.

"Thank you for dinner," Marco said, turning to Madame Dubois.

"Of course," she said. "And tell your mother she must come to the country."

The kiss went smoothly this time, Marco's cheeks lightly touching Vidalia's.

"À la prochaine," Marco said. *See you next time.*

And then, finally, he was gone, and Vidalia could go to bed without breaking some French law that you have to sit with people and kiss them and be insulted by them even when you're beyond exhausted.

Madame Dubois started stacking plates and dishes at the dining-room table. Vidalia was about to say good night when Monsieur Dubois spoke.

"This Marco is very brilliant," he said.

Was he talking to her or to himself?

"I expect great things from him." He raised his glass, newly poured with scotch or whatever he was drinking.

"Oh," said Vidalia, and then because she didn't know what

else to say and also because she was curious, asked, "Where are you going tomorrow?"

"To Brussels," said Monsieur Dubois with a smile. "To conduct some business meetings. Nothing that would interest a young artist, I'm afraid."

"Well . . . good night," said Vidalia.

"Good night, Vidalia," he said.

"Good night," echoed Madame Dubois as she swept off to the kitchen, her arms full of dirty plates.

CHAPTER

 **6**

"YOU WILL ALL WORK on figures in your copies," Monsieur Benoît told the group of students at the beginning of Friday morning's class. They'd spent the week sketching hands and feet and heads from nine A.M. to noon every day. Though Monsieur Benoît hadn't been mean to Vidalia after that first day, the class still wasn't exactly fun. Actually, a lot of it just felt tedious. This morning, though, something new was happening. Vidalia and the rest of the students stood in front of easels and sketch paper. On a platform at the front of the room sat a naked woman.

"Today I want you to think about the body, the shape of the muscles, the forms that underlie what will mostly be, in your paintings, clothed figures. Of course we could spend an entire course on life drawing. Our time is limited, however, so be sure to take advantage of these pleasures of the flesh before we move on to the museum."

The class tittered at the joke. Caroline turned and rolled her eyes at Vidalia, who smiled. Vidalia was pleased that Caroline didn't want to speak English with her. *"Mon anglais est affreux"*—My English is awful—she'd said. Everyone else Vidalia met in Paris seemed to speak near-perfect English, so art class was the one place she really got to practice her French. Caroline had said that she and the other students were all in high school, too, and that they were all hoping to get into the École nationale supérieur des beaux-arts for college.

Vidalia drew tentatively at first, afraid to look too long at the woman in front of her. She'd never drawn a naked model before, and she felt rude staring at her. The other students' pencils scratched against paper. The model lay sideways on stacked pillows, her chin in her hand. After a few false starts, Vidalia sketched more quickly. She began to see the model not so much as a naked woman but as a series of forms, like Monsieur Benoît had said.

Twenty minutes before the end of class, Vidalia was done. In her opinion, the sketch she'd done looked a lot like the model.

Just for fun, and to use up the rest of class time, Vidalia changed the expression on the face. Now the woman in her drawing winked out at the viewer with a lecherous curl to her mouth. Vidalia grinned and stood back. Her drawing had personality. Next, she erased the hand that lay flat along the woman's leg, bent the arm at the elbow, and pointed a finger at the viewer. It was Uncle Sam's "I Want You" with a twist.

Monsieur Benoît paused by Vidalia's easel for the first time that day. She turned, nervously pleased with what she'd done, but Monsieur Benoît only scowled.

"If you want to draw cartoons, there must be a school for that somewhere in the United States," he said, his voice harsh.

Vidalia's smile fell away.

"But if you want to work with us here at the Beaux-Arts, then I would ask you to leave your *creativity* at home and concentrate on learning the skills that I am here to teach you."

Vidalia looked back at her sketch, wanting to melt into the ground, but Monsieur Benoît wasn't done.

"Shading, for example," he said. "Of which you seem to have a very poor grasp. Please take the rest of class time to look at the other students' work so that you may see what we are really working on here."

For the next ten minutes, she forced herself to walk around the room. Most people had left the face out entirely, concentrating instead on the contours of the figure and the shading, like Monsieur Benoît had said. The others had drawn the way the light fell from the high windows onto the model's shoulders, how her upper body shielded her torso, making it darker. Bruno, who was obviously the star of the class, had done an especially good drawing. All too clearly, she saw what Monsieur Benoît had seen, that her sketch was about a million miles behind everyone else's.

That afternoon as she sat in the darkened art history room looking at slides, Vidalia started to wonder what she was going to do with her Friday night. Madame Dubois had told her that morning that she and Clara would be going to Clara's grandparents' house for dinner. Monsieur Dubois, of course, was out of town. Vidalia had been surprised that Madame Dubois didn't invite her. The Dubois were turning out to be nothing like the second family she'd imagined. In fact, she'd started wondering why they'd even bothered to host her. Madame

Dubois had said it was to have someone for Clara to practice her English with, but considering how little time Vidalia actually spent with Clara, and how seldom Clara wanted to talk with her when they did spend time together, the whole thing seemed strange.

Madame Zafar flipped the lights on and clapped her hands as everyone in the room started standing and talking.

"Class, remember the reading you're to do for tomorrow. And don't forget that the entire institute will be going to Versailles next Monday afternoon, so our class will be canceled. That does not mean, however, that you don't have homework. On Monday, I will collect your paragraphs responding to one of the architectural forms we've discussed."

Vidalia walked out into the courtyard with the rest of the class. Becky kissed the skater guy—whose name was Kenji and who was from Boston—on the cheek and walked over to Vidalia. She sighed dramatically.

"Kenji's not coming," she said.

"To Avignon?" asked Vidalia. Becky and Heather were leaving with the Avignon group today.

"Yeah," said Becky. "I guess absence makes the heart grow fonder, though, right?" She smiled brightly. "Where's Heather?" she asked, looking around the courtyard. "We have to go soon." She turned back to Vidalia. "It's too bad you're not coming."

Becky looked closely at her.

"Why don't you want to?" she asked. "Is it because of Heather?"

Vidalia looked at her, startled.

"No," she said, feeling defensive and wondering what Heather had said to Becky about her. "I came here to be in Paris. I don't *want* to go away."

"What's up with you guys, anyway?" Becky asked, ignoring Vidalia's excuse. "I mean, Heather told me you used to be friends, but the two of you act really weird around each other."

"Nothing," Vidalia said, relieved to hear that that was all Heather had said. "We just stopped being close, I guess." If Heather wasn't going to tell Becky what had happened, then she certainly wasn't.

Just then, Heather walked into the courtyard. Becky waved energetically to her.

"Have a fun weekend," Vidalia said as Heather approached. "See you Monday."

"See you, V," said Becky. "Don't do anything I wouldn't do." She winked at her before turning to Heather.

Vidalia walked toward the back of the courtyard, trying to fit her art history notebook into her bag and find her sketchbook at the same time. She thought maybe she'd draw the trees, or the line of the roof against the sky, or the tables with the glass doors reflecting the late-afternoon light behind them. She didn't look up until she was just a step away from the farthest table to the back. And that was when she saw him. For a second she thought maybe she was hallucinating, but then he leaned back and smiled that same half-mocking smile at her.

"Hello, Vidalia," he said.

"Hi, Marco," she said.

"It's a nice courtyard," he said, looking around briefly.

"Yeah," she said. "It is." And she just stood there, waiting for some explanation, her arm still half-inside her bag.

"You don't go with your friends?" he asked, tilting his head toward the front of the courtyard.

Vidalia turned to see Becky and Heather walking out the door that led from the courtyard to the street.

"They're not really my friends," she said.

"Why not?" he asked.

"I don't know—I mean, I guess they are." She sat down at his table. He was leaning back, looking at her like he was waiting for something. "What are *you* doing here?"

He smiled.

"I come here to read sometimes," he said. "You made me remember when we meet at the Dubois' that evening." He paused. "And then I thought maybe I will see you again, too," he added, meeting her eyes quickly as he said "you."

In spite of herself, Vidalia's stomach did a tiny flip. What was going on here? She'd never gotten as much attention from guys in her life as she had in the past week.

Marco tapped his pack of Marlboros against the table and took one out. Then, hurriedly, like he'd caught himself being rude, he extended the pack to her. She started to say no, but then thought, *why not?* and took one. When she put it to her lips, he leaned toward her with his lighter. Their eyes met as the cigarette flared between them.

"So," she said, taking a drag and instantly remembering why she didn't smoke. "What do you do besides hang out in courtyards waiting for girls you don't know?"

He smiled.

"I do what I like to do," he said.

"Hmm," she said. "And how do you know the Dubois again?"

Marco took a drag from his cigarette. "They are very nice with me," he said. "Our families have known one another for a long time. Monsieur Dubois tries to help me." He shrugged like it didn't matter. "But what I want to ask," he said, "is are you interested in galleries? I am going to a show today, and I think you like art."

"Galleries?" she asked. "You mean right now?"

"Yes," he said. "Maybe it's too much for me to come here and ask you. . . ."

"No . . ." Vidalia started to answer. She was flattered and curious, about the gallery and about him. Marco seemed a lot nicer now than he had at the Dubois'.

"But I don't know a lot of people who want to go to these shows with me. I thought since you are new to Paris and you are an artist, maybe you will like it."

He shrugged and, for the first time, Vidalia thought he seemed nervous.

"Okay," said Vidalia, feeling more confident. "Why not?"

"You will come then?" he asked.

"Yeah," she said. "I'll come."

Marco smiled.

"*Allez,*" he said. "Go."

CHAPTER 7

THEY TOOK THE MÉTRO north, to a point on the map that Vidalia hadn't been to yet but that Marco told her would drop them off in Montmartre.

"It is where the artists stayed in the beginning of the century," he told her when they were standing on the Métro, holding on to the metal pole in the middle of the car. "Renoir and Picasso and Modigliani, all these guys."

"Oh," Vidalia said. "So no *real* artists." She was remembering what Marco had said to her about East Hampton when they met at the Dubois'.

He turned with a startled expression before he realized she was kidding, and then he laughed.

"No," he agreed. "Just a few little ones."

The Métro was running aboveground here, and Vidalia looked out at the buildings and trees as they passed. Unlike in New York, there was no air-conditioning on the train, so it was hot. The little glass windows were pulled open, and the breeze that blew in felt good. She moved her thick hair over one shoulder to let the air cool her neck.

"Anyway," Marco said, "this area once was very bohemian,

full of artists. It's still nice but it's very touristic, too."

"It's where that movie *Amélie* took place, isn't it?" Vidalia said, remembering the little cafés and narrow cobblestone streets of the film. She'd loved that movie, though more because of how much it made her want to go to Paris than for the story. The main character had been a little too goody-two-shoes for her taste.

"Yes, *exacte*," said Marco, smiling at her. Now that they were standing close to each other in the crowded train car, Vidalia noticed a scar on Marco's lip that folded when he smiled. Maybe he hadn't been mocking her with those crooked grins all along.

When they got off the train at Anvers, Marco led her down a cobblestone street, past white houses with cracked walls covered with vines and windows filled with boxes of red flowers.

"This is the touristic part," said Marco as they turned onto a cobblestone square. "La Place du Tertre."

The square was filled with café tables, where people sat under the trees, drinking espresso and glasses of beer, smoking cigarettes, and talking. Artists with easels and chairs surrounded the square on all sides, painting the buildings around them or drawing pencil portraits or caricatures of tourists, who sat very still in front of them.

"What are those?" asked Vidalia, approaching one vendor who was cutting a shape out of black paper.

"It's, how you say, a *silhouettiste*," said Marco.

"Oh, it's a silhouette," said Vidalia, walking closer and

seeing that, indeed, the older man was cutting out a perfect silhouette of the brown-haired woman who sat in front of him. Next, he did the woman's daughter, a little girl with curly red hair holding a doll.

"It looks just like you!" the mother said to the little girl, who laughed. They were American.

"It's not great art," said Marco apologetically.

"It's cool, though," said Vidalia. "So where's the gallery?"

"This way," Marco said with a shy smile.

They walked up a steep set of stairs, the white church of Sacré-Coeur looming over them, until they reached the top. It was hot out, and Marco and Vidalia were both breathing hard at the end of their climb. They paused and looked out over the city, hazy in the summer heat, while Marco smoked a cigarette.

"Wow," said Vidalia. "You can really see everything from up here, can't you?"

"Yes," agreed Marco. "There is the Louvre." He raised his hand and pointed. "And there, les Champs-Elysées."

Vidalia followed his pointing finger with her eyes.

"The Eiffel Tower," she said. Then she spotted a large blue building with red piping running along its side and asked, "What's that?"

"Ah, this is Beaubourg," Marco said. "You haven't been to this museum?"

"No, not yet," said Vidalia.

"We go there sometime," Marco said.

Vidalia's heart fluttered as she nodded. He was making plans with her.

"Ready?" asked Marco when he'd tossed his cigarette to the ground.

Vidalia nodded and followed him behind the church of Sacré-Coeur. Here, the streets were quieter. There were no artists painting portraits, and there were fewer tourists. After they'd walked a ways, Marco said, "Here," and led Vidalia into a gallery. Inside, giant yellow and black balloons of different shapes filled the space. Vidalia and Marco wandered among them, laughing at the funny shapes. At the next gallery, just down the street, they saw photographs of dirty-looking guys in dirty rooms. Marco made cynical comments about these, and said they were a little too *branché* for his taste.

"*Branché?*" asked Vidalia.

"You don't know *branché?*" Marco asked. "It mean very cool, you know, too much style."

"*Branché,*" Vidalia repeated again. She was learning new words every day.

The third gallery was showing old paintings in ornate frames that the artist had found and then "redecorated." He'd splashed brightly colored paint over their surfaces and tossed bits of yarn and broken glass on top. The darkened images of the originals peered out from around the edges of these additions.

"I like this guy," said Marco, standing in front of one where crimson paint had dripped over the edges of a small gold frame. "What do you think?"

"It's okay," Vidalia said, thinking about the paintings they looked at in art history and the busts in Monsieur Benoît's class. All she'd thought about since she'd gotten to Paris was classical French art. "I like how he's mixing old and new kinds of art," she said. Marco nodded, looking at the piece on the wall. There was a razor blade that looked like it was crusted with blood buried in the canvas. She could just see the head of one of the hunters from the original painting looking up from underneath it.

"Artists have always had to destroy the past to make something new," Marco said. "Everyone wants to preserve the past, put it carefully in glass cases, but the whole point is just to break the case." He met Vidalia's eyes, with that half-serious, half-mocking look.

She nodded slowly, thinking of Monsieur Benoît. What would he say about that? Come to think of it, she didn't really want to know.

"We go?" Marco asked. "There is just one more show I want to see."

In the next gallery, video monitors lined one long wall, each with a different person's face up close, looking at the camera. One guy with curly brown hair darted his eyes back and forth. A small woman with a colorful knit hat and a red nose sniffled. Vidalia and Marco walked the length of the gallery in silence, pausing in front of each face.

About halfway down, Marco turned to her and said quietly, "I wish they stop looking at me."

Vidalia giggled. It *was* kind of disconcerting to have all these faces staring out of the wall. They stepped past a black curtain into the next room, which, unlike the first, was noisy.

Here, the people on the screens were singing Madonna's "Like a Virgin." There was no background music, and every one of them sang at top volume, their voices joining in a cacophony of off-tune eighties pop.

One guy waved his arms over his head as he sang. A girl pumped her fists up and down. An older woman stood perfectly still and sang very seriously. Vidalia smiled shyly at Marco. He raised a skeptical eyebrow in response.

They walked through another black-curtained doorway into a darkened room with benches. On a screen in front of them, Katharine Hepburn slapped a man with his back to the camera across the face, over and over again. Vidalia and Marco sat down on one of the benches. They were the only people in the room.

"What do you think?" Marco whispered to her.

"I like it," Vidalia said.

"Really?" Marco didn't seem convinced.

"It's kind of a relief to see something modern," Vidalia said. "After all the classical stuff in art history. I mean, I love that, too, but this is . . ."

"More energy?" Marco asked.

"More . . . direct," she said, thinking of the cathedrals and the medieval paintings and how many secrets they seemed to hold.

Marco nodded like he was thinking about that.

Vidalia looked up at the film loop and felt its pure aggression. She thought of Monsieur Benoît and all his techniques. She thought of Jackson Pollock and his drip paintings. She thought of the slides Madame Zafar had shown them of the rose window at Chartres. It was all art. But how did it all fit together?

"Vidalia."

She turned to Marco, thinking maybe he was going to answer her question.

"You like Moroccan food?" he asked.

She paused for a moment, pulling herself out of her thoughts.

"I've never had it," she said.

Marco smiled.

"I think you like it," he said.

Vidalia didn't bother calling Madame Dubois to tell her she'd be late since the whole family was out tonight anyway. When she and Marco got off the Métro at Beaubourg, it was almost eight, and the bars and restaurants they passed were filling up. Marco led her to a restaurant that opened onto the street, its tables spilled from the inside out onto the sidewalk. Once they'd sat down just outside the restaurant's interior, Marco ordered a half carafe of white wine and dinner for them both.

"It's okay I order for you?" he asked. "You like lamb?"

Vidalia nodded, feeling flattered that he was taking such good care of her. None of the guys she'd gone out with at home had ordered for her when they got sandwiches at the deli in East Hampton. She almost laughed out loud at the thought.

Marco held up his glass, and Vidalia smiled as their glasses touched and their eyes met. She'd never been that interested in drinking cheap beer at keg parties in people's basements or on the beach, but this was nice. This was civilized.

"So, are you in college?" Vidalia asked.

"No." Marco held his pack of Marlboros out to her and she shook her head. "Everyone thinks I should go, but I stopped."

"How come?" Vidalia asked.

"Just bored," he said with a shrug. "Everyone say you have to do this, you have to get this diploma, you have to get this job—but I'm not learning anything, so what's the point? I guess I don't believe in the French way."

"Oh," said Vidalia. She had the opposite problem. She wanted to go to college but she was afraid she wouldn't be able to because of money, because of her mother.

"I want to do a gallery," he said. "Like your mother."

She glanced quickly up, but he was looking out at the street. Maybe she'd imagined that knowing look he'd given her at the Dubois'.

"But it takes a lot of money, and I don't have that," Marco continued.

Vidalia was surprised. She'd thought because his mother was friends with the Dubois and because of how new and crisp his black collared polo shirt was—open at the neck and snug around his lean torso—that he had enough money to do whatever he wanted.

"I'm starting now to sell some art," he said. "One piece here or there. That way I have some clients, make some money for the gallery when I'm ready." He smiled.

"Who do you sell to?" she asked.

"I try to meet collectors, make friends everywhere. The

Dubois bought one piece," he added, stubbing out his cigarette and looking around the restaurant.

"Really?" Vidalia said. "I guess they do have a lot of paintings at the apartment."

Marco nodded.

Just then the waiter arrived with the food. He placed a clay dish in front of Vidalia, lifting its cone-shaped top to release a cloud of spicy steam.

"It smells delicious," she said.

"Bon appetit," said Marco, lifting his fork over his plate and smiling at her.

"I told you me," Marco said once they'd each tried their food. "Now what about you? What is your art?"

"On Monday I'll start copying a painting at the Musée Apollinaire," she said.

"But I want to know what you do yourself," Marco insisted. "What is your own art?"

"It's hard to describe." She sighed. "They look cooler than they sound."

"Okay," he said, smiling, watching her, waiting.

"I spent the whole past year doing a series called *Rabbit House*," she started.

"Rabbits?" He laughed.

"Yup," she said, meeting his eyes across the table. "Bunny rabbits."

"Okay," Marco said. "Bunny rabbits."

She laughed at how that sounded with a French accent. But he was still looking at her, waiting for her to explain. So she did.

"I love this," Marco said when she'd finished describing the houses.

She gave him a skeptical look.

"It sounds funny and . . . real," he said. "Where does it come from?"

"What do you mean?" she asked.

"I mean, why do you make them? What is it inside you that says to you, 'Vidalia, make a house for bunny rabbits'?"

He said the last part in a deep voice and Vidalia laughed, but she could tell that he was really asking, too.

"I don't know," she said. "I started doing one in the fall, just for fun, and then I got totally into it. I'd think of an idea for one and it would lead to another idea, and then all of a sudden I'd be stenciling designs around the top of a wall in one room and filling another one with, like, heavy-metal posters. I mean, my mom has always been really into . . . interior design, so maybe it started with that." She didn't mention that her mother's version of interior design was to move ancient furniture from room to room, coming up with fanciful themes for the living and dining rooms, and had nothing to do with decorating magazines or fancy furniture stores. Once when Vidalia was little, they'd turned the dining room into an underwater scene. Vidalia had cut pictures of fish and sea life out of magazines, and her mother had arranged them on the newly painted blue walls.

Marco was nodding.

"It's interesting," he said. "I can see that houses are very, how you say, *évocatrices*?"

"Evocative?"

"Yes," he said. "Maybe especially when it is a family's house. There is a whole world, a whole past and future that exists there."

"Yeah," Vidalia said. "Exactly. It's like every house is its own universe, with its own rules, and everything in it depends on the people who live there. I always figured out the family first—how many kids there were, if both parents were around, if there were grandparents. In a way it was really about inventing those families and their stories more than anything else."

"This must be exciting," Marco said.

"It was," Vidalia said. "It was all I could think about for so long." She paused. "That's what I miss with what I'm doing now. I thought I'd feel that way again in this class, but instead it's like I go in there every day and I'm just trying to follow the rules. I feel trapped."

"Maybe this will change," Marco said. "Maybe it gets easier to break the rules."

He smiled at her and his lip curled on one side.

"Yeah," she said. "I hope so."

When they'd finished their food, Marco leaned across the table and spoke quietly. "You want to go?"

"Okay," she said, looking around for the waiter.

"The server, we haven't seen him for a long time," Marco said, looking at her, his eyes warm. "Let's go."

"Go . . . ?" Vidalia looked at him, confused.

"They make a lot of money here tonight, no?" He looked back at the full restaurant. It had gotten dark since they'd been sitting there, and more and more people were filling the place. "You think they need ours?"

Vidalia looked uncertainly at him.

"Allez," he said for the second time that day.

And, without really thinking about it, but ready to follow him, Vidalia said, "Okay."

They stood and moved through the cluster of tables to the sidewalk. Vidalia didn't dare look back as they walked to the corner. When they turned onto a small side street, Marco said, "Run!" and Vidalia stifled a scream in her chest as she ran alongside him. He grabbed her wrist and they turned a corner onto another narrow street and kept running, their feet hitting the cobblestones together, until, finally, they reached a big boulevard, and burst out into the light of the cafés and the cars and the streetlamps. Vidalia saw some faces turn curiously to them as they bent over, laughing and gasping for breath.

"What . . . ?" Vidalia laughed. "Why did . . . ?"

Marco stood up and smiled at her.

"You are a good runner," he said.

"Thanks," she said. "You're not so bad yourself."

Marco stepped toward her and she straightened, her laughter slowing as he looked at her with an intensity that made her go numb. He pushed a piece of hair back from her forehead, standing close to her.

He's about to kiss me, she thought.

But then Marco stepped back.

"Bon," he said. "Thank you for this night."

"Oh, yeah, I mean . . ." Vidalia stumbled.

"You know how to get home from here?" he asked.

Vidalia looked around. Was he really about to leave? They

were standing by the Filles du Calvaire Métro stop. She'd figured out how to follow the Métro map and she was pretty sure
that she wasn't far from home. She nodded, still breathing
hard, still confused.

"Better not to tell the Dubois that you saw me," he said,
taking another step away from her, and now his smile looked
mocking again.

"I won't," she said.

"Good night, Vidalia." Marco raised one hand.

"Good night," she answered, and then he turned and
walked down the crowded street, leaving her breathless, and
alone.

When she got back to the Dubois', it was just a little before
eleven and Vidalia decided to try going up the back stairwell
that Clara had told her about instead of through the apartment. No danger of the Dubois smelling wine on her breath
that way. Slowly, she walked up the creaking, narrow stairs,
all the way to the top floor.

Vidalia just wanted to get into bed and close her eyes and
think of Marco, but when she took out the phone Clara had
given her to set the alarm, she saw that she had a message.

"Vidalia . . ."

It was her mother's voice. From the sound of it she wasn't
far from a meltdown.

"There's . . ." Her mother paused, and Vidalia could hear
her holding back tears. "Something's gone a little . . . wrong."
Another choky pause. "Please call me, darling. I might need
some advice from you."

Her voice rose at the end like she was trying to sound cheerful, like whatever this was, it wasn't a big deal. Which was bullshit. Vidalia knew perfectly well this was an SOS. She turned off her phone and gave a frustrated groan.

Did she have to return the call now? Couldn't she just wait until the next morning?

But her mother was probably waiting by the phone. No, she had to call, if only because Vidalia knew she'd never get to sleep until she did.

"Hello?"

"Hi, Mom."

"Oh, darling!" Her mother's relief came crashing through the phone.

"What's going on?" Vidalia asked. "I just got your message."

"Happy Fourth of July!" her mother cried. "I don't suppose the French are celebrating?"

"Oh, no, I completely forgot about it. But Mom, you sounded upset in your message."

"Oh, well . . ." Her mother's voice grew tentative, almost shy. "There's a little problem with the . . . lights."

"With the *lights*? What, you need Mr. Nichols to change a bulb for you?"

"No, no, it's *all* of the lights." Her mother's voice was frightened. "They're off."

Vidalia paused.

"All the lights are off," she echoed.

"Yes." Her mother sounded relieved now that Vidalia understood the situation.

"And they won't go back on," Vidalia clarified.

"No, darling, that's what I'm telling you, the *electricity* has been shut off!"

"How can the . . . Oh, no. Did you send that check?"

"What check?"

"Mom, the check I told you to leave out for the mailman. The one for the electricity. Did you do that?"

"I don't . . . I don't think so." Her mother sounded like a wilting violet again.

"So you *never* sent it? Like, it's still sitting on the table in the front hall?"

She could practically see her mother peering around the corner at the table.

"Yes," her mother said, confident now. "Here it is."

"Okay," sighed Vidalia. "What time is it there?"

"Just a little before five," her mother said hopefully, like she was trying to get the right answer in class.

"There might still be time to call them," Vidalia said, reaching into her bag for a pen and her art history notebook. "Find the Long Island Power Authority number on the bill in there."

She could hear her mother obediently tearing the envelope.

"Here it is, darling." She was all business as she read the number. Vidalia scrawled it down in her sketch pad.

"I'll see if they can take care of this today. I don't know, though. It's pretty late and tomorrow's Saturday. Ugh, I'll call you back, okay?"

"Yes, darling, whatever you think is best. I trust you."

Vidalia rolled her eyes. She hated hearing her mother go all docile and little-girly like that. It made it seem like Vidalia would have to take care of her forever.

Once she made it through the voice-mail maze and got a person on the phone at the Long Island Power Authority, it took a few minutes to figure out what had happened.

"We haven't had a payment since May third," the woman on the other end of the line said. "We sent out several notices. The power gets turned off after eight weeks, you know, that's just how they do it."

"Not since May?" Vidalia was stunned. "How is that possible? The check must have gotten lost or something. I'm sure I paid it." But then she wondered if during exams and the spring art show preparations, she *had* forgotten. Which would mean that when her mother hadn't paid this one, it had been two months, not one.

"All I can tell you is that we did not receive payment," said the woman.

"Okay, well let me pay you now then." Vidalia gave up trying to understand and just read the account and check number over the phone. "When will the lights go back on?" she asked when the process was finished.

"It usually takes a few hours, but it's Friday night. There's no telling if they'll do it before Monday." She sounded regretful. "You'd better tell your mother to get some candles out."

"Thanks," Vidalia sighed. "I'll do that."

After she hung up, she wondered if her mother even *had* candles. She called Mr. Nichols and asked him to bring some over. Then she called her mother again.

"I don't know exactly when the power will be back on, Mom, but Mr. Nichols is coming over to give you a flashlight and candles."

"Oh, Kirby's coming?" Her mother's voice got high and excited. Vidalia rolled her eyes. "I'll have to make him something to eat."

"Well, if you can cook in the dark, then go ahead," said Vidalia. "I'll call you tomorrow to see if the lights are back on, okay?"

"Yes, of course," said her mother. She sounded distracted, and Vidalia knew she wanted to go get ready. Since Mr. Nichols was the only guest she could stand to have, it was always a big deal when he came by.

Vidalia lay awake in bed. She tried hard not to think about her mother, replacing the image of her in the dark with one of Marco. She pictured him stepping toward her, touching her hair. Why had he walked away? And what had his smile meant? All Vidalia knew for sure was that even though her mother's crisis was under control, she wasn't getting to sleep anytime soon.

CHAPTER

 **8**

MADAME DUBOIS WAS ABOUT to take Clara to her horseback-riding lesson when Vidalia came downstairs on Saturday morning.

"Did you have a good evening last night?" Madame Dubois asked.

"*Oui*," said Vidalia, the image of Marco across the table flashing through her mind. "I had fun." She wondered if Madame Dubois would ask her what she'd done and quickly tried to think of some school thing that would sound right. But Madame Dubois didn't seem curious at all about Vidalia's nighttime activities.

"Again tonight we will not be here," said Madame Dubois. "Clara will stay with a friend, and I have a dinner engagement. Monsieur Dubois is away until Tuesday."

Vidalia thought she saw Clara scowl under her riding helmet.

"Okay," said Vidalia.

"I've left some food in the refrigerator for you, and there is bread and cheese."

"Great," said Vidalia.

"Call me if you need anything," finished Madame Dubois.

When they were gone, Vidalia drank her coffee and sketched for a while before taking the Métro over to the bookstore.

"Vidalia!" Julien cried when she walked in the front door.

"Julien!" she cried back at him.

"I'm sorry," he said right away. "I didn't have your phone number, but I have to work until six today after all. Someone called in sick this morning, and no one else can do the register."

He looked really sorry.

"Oh." Vidalia was disappointed. "Okay, well . . ."

"But I'm having people over to my place for dinner tonight," he continued, brightening, "and I hope you can come for that."

"That sounds good," Vidalia said. "How do I get there?"

"Can you meet me back here at six?" he asked. "Then I can just show you and it's easier. You can help me to do the shopping, too," he said with a smile.

"Oh, I get it," said Vidalia. "You just want me to carry your bags for you."

"*Ah, non!*" he cried, but Vidalia was already halfway out the door, laughing.

"See you at six," she said, and stepped back into the hot afternoon.

With several hours to kill, Vidalia decided to take the Métro to the Louvre. Monsieur Dubois had pointed out the magnificent glass pyramid in front of the museum as they drove by on the way from the airport that first day, but Vidalia had yet to venture inside. She entered the pyramid with a crowd of

English tourists and took the escalator downstairs. She hardly noticed the time passing, and at the end of the afternoon, she felt like she was on a cloud, floating among mythological battles, shafts of light that fell across babies' foreheads and dancing nymphs.

Emerging again into the heat of the late summer afternoon, Vidalia remembered that she wanted to call her mother to make sure the lights had gone back on. She found a phone booth and took her calling card from her bag.

"Everything is fine now, darling," her mother assured her, obviously in a good mood. "Kirby was here. Oh, we had a wonderful time with the candles and everything!"

Vidalia was relieved to hear that things were back to normal.

When she got to the bookstore just after six, Julien was ready for her.

"Hey, Vidalia." It was Margie, walking in with a stack of books in her arms. "You doing the shopping with Julien?"

"Looks like it," she said.

"Let's go," Julien said. "You'll meet us at my place later, okay, Margie?"

Vidalia followed Julien from store to store, watching him choose the perfect tomatoes from the vegetable stand and point out the loaf of bread he wanted at the bakery. At Monoprix, a big grocery store, they bought butter, cream, bacon, and dark chocolate.

Julien made her laugh on their way back to his apartment by describing how unpredictable Henry was. For one thing, he'd recently decided that Julien was the only one who could run the cash register other than himself. Henry's trust in him made Julien's life kind of hellish, though, because it meant he wanted Julien there all the time.

"I practically had to wrestle him to get the night off," Julien finished with a sigh. "It's why I had to cancel this afternoon. He just wouldn't let me go."

"Well, at least you know your work is valuable to him." Vidalia laughed.

"It's a crazy place," Julien said. "But Henry really loves it, and that gives it a lot of life, a lot of energy."

Julien lived on a narrow street halfway up a hill. When they reached his building, they walked up the five flights to his tiny top-floor room. It was a *chambre de bonne* just like Vidalia's, except that the window looked out over the street instead of up at the sky. A cow with wings hung from the ceiling. Julien swung it at Vidalia as she walked in.

"How do you cook in here?" Vidalia asked, looking around at the absence of a kitchen.

"Just a hot plate," he said, pointing. "But I have a beautiful dining room."

Vidalia looked around, confused.

"Up on the roof!" said Julien.

"Ah," she said, sitting at the desk as Julien unpacked groceries onto a small table.

"Here," he said. "Chop."

Vidalia turned to find a cutting board and garlic in front of her on the desk.

The garlic was sizzling in oil on the hotplate when Margie

and Andy, the poet from the reading, appeared. They squeezed into the room.

"Oh God, Julien, that smells so good," said Margie. "I don't know how you cook in here. All I can do in my room are sandwiches."

"Up to the roof," said Julien, handing them dishes and silverware to carry. "It's almost ready."

Margie led the way out of the room, up a narrow staircase, and through a door onto the rooftop. There was a table in the middle and a view of the city skyline in front of them. Julien came after with a tablecloth thrown over one arm and a bowl of cream-drenched pasta flecked with bacon in his hands.

"Henry was going mad after you left, Julien," Margie said, taking the tablecloth and spreading it over the little table. "You saw him, right, Andy?"

"I did." Andy took an enormous forkful of pasta as soon as Julien served him.

"What's the problem?" Julien asked.

"Oh, the orders are off and everything's wrong for the whole next month. You know, he just flips out every time you leave the store. That's all there is to it."

"You've got the magic touch, Julien," said Andy.

"Yeah, and *you* don't have to do a thing, *Monsieur le poète*," said Margie. "Sitting up there at your desk while the rest of us scurry around doing Henry's bidding."

"I'm the writer-in-residence, that's what I'm supposed to do," Andy said plaintively. "Besides, I'm no good at shelving." He grinned at Vidalia.

"Scribbling verse," Margie said in a fake-disgusted voice.

They sat for a long time over dinner, and Vidalia couldn't help thinking how pleased her mother would be if she could see her here, hanging out with literary types on a rooftop in Paris. But even though she felt happy and comfortable, something was missing. It was Marco, she realized. She missed the excitement of the night before.

When dinner was finally done, Margie declared that she had to go meet Michel, her French boyfriend.

"Why didn't you bring him?" asked Julien.

Margie waved a hand. "Oh, you know, he's always having dinner with *Maman*. These French boys don't know how to cut the apron strings."

"Oh!" cried Julien. "That's a lie."

Everyone laughed as Andy and Margie both stood to go. Soon, Vidalia was alone at the table with Julien. They sat in the dimming light, eating squares of dark chocolate and drinking espresso. Julien was across from her at the table, his legs up on a chair.

"What's your home like?" he asked. "In New York?"

"Kind of crazy," she sighed.

Julien laughed.

"What does that mean?" he asked.

"We live in this big old place," she said. "It's been in my family for generations, and it's packed full of stuff."

"You and your parents?" he asked.

"It's just my mom and me," said Vidalia. "I guess she's the one who's crazy, more than the house."

"Oh?" Julien asked, looking at her across the table. She

couldn't see his face that clearly now. She traced the rim of her water glass with her finger.

"What kind of crazy?" asked Julien after a minute.

"She's kind of . . . helpless," Vidalia said. "She doesn't go out much." Vidalia looked up at Julien, but all she could see was the shape of his curly hair and his arm on the table, his reassuring square hands, the line of rooftops behind him. "Or ever, actually."

"For how long?" he asked, not sounding shocked the way Vidalia always thought people would if she told them.

"Well, it happened kind of slowly," she said. "But the last time I remember her leaving the house was in September. She drove to the farm stand for vegetables."

"September?" Now he did sound sort of shocked. "That's almost a year."

"I mean, it's possible she's gone out while I was at school or something," she said. "But I doubt it."

They sat in silence for a minute or two until Julien spoke again.

"Why?" he asked.

"I don't know," Vidalia answered. "I mean, even when I was little she didn't like going out." She was surprised by her desire to tell him. "I never really thought about it, but as soon as I was old enough to bike home from school, I started doing that. And she'd never go to teacher conferences, stuff like that."

Vidalia paused to drink the last cold sip of espresso from the bottom of her cup.

"It got really bad right when I was about to start high school. There was an orientation day where the parents came and met the teachers. She was acting weird all day, like she kept trying to hold my hand. It was totally embarrassing, you know? To be starting high school holding my mom's hand."

She shook her head.

"Then, at the end of the day, there was this big assembly where the principal talked. The whole place was full. I could feel her getting more and more freaked out next to me, like looking around and stuff, and then she just stood up. Everyone was staring at her, and the principal stopped talking. I whispered to her to sit down, but instead she pushed her way past all these people and ran out of the auditorium."

"What did you do?" asked Julien.

"I just kind of sank down in my seat."

Vidalia laughed even though it wasn't funny.

"Once the principal started talking again, I got up and went after her. I found her in the hallway, crouched down against the wall, all by herself, crying. I was terrified. I wanted to get the nurse or something, but she kept saying, 'Take me to the car, take me to the car.' So finally I did." Taking a bite of chocolate, Vidalia continued. "She got it together enough to drive home but then didn't go out for maybe a month afterward. Then things got better for a while after that, and she'd go out for groceries and things. It comes and goes."

"What about your father?" Julien asked, hesitating slightly.

"Oh," said Vidalia dismissively. "I don't have one."

"Well . . ." Julien said with a smile.

"Yeah, I mean, I guess there had to be one, but I've never met him. My mom says he was a ship that passed in the night." She spoke in a singsong voice, mimicking what she'd heard her mother say more than once. "He had no interest in meeting me or anything, and I've never really cared enough to try to find him. I feel like I've got enough parental issues without going looking for more."

Julien laughed and nodded.

"So you take care of her?" he asked after a pause.

Vidalia nodded.

"Only you?" he asked.

She nodded again.

"I have an aunt who lives kind of nearby, but she and my mother had some big fight a few years ago, so we hardly ever see her. Mom's afraid she'll try to take the house away from her or something. But Aunt Pat can give me rides places if I have to go somewhere far or get things at the big stores for us. Still, my mom doesn't want Aunt Pat knowing that she doesn't go out anymore. That's a secret."

"It sounds like a lot of work," he said.

"I guess," Vidalia said, shrugging. "I'm pretty used to it. I've looked things up online—you know, psychological conditions." She put on a serious voice. "My diagnosis is agoraphobia with bipolar tendencies."

"It's too much," Julien said softly.

Vidalia didn't answer. Too much or not, it was just the way it was. What did he think she should do? Call the authorities?

Have her mother put in a mental hospital? Get sent to live with uptight Aunt Pat and her spoiled-brat cousins in Hampton Bays? She heard a siren in the distance.

"This is the first time I've ever been away from her," she said, looking down at the tablecloth and smoothing it with her thumbnail. "I mean, I went on trips with my aunt and my cousins a couple of times when I was a kid, but . . . I don't really know how this is going to turn out."

"Why?" he asked. "What's wrong?"

"I don't know," she said, cringing. "My mom left me this message last night and the electricity had gone out. I had to make all these calls. . . ."

Julien nodded and reached out to put his hand over hers. It felt reassuring, not romantic. To her surprise, Vidalia realized she was about to start crying. She bent her head and tried to stop it but the tears were already rolling down her cheeks.

"It's okay," said Julien, keeping his hand on hers. "It will be okay."

She gave up and let herself cry, feeling safe here on Julien's roof, with the city down below and his warm hand on hers. She nodded through her tears, trying to believe that he might be right, that maybe, somehow, it *would* be okay.

CHAPTER

 **9**

MONDAY MORNING, VIDALIA TOOK the Métro to the Musée Apollinaire, which was in an old church at the southern edge of the city. She'd spent the day before at the Musée d'Orsay and this museum was nothing like that one, where marble statues filled the long hall of what was once a railway station. Walking in through a little garden, Vidalia passed a guard, who waved her inside when she showed him the student ID that meant she didn't have to pay. Inside, paintings lined the walls and light from the stained-glass windows made patterns on the floor. All the pews had been taken out and walls had been erected where the aisle would have been, adding space for more paintings. It felt mysterious and almost magical, nothing like the grandiosity of the Louvre. For the first time since she'd started her art class, Vidalia thought maybe something good could come out of it.

"This museum houses a small medieval and Renaissance collection," Monsieur Benoît said when they'd all gathered around. "It is not bad. There are some interesting paintings, and it is quiet, a good place to work."

He looked around at the group.

"Now, you will begin by choosing a painting to copy. And

don't trouble yourselves too much about which one you select. If your painting is a failure, you will do another one after."

He gave a dismissive wave and the class dispersed. Vidalia hoped hers wouldn't be a failure, though the way things had been going, she didn't have a lot of confidence.

Most of the paintings were smallish portraits. The first one Vidalia looked at was of a smooth-skinned bald man. He wore a blue-and-gold hat and a red shirt that puffed out at the shoulders and cinched in at the waist. He looked haughty and disapproving, not like someone she wanted to spend five weeks with. The next was of a girl with pale skin and a sweet expression. Her yellow dress had intricate lace at the collar, and she held a string of beads wrapped around her fingers. This one might be fun, but Vidalia figured she'd look at the others before deciding.

She held her sketchbook under one arm and walked away from the other students, who were gathered by the portraits. Caroline had already taken out her pencil and pad and was sketching. Bruno was talking and gesturing to Monsieur Benoît, who nodded seriously at him. Going toward the back of the church, Vidalia saw that one painting hung alone at the center of the far wall. It was bigger than the portraits, maybe five feet across and four feet tall.

In the foreground, a girl sat on a patch of green grass. She had long brown hair that fell in soft curls over her shoulders. Her heavy purple dress was embroidered with gold. Her head turned slightly to one side as she looked down at her lap, where a small, goatlike unicorn rested its head. The animal gazed up at her, its long horn crossing her torso. Her hand, fingers outstretched, wrist delicately bent, stroked its neck. The grass of the clearing where they sat rose steeply behind them to a dark thicket of trees. Overhead, the blue sky was dotted with puffs of cloud, and in the top left corner, an icy, bluish cathedral seemed to hover over the scene.

"This is a late medieval work," said a voice behind her. Monsieur Benoît. He stood with hands behind his back, feet apart. "It is the best painting in the collection."

"I want to paint this one," she said.

"It is too difficult," Monsieur Benoît said. "You should choose one of the portraits like the others." He gestured to where the other students were setting up easels behind them. But even the girl in the yellow dress looked stuffy and dull to Vidalia now.

"No," she said with a hint of desperation. "I want to do this one."

The teacher looked at her, his face unreadable. Vidalia had to struggle to hold his gaze, but she knew she couldn't spend the summer with one of the portraits, even the girl in the yellow dress—not when this painting was here. Finally, Monsieur Benoît turned his eyes back up to the painting.

"It is your choice," he said. "But you may have a lot of difficulty with this."

She nodded, wishing she could promise to do a good job. If she'd learned one thing in this class so far, though, it was that she couldn't guarantee that her work would please *le Maître*.

Monsieur Benoît nodded, then stalked off to the other side of the room. Vidalia breathed a sigh of relief. Before opening her sketchbook, she leaned over to read the name of the painting on the small brass plaque: *La jeune fille à la licorne—The Young Girl and the Unicorn.*

That afternoon, when she came out of art history, Vidalia took three steps before letting herself look toward the back of the courtyard. And even though she'd been telling herself all day that Marco wouldn't be there, she felt a dull thud deep inside her chest when she saw the empty table. It was the same on Tuesday. It didn't matter how many times she told herself that she didn't really want to see him—that he was weird and dishonest and she'd rather hang out with Julien—when he wasn't there, she felt like crying.

By Wednesday, she was nearly over it. It had been five days since her date (was that what it was?) with Marco, and she told herself not to care that he wasn't coming back. She was so determined that she didn't let herself look toward the back of the courtyard when she came outside, stopping instead to talk to Becky, who was already seated at a table in the middle of the courtyard.

"What about Brittany, Vidalia?" Becky asked. "Can we convince you to come with us this time?"

Vidalia started to say something noncommittal, but just then Kenji walked up behind Becky and started rubbing her shoulders.

"Kenji's coming, right?" Becky said, tilting her head back to look up at him.

"Where, Brittany?" he said. "Totally." He gazed adoringly down at Becky, who winked at him.

"See, V?" Becky said. "You should come."

"I'll think about it," Vidalia said.

Becky and Kenji started cooing and whispering to each other then, so Vidalia thought it was a good time to remove herself. Casually, she turned to look to the back of the courtyard, just to confirm that Marco wasn't there. And there he was, looking right at her, smiling, waiting.

"See you later," Vidalia said as she walked away from the table, ducking her head so that Marco wouldn't see how giddy she was. He smiled up at her, his blue eyes creasing at the corners. Somehow, the second she saw him, she knew that whatever they'd started last week hadn't ended at all.

"Nice courtyard, huh?" she asked, pausing in front of him.

"Very nice," he agreed.

"A great place to read," she added, sitting.

"The best," he said, holding up a thin paperback. He leaned forward and linked his index finger around hers. "And not bad for meeting a pretty American, too."

Vidalia felt herself blush.

"What are you doing today?" he asked.

"I don't know," she said. "What are you doing?"

"A new artist," he said. "Her first show. You want to come?"

She leaned back and looked at him, pretending to think about it.

"Yeah," she said. "I'll go."

They walked slowly to the Luxembourg Gardens after leaving the institute, through the big metal gates and past the apiary, where bees hummed around their wooden hutches. There were other people walking slowly and sitting in the chairs and benches reading or just watching pedestrians go by. Vidalia and Marco walked a few feet apart, weaving closer every once in a while, then apart again.

"What'd you do over the weekend?" she asked him as casually as she could. She didn't want to say, *Why didn't you call me?* but he must have caught something in her voice because he looked quickly up at her.

"I'm sorry I didn't call," he said. "I had a trip that came up suddenly, and I never got your phone number last week." He looked worried.

"That's not what I meant," she said, even though it had been.

"I didn't think it was a good idea to call Roger and Catherine and tell them, 'I'm looking for your little American, please.'" He said this in a goofy voice that made her laugh.

"What was the trip?" she asked to change the subject.

"To Geneva," he said. "An old guy died. He was from an important family. Sometimes you find interesting things in the estates."

"Oh, yeah?" she said, looking up at him. So he really did travel around buying art. "And did you?"

He shrugged.

"Three little country paintings. Nothing exciting, but I can sell them."

Vidalia felt her phone vibrate in her bag. When she took it out, she saw the number from home flashing on her screen. Her mother. She hadn't talked to her since checking in on Saturday morning to make sure she'd gotten through the night.

Vidalia had been meaning to call again, but she didn't want to talk to her now. She pressed DECLINE and dropped the phone back into her bag.

"Who will you sell them to?" she asked.

"There is one buyer I know who takes a lot. He sells to museums, bigger collectors. Maybe him."

Just then Marco's phone beeped.

"I take this," he said, looking at his screen. "Excuse me."

He wandered off to the side of the path under the shade of one of the big trees. Vidalia walked to the opposite side and sat on a bench. She glanced up to see him talking and gesturing.

After taking out her phone, she dialed to listen to her messages.

"Vidalia," her mother's voice said shakily. "Please call home. I have to speak with you." Then she tried to sound cheery. "The lights went back on." Her voice sank again. "But there's something else. Call me, darling."

Vidalia looked over at Marco. He was facing away from her, with his head down. She didn't want to call, but the thought of her mother alone in the house, waiting by the phone, was almost nauseating. She pulled out her phone card and dialed. Her mother picked up right away.

"Hello?"

"Hi, Mom," she said. "I got your message."

"Oh, baby," her mother said. "I'm so glad you called." She paused.

"What's up?" Vidalia asked, biting the side of her lip and

leaning forward slightly. Whatever it was, she wanted to get the conversation over with and get on with her evening.

"It's about the groceries," her mother said.

Vidalia waited.

"They came three hours later than they were supposed to, and the herbs were no good at all." She sounded like she was about to cry. "The basil had brown spots! Vidalia, I can't stand going through the summer without having fresh produce from the farm stands." She ended with an outraged half sob.

"So go to the farm stand," Vidalia said slowly.

Her mother seemed not to have heard her.

"Darling, I know you're having a good time over there, but I was thinking maybe you could come home a little early."

"What?" Vidalia looked at the garden around her, at the people moving slowly through the dappled sun that fell through the leaves, at Marco leaning against the broad pale trunk of a tree, talking. He looked up and raised his hand to her.

"You help me so much. I don't know what to do without you," her mother said.

"Mom, I've only been here a week and a half." Vidalia felt herself getting angry. "I can't come home yet."

"I guess I just wasn't prepared for you to go. But if you could come home and help me now . . ." Her voice was tearful. "I just thought if you did that, then maybe you could go back to Paris next summer, for the whole year even."

Marco was walking toward her across the gravel path.

"I'll think about it, Mom," Vidalia lied. She was pretty sure her mother would get over this if she just humored her for a little while.

"All right," her mother said weepily. "I suppose that's all I can ask."

"I'll call you later," Vidalia told her. "I have to go now, though. Bye, okay?"

Marco was next to her. She dropped the phone back into her bag.

"Something's wrong?" he asked, stopping in front of her and looking into her eyes.

She took a breath and tried to relax as she smiled. "No," she said. "Everything's fine."

"Good." He nodded and smiled back at her in a watchful way.

Vidalia stood, almost choking on a wave of anger that rose up unexpectedly. How could her mother do this to her? She always needed so much—*too* much, like Julien had said. Well, Vidalia had earned this summer, and she wasn't giving it away just to go to the farm stand for her mother.

"Let's go," she said. Marco nodded, and they walked down the path to the big iron gate that led out of the garden.

They stopped at a café before going to the art show, and by the time they got to the gallery, it was almost nine and the place was packed. Marco led Vidalia inside through crowds of people to a table off to the right, where a skinny guy in a black T-shirt and black-framed glasses was pouring wine into plastic cups and looking frantic.

"Leila!" he called. "I need more red!"

Marco picked up two cups and handed one to Vidalia, then led her by the elbow to the other side of the room.

"You want to look at the art?" he asked close to her ear. She nodded, feeling his breath on her cheek.

They pushed through the wall of people so that they were in a narrow alley between the crowd and the walls. The paintings were black and blue and pink, and they were all of little girls—girls with rounded bellies wearing tube tops, girls sitting on the floor and talking on telephones too big for their ears, girls lying on beds looking up at the sky, girls leaning into one another's arms. Looking at them, Vidalia felt the same spark of excitement that had kept her going on the rabbit houses for the whole year. This was art the way she knew and loved it. This had nothing to do with the tedium of class or the tyranny of Monsieur Benoît and his old masters. She missed the flights of inspiration and the thrill of what she'd done before. They moved along the wall until they reached a door at the back. Here was a small closetlike space with just a few paintings in it. Vidalia and Marco were the only ones inside, the crowd just behind them in the main gallery.

"You like them?" Marco asked, his voice low and close.

"Yeah," she said. She could understand these girls, she thought, how they were bored or lonely or tired, and how there was no escape from feeling that way, no escape from themselves.

"Me, too," Marco said, and he took her hand and squeezed it.

The warmth of his hand and the thrill of his closeness combined with the excitement of the paintings on the walls. They were beautiful, she thought, and Marco got it. The voices and the heat were like a heavy curtain around them. For no reason except that she could, Vidalia reached out and touched the painting, running her finger along one girl's curved back. When she turned to Marco, his eyes had the same shine she'd seen at the restaurant last Friday.

"It's so small," he said. "You could fit it in your bag." He smiled like he was teasing her, but was he? Or did he mean it?

He was right—it would fit in her bag. Vidalia held his gaze as she reached her hand to the wall and touched the edge of the painting again. They were alone together in this little room. How would she have felt, she wondered, if someone had taken one of her rabbit houses at the spring art show? It would have been bad, she thought, but it would have meant that someone wanted it, too—maybe even needed it—and that was flattering. She looked at Marco. He thought she should do it, she could tell. Her hand was tentative at first, then more confident as she lifted the canvas from the wall. Marco's eyes were bright with excitement. She felt the air get sucked out of the room. People were talking, laughing, drinking in the bigger gallery, but nobody saw Vidalia and Marco, who stood close together, their bodies shielding the painting from view. It slid easily into her bag. She turned to Marco and smiled, and the sound broke over her like a wave, the world around her suddenly felt real again. Marco took her hand and pulled her through the crowd.

"Let's go," he said. Vidalia nodded and followed him as he moved, unhurried, through the room. Before they reached the door, Vidalia felt someone push in beside her. It was a girl with olive skin and wavy black hair.

"Marco," the girl said, and she looked glad to see him in a way Vidalia couldn't help hating.

"*Salut, Leila,*" he said. Vidalia turned to Marco and then back to the girl.

"Vidalia, this is Leila, an old friend," he said. "Leila, this is Vidalia."

Leila looked Vidalia up and down with a tight smile, and Vidalia, her heart racing, smiled back at her as coolly as she could.

"Leila is an assistant in this gallery," Marco said.

"*Enchantée,*" said Vidalia. She was surprised Marco hadn't told her before that he knew people here. Leila looked like she was about to say something, but just then a small blonde woman in a silver dress appeared next to her.

"Leila," she said breathlessly. "Help me—I don't know what to say to these people." Her blue eyes darted over the crowd and then came to rest on Marco and Vidalia. She spoke with some kind of an accent. Leila nodded to her.

"This is Ruby," she said, more to Marco than to Vidalia. "It's her show tonight."

Vidalia felt herself go hollow as she looked at Ruby. Somehow she hadn't thought about the person who had made these paintings, a person like her, a person who would be really upset when she found out that one of them had been stolen.

"Uh, hi," said Vidalia. *Chill,* she thought, *just chill.* But she felt like her bag was about to burst into flames at her side. "I like your work." She smiled in a way that she hoped didn't look like she was going to puke.

"Thank you," said Ruby. She turned back to Leila. "They all want to talk about money," she whispered in French. "I don't know what to say. Am I supposed to negotiate prices?"

"No," said Leila firmly. "Tell them they have to talk to Anne."

Ruby looked back at Vidalia and shook her head.

"It's my first show," she said apologetically in English. "I'm a nightmare."

Vidalia smiled nervously.

"Come," said Leila. "We'll talk to Anne."

She leaned over and kissed Marco quickly on each cheek.

"Call me," she said in French, and she gave Vidalia a hard look.

Leila and Ruby pushed off into the crowd.

"We go," Marco said, pulling her by the hand.

They walked down the curving cobblestone street and turned onto a street with a river running down the middle of it. Marco led her up the steps of a footbridge, and they stopped at the top.

"Is this the Seine?" Vidalia asked. She felt numb and confused.

"No," he said. "The canal. See, it's too still for the river."

He was right. The water below was almost perfectly smooth, a sheet of slippery darkness reflecting the deep green of the trees and the dark sky above them. Vidalia leaned over the railing and gazed down. The feeling came then, a slow stream of guilt and fear that pooled inside her, steadily filling her up.

"I have to give it back," she said.

Marco shook his head.

"Too late," he said, watching her.

"I can mail it to her," she said. "At the gallery."

He shook his head.

"Well, what do *you* think I should do with it?" She wanted to throw it in the canal.

"I sell paintings, remember?" he said. "We can make some money." He turned back to the river, his hand running up the back of her arm. "Anyway," he said, "you did a good job." He turned and smiled teasingly at her. "You've done this before?"

"No!" she said. "I feel bad." She winced. "Ruby . . ." But now she was thinking of his hand on her arm, thinking that he was really close to her.

"Don't worry about Ruby," he said, leaning back against the rail and pulling her in front of him. "You don't think she makes five of those in a day? She doesn't lose money. It's when she sells one that she *makes* money."

Vidalia looked at him suspiciously. It made sense, sort of.

"The market is strange for art. You must know this, with your mother."

Vidalia nodded slowly as if, yes, she did know.

"There is no real price," he said, drawing her closer to him, his hand on her elbow. "Art is just some paint and some canvas. The value is all in their heads." He ran his hand up the back of her arm again, and she hoped he didn't feel the goose bumps on her skin. He pulled her closer to him and pushed her hair away from her forehead the way he had the other night. "And Ruby knows that," he said.

Vidalia thought of Ruby asking Leila about the prices. She thought of her mother begging her to come home. She thought maybe Marco was right.

He smiled and pressed his forehead to hers.

"Okay?" he said, sliding his fingers up around the base of her skull.

What he said made sense in a way, but it was the closeness of his body, his skin, his mouth, that really convinced her.

"Okay," she breathed. And then the warmth of the kiss closed over her, and she forgot whatever it was that had told her this was wrong.

CHAPTER

🕊 **10** 🕊

VIDALIA HAD HOPED HER art class would get better when they started at the museum, but so far she'd felt pretty much the same way she had at the atelier, like everyone else knew something she didn't and she was struggling just to keep up. They repeated the lessons they'd done in class the week before, this time using their paintings to work on shading, depth, perspective. Today, Thursday, they were working on the figures. Vidalia drew the girl and the unicorn over and over, going through sheet after sheet of sketch paper, trying to make them look comfortable together, the way they did in the painting. But no matter what she did, they looked awkward and lopsided. She walked around to look at the other students' work, to see if they were doing anything she hadn't thought of, the way they had been with the live model at the atelier. She took note of how they were all working and tried to imitate them when she sat back down in front of her easel.

It didn't help that she kept thinking about the night before. Even while she was drawing, she'd see herself putting the painting in her bag, and Ruby's open, nervous face. Marco had taken the painting with him at the end of the night, and she'd been glad to get rid of it. She felt worse and worse as the day went on, and by the time class was over, she was more frustrated and depressed with her work than she'd been since she'd started Monsieur Benoît's class. Mrs. Greenberg hadn't known what she was talking about. Vidalia should just get back to her little dollhouses. She obviously wasn't the right kind of artist for this.

"Class," Madame Zafar said at the end of art history later that day. "Remember that tomorrow we discuss the cathedral that you've visited on your own. Which means, if you haven't gone to one yet, then you'd better go right now. And don't forget that we will be meeting earlier than usual on Monday, at noon, when we will go to Versailles."

Vidalia felt depressed knowing that Marco wouldn't be there to meet her today. He'd told her last night, when he'd walked her to the Dubois' building, that he was having dinner with his mother tonight. But Vidalia had told Julien she'd go by the bookstore after class, so it wasn't like she didn't have anything to do.

When she walked through the front door of Shakespeare and Company, Julien was already looking up from the register.

"Hi, Vidalia," he said.

"Hey, Julien," she answered, sitting down in a wooden chair next to the register.

She was glad to see him now that he was right in front of her. She'd forgotten how easy it was to hang out with Julien. He was so mellow.

"So, what are we doing this afternoon?" he asked.

"How about Notre-Dame?" she said. "I have to go see a cathedral for my art history class."

"Okay," he said, leaning back. "But maybe we should go to the Sainte-Chapelle instead. It's just as beautiful and not as crowded."

Margie burst through the front door.

"I'm here, Julien!" she cried. "I'm not late!"

Julien made a show of looking at his watch.

"You mean, you're not *very* late," he said.

Margie rolled her eyes and dropped her bag on the counter.

"Hullo, Vidalia," she drawled. "Let me guess, you're the reason Master Julien is so eager to leave today. Normally, you can't *drag* him out of this place."

Embarrassed, Vidalia leaned over and retied her left bootlace.

"Better ask him," she said, hoping they could drop the subject. But Margie wasn't through.

"Oh, I don't need to ask," she said. "I can read him like any one of the books in this place. And he is *very* happy to see you."

Vidalia remained bent over her boot. When she finally sat up again, Julien was looking seriously through a stack of receipts, and Margie was grinning diabolically.

"Anyway, let's go," said Julien, and she saw him kick Margie in the ankle as they traded places at the register.

"Ow, that hurt!" Margie cried with that questioning Australian upswing.

"Okay." Vidalia shrugged. "Bye, Margie," she said, putting her sunglasses on as she followed Julien to the door.

When they got outside, Julien looked off into the distance. He squinted and pointed toward the Seine.

"It's this way," he said.

As they walked to the cathedral, Julien asked Vidalia about her class and she told him what she'd learned about cathedrals from Madame Zafar. It wasn't long before they arrived at a cathedral that looked a little smaller and less impressive than Notre-Dame. When they entered, they walked down the long center aisle together.

"Will this work for your class?" Julien whispered to her.

"I guess," she said, looking sideways at people kneeling in the pews nearby. "But it's not as fancy as the ones we've been looking at."

"This way," whispered Julien, leading her off to the side. Vidalia followed him up a dark set of stairs. When they got to the top, she understood. The walls were maybe thirty feet high and they were all stained glass. Shifting, jewel-like color poured through them. She felt like she'd stepped into a kaleidoscope.

"Wow," she whispered.

"It's better without sunglasses," Julien whispered back. She took them off, and he was right, it was better.

"You like it?" Julien asked.

"It's incredible," she said. "It makes me feel . . . holy or something."

He looked up at the rose window and tilted his head. "You can understand why religion worked for so long. All the pretty colors to hypnotize the people." He smiled at her.

"It's so beautiful," Vidalia said, looking up at the shafts of light coming through purple and green and yellow glass.

Julien walked ahead of her, and Vidalia gazed raptly at the beautiful windows until she felt her phone vibrate in her bag. It was Marco's number on the screen.

"Hello," she whispered, stepping into the corner and hoping that no one in the church would notice. She hadn't expected to hear from Marco today.

"Hi," he said. "How are you?"

"I'm fine," she said uncertainly, wanting to know what he was thinking about last night but not sure how to ask. "You?"

"Good," he said, and his voice was warm. "But I miss you." Vidalia felt herself relax. "Where are you?" he said.

"I'm at Sainte-Chapelle, the cathedral." She looked up at the bright windows. "It's really beautiful."

"You're alone?" Marco asked.

Vidalia looked at Julien sitting ten or twelve yards from where she stood. He was leaning back with his eyes closed.

"Yeah," she said, looking away again.

"What are you doing this weekend?" he asked.

"Uh, nothing," she said, glancing around. Julien's eyes were open now, and he was watching her.

"Can you go away with me?" Marco asked.

"Really? I mean, maybe," she said. "Where?"

She turned toward the wall and thought quickly. *Could* she go away with him?

"Cannes," he said. "What do you think?"

"Yeah," she said. She'd figure something out. "Yes." She felt another rush of excitement as she said it. "But I have to be back for class on Monday." She couldn't afford to miss any of

Monsieur Benoît's classes, however miserable they made her, and then there was the Versailles trip with the institute in the afternoon.

"No problem," he said. "We come back Sunday. You can leave with me tomorrow, one o'clock?"

"Yes," she said, thinking fast. She could skip art history this once and meet him right after art class.

"Meet me at the train station at Gare de Lyon at one o'clock tomorrow. You know where is it?" He sounded rushed.

"Yes," she said. She'd seen the stop on the Métro map.

"Okay, see you there," he said. "Vidalia, I have to go now, but I look forward to see you."

She felt her face get warm.

"You, too," she said. "I mean *me*, too." She blushed.

"*À demain*," he said, and she thought she heard an affectionate laugh in his voice.

"See you tomorrow," she said.

And then she was back in the cathedral with colored light falling all around her.

She tried to stop smiling before she turned and walked over to Julien.

The next day, Monsieur Benoît's class was back at the atelier near Saint-Michel. They had finished with their preliminary sketches at the museum, and on Monday they would start painting. Vidalia was dreading today's class. She'd avoided any direct contact with Monsieur Benoît over the past week at the museum, but somehow she was sure that she was going to fall back into his sights today.

She walked down the long hallway just like she had the first day and pushed open the door to the big, dusty studio. There was Monsieur Benoît, and next to him, Bruno was talking and gesticulating. Caroline and the other students all held wooden frames and strips of canvas. Vidalia's heart sank. They were stretching canvases. She walked slowly toward the group, but Monsieur Benoît intercepted her in the middle of the room.

"Vidalia," he said. "Come with me."

She followed him to where the rolls of canvas leaned against the wall.

"You need to make your canvas," he said.

"I, uh . . . don't know how," she said. "I've never done it before."

"I know," he said as he cut a strip of canvas from the roll with big scissors. "That's why I'm showing you."

Chalky dust floated into the air. He picked up an empty frame from the floor and handed it to Vidalia.

"Put it on the ground," he said.

She knelt on the floor, balancing on the balls of her feet, and put the frame down in front of her, then looked up at him, not sure what she was supposed to do next.

"Take this and place the frame in the center," he said, handing her the canvas. She took it and laid it down on the ground and then placed the wooden frame on top of it.

"Now." Monsieur Benoît knelt next to her and pulled her canvas hard with a pair of pliers. "Take this," he said, "and pull it tight."

Vidalia took the pliers from Monsieur Benoît, leaning across him as she did. Gingerly, she avoided touching his arm with hers.

"Pull!" said Monsieur Benoît, grabbing her wrist and pulling it upward. Vidalia gripped the pliers until her knuckles went white. Up close, she could smell Monsieur Benoît's cigarettes and maybe a faint whiff of alcohol.

"Okay," he said. "Now put your knee here." He indicated the right side of the frame. She slid her knee onto it and leaned down where her hand had been gripping the canvas. "Here."

He handed her a big stapler splashed with dried paint.

"Put it there." He pointed to the side of the canvas she was still holding with the pliers. He'd let go of her wrist now, and she was holding the canvas herself. She put the end of the stapler where he'd said and leaned forward onto it, stapling the canvas to the wood at the corner.

"Now the other side," said Monsieur Benoît.

She pulled the other side with the pliers and stapled there, too.

A few minutes later he'd shown her how to fold the corners neatly and staple them. She stood up with a stretched canvas in her hand. Monsieur Benoît pulled himself up, leaning one hand on his knee.

"Now," he said. "Do three more just like this." And he left her standing there, feeling ridiculously proud of the neatly stretched rectangle in her hand.

CHAPTER
11

MARCO WAS STANDING BY the ticket counter when Vidalia got there that afternoon. He was smoking and leaning against a concrete post, the one still point in a crowd of rushing people. She felt a flash of pleasure. How lucky was she to be the one who was walking over to join him?

He smiled and pulled her quickly to him, kissing her on the lips and then whispering, "I got the tickets."

She wanted to ask him a million questions, but he was leading her toward the station doors. She figured they'd have time to talk on the train.

"I told Madame Dubois I was going to Brittany with people from school," she said once they were settled in their seats, their bags stowed overhead.

Madame Dubois had barely reacted when Vidalia told her that she was going away.

"That sounds lovely," she'd said, looking down at her mail.

Vidalia couldn't believe how easy it all was.

"Where are we going to stay, anyway?" she asked Marco.

"Some friends of mine have a villa," he said. "By the water. They don't use it this weekend."

"Is the Mediterranean really as blue as it looks in pictures?" Vidalia asked.

"More blue," he said, looking at her and pushing a strand of hair away from her eye.

"I can't wait to see it," she said.

Marco smiled at her.

"It can't wait to see you," he said.

When they arrived in the station at Cannes, it was dark. They took a cab up a hill, passing palm trees along the way. When they got out, Marco told her to wait for him before disappearing behind the house. There was an expanse of mown grass leading up to the house, which was made of brown stucco and had the same kind of wavy tile roof she'd seen out the train window on the way south. Flowering vines climbed the façade and wrapped around the windows with their brown wooden shutters. Vidalia closed her eyes and smelled the ocean. It was familiar and foreign at the same time.

"They hide the key," Marco said when he came back.

Vidalia followed him through a side door into a dark kitchen and up carpeted stairs, down another hallway, and to a bedroom. Marco dropped their bags and, together, they walked across the room to a set of glass doors. Vidalia turned the handle and stepped out onto the balcony.

She looked down at the garden and a pool beneath her; at the sea down the hill, stretching out into the darkness; at the mountains on the other side of the water; at the boats in the harbor. She thought of the painting in the Musée Apollinaire, the girl and her unicorn hidden from view, safe from the world, the cathedral behind them all icy and eternal. This was her eternity then—the Mediterranean, the night sky, the warm breeze, and then Marco, behind her, putting his hands on her waist.

"You want to go out tonight or stay in?" he asked softly in her ear.

Vidalia had thought about this and she already knew what her answer was. She turned to him and put her arms around his neck and pressed her forehead to his, looking into his eyes.

"Stay in," she said, and she smiled even though she was a little nervous about what would happen next. Marco smiled back, and they kissed. His mouth was warm and soft, his tongue finding hers. She leaned into him, the kisses more liquid and ecstatic than any she'd ever experienced.

They pulled apart, and Vidalia found herself out of breath, her heart racing. She was scared and happy and alive. They moved together to the bed, then they were in it, falling all over each other, their mouths, their bodies perfect and natural together.

She pulled away to raise her arms so that he could lift her shirt over her head, then did the same for him. And they were in the bed and on top of each other.

"Hold on a minute," he said, and he reached into his bag for a condom. And then he was inside her, and everything in the world was his soft skin all over her, his hot mouth, this feeling of so much pleasure. *This is how it's supposed to be,* she thought. *Just like this.*

When it was over, Marco pulled her hair aside and she turned to face him, looking into his eyes.

"Oh my God," she said, and she laughed.

"Yeah," he said. "Me, too." He was smiling at her in the moonlight coming in through the window.

They looked up at the ceiling together, their hands interlaced.

"It wasn't your first time?" he asked finally.

Vidalia laughed again.

"That was so much better than any first time," she said, rolling toward him.

"Yes," he laughed. "It's true."

He smiled at her in the dark. She could see his eyes and the scar at the corner of his mouth. She touched her finger to it lightly.

"How did you get this?" she asked.

"A dog," he said. "When I was small."

"It must have hurt," she said.

"Yes," he said. "It hurt."

He pulled her close and she felt safe and warm. *This is what it's like to be in love,* she thought.

After a while, she stood and wrapped the sheet around her, leaving Marco sitting in the bed, watching her as she crossed the room to the window.

"So who are these friends, anyway?" she asked as she walked into the bathroom to get a glass of water.

"What friends?" he asked.

"The ones whose house we're in, duh," she said. Marco

was quiet until she came back out to the room. She leaned against the doorjamb and took a sip of water.

"You know, Vidalia," he said. "I don't have a lot of friends, really."

"Well, the ones you do have are good enough," she said, looking around at the big room with its soft white rugs and abstract modern paintings on the walls.

Marco just looked at her from the pillow, the light from the moon reflecting in his pale eyes. He shook his head and half smiled, and Vidalia felt something twist in her stomach.

"This is your friend's house, right?" she asked slowly.

"No," he said. "It's just someone's house."

Her stomach twisted harder.

Marco looked up at her from where he lay, watching her. She stared back at him.

"You mean . . ." she said. But she knew what he meant. "How do you know they're not coming back?"

"I know who they are," he said. "They won't be here this weekend."

Vidalia nodded and looked around again. This room, which had felt like a safe hiding place away from the world just a little while ago, suddenly felt like a minefield. One wrong move and it would all go up in flames. Crossing the room, she sat down hard on the end of the bed. It struck her that this wasn't all that much of a shock, that after the dinner, and the painting, she might have even half expected it. And there was her surprise when she'd first seen Marco in the courtyard at the institute that day. A jolt that made her ask, *What is he doing here? What does he want?*

"Do you mind?" he asked. He leaned over and trailed his fingers down her forearm. "Are you angry?"

He was looking at her questioningly, his eyes worried. And as she met his gaze, Vidalia saw that everything that had passed between them so far, the whole deep river of under-standing and laughter and connection, was still right there. All she had to do was jump back in.

"No," she said. "But we'd better not get caught or I'll be going home sooner than I planned."

"Okay," he whispered. "We don't get caught." Then he kissed her again, and she sank back into him, closed her eyes, let the dark envelop her.

CHAPTER 12

VIDALIA WOKE UP BEFORE Marco. She opened her eyes to see his sleeping face on the pillow next to hers, his lips parted, one arm thrown over her. The night before, they'd scavenged food from the kitchen, keeping the lights out as they searched so that nobody would notice them from outside. When they'd gone back to bed afterward, Marco had fallen asleep quickly, but Vidalia had lain awake for a long time, hearing tiny noises in the house, sure the police were about to break down the door.

But now the sun poured into the white bedroom through the glass doors to the balcony, and when she looked at Marco sleeping next to her, everything that had felt scary the night before felt okay. It wasn't so serious, after all, she thought, touching her thumb to his jaw and tracing the line of it. They were just having fun. They were just falling in love.

Marco opened his eyes and made a sleepy sound as he wrapped his fingers around her wrist and pulled her hand under his cheek.

"*Salut*," he said, his eyes still shut.

She loved how entangled they were.

"*Salut*," she said.

He snuggled into her, pressing his forehead against hers.

"What you want to do today?" he asked.

"I don't know," she said, looking at his eyelids, his long lashes, the smooth, olive skin under his eyes. "Go to the beach, I guess."

"Yes," he said. "The blue, it wants to see you." He smiled, his eyes still shut. Then he lifted his hand and cupped it around the back of her head, weaving his fingers through her hair. Vidalia closed her eyes and let him hold her in the white morning sun.

A little later, they were downstairs in the big kitchen, the black and white tiles cool on the soles of Vidalia's feet.

"What do you eat for breakfast?" Marco asked, glancing over at her with a smile. "Lots of eggs and bacon?"

"I usually just have cereal," she said.

Marco laughed as he opened a packet of coffee and sniffed it.

"I don't think you're really an American," he said. "I think you lie."

"What, just because I don't want eggs?" Vidalia asked.

"Not only that," he said, finding an espresso pot and pouring the grounds into the metal basket. "You don't look like an American. You don't dress like one or talk like one." He shook his head and turned to her as he filled the pot with water.

"Maybe I don't know what a real American is then," said Vidalia, sitting down at the round white table in the middle of the kitchen.

"Yes," he said, still making the coffee. "I think this is why I like you." He turned from the coffee and smiled at her. "You're not a real American and I'm not a real French. We are both from nowhere, making ourselves what we are." He opened a cabinet. "No cereal," he said. "But we got *craquottes*." He took a box in one arm and went to the refrigerator, where he got butter and a jar of jam.

When Marco brought the coffee, which he'd poured into two bowls, adding copious amounts of milk, she was spreading a hard, dry piece of toast from a box with butter and then jam. It was like eating crackers for breakfast. Strange, but not bad.

"Have you been here before?" she asked him.

"To Cannes?" he asked, reaching for the dish of sugar cubes in the middle of the table.

"No," she said, watching his face. "This house."

"Ah, the house," he said, glancing up at her with a smile, and then leaning back, his bowl of coffee held in two hands. "No. It's my first visit."

"How did you know where to go?" she asked. "I mean, I hear about people doing this in the Hamptons sometimes. Like, summer people will come and find out that someone's been living in their house over the winter. But I never understood how you could be sure that the place would be empty." She looked up at the kitchen's high ceiling.

"I make a point to find out," he said with a smile. "Research."

"Huh," said Vidalia, thinking that it didn't explain much. "Well, who are they, anyway?" She felt a tingly sensation, thinking of the people who usually inhabited these rooms.

"Some rich people," he said. "They own maybe five houses."

He looked around the kitchen. "This one is empty most of the time."

He gave her his crooked smile.

"What do they care?" he asked. "We don't hurt anyone."

"But still," she said slowly, looking down at her bowl of milky coffee. "It is *theirs*. It belongs to them." It was true that she felt better this morning, but Vidalia still wasn't seeing how breaking into a person's house and eating their food was A-okay. She looked up at Marco. He seemed so at ease here.

"I understand what you say," he said seriously, "that it is personal property. But the world is full of personal property, and it all belongs to the same people. There are so many poor people who stay poor living in shit, and the rich people have this." He gestured at the big room. "It's a couple that owns this house, Vidalia," he said. "One man and one woman. Do they really need it all for themselves?"

Vidalia shrugged and looked around at the gleaming white counters, the shiny appliances. No, she thought, probably not, but did that make it okay to break in?

"If we're smart enough to take a little piece of this for us, just for one weekend, what's the problem with that? We don't take food from children, we don't"—he pulled out a pack of cigarettes—"bomb the shit out of peasants or make people work in a factory." He lit his cigarette and gave her an ironic smile. "We just have a little breakfast, go to the beach. There's nothing wrong with that, not in the big scale of things that are wrong with this world."

He looked at her, and Vidalia nodded. What could she say? He was totally right.

"They won't come home, don't worry," he said, taking a sip of his coffee. "We got until tomorrow morning."

"All right," Vidalia sighed, leaning back in her chair. "Let's go to the beach then." She dunked her cracker in her coffee, like she'd seen Marco do, and took a bite. It tasted better that way.

They spent the whole day swimming and lying on the beach. Vidalia was amazed at the gleaming, barely clothed, bronzed bodies that extended as far as she could see. The sand was even more tightly packed with people than it was in East Hampton in July.

Back at the house that night, Marco suggested they go into town to eat. Vidalia wore her standard boots and miniskirt, but she put on the one dressier shirt she'd brought, a purple V-necked tee that fit her snugly. It was one of the few items of clothing she'd bought new, on sale at the Gap in Bridgehampton in the spring. Marco wore a striped button-down shirt open at the neck, just like on the first night she'd seen him. Somehow, the more time she spent with Marco, the more Vidalia found herself questioning her own style. Not that he said anything about it, but just being with him made her want to look more sophisticated, more glamorous, maybe just more beautiful. Well, there wasn't much hope of that, she thought. She was cursed with skinny-ugly-duckling looks, but at least the T-shirt she was wearing wasn't ripped.

All of the cafés were overflowing with people. Marco pointed to one and they sat at a table outside, where they could see the well-dressed crowds passing by. Marco held her hand while he ordered a bottle of wine. Vidalia smiled at him and felt a rush of pleasure at being here with him, drinking wine in the south of France. It was everything she'd wanted—it was more.

They looked at the menus, and, when the waiter came back with the wine, they ordered—Marco, a rabbit dish, *lapin à la moutarde*, and Vidalia, lamb, *navarin d'agneau*. Then Marco turned to her with a strange hesitation.

"What?" she said.

"I want to tell you," he said. "I did something about this painting."

Vidalia's awful guilt came flooding back.

"Ruby's painting?" she asked.

"Yes." He spoke carefully, like he was afraid of upsetting her. "I found someone to buy it," he said. "Someone I sell to every once in a while." He paused.

"Oh," Vidalia said. She was thinking of Ruby's nervousness at her first show, at how disappointed she must have been later when she realized the painting had been stolen.

"He paid quite a bit," Marco said. "About one thousand euros."

Vidalia looked up.

"That much?" she said.

Marco smiled, but he was still watching her, speaking carefully. "Yes," he said. "It's a good price."

She was still staring at him.

"Well, what are you . . . What are we going to do with it?"

"I have the money at home," he said. "I didn't want to bring it to you here. But I thought half and half, is that okay?"

She nodded. Of course it was okay. Did he think she was in the habit of negotiating cuts with the people who sold her stolen paintings?

"Wow," she said. "That's . . . great."

"I think so," he said.

Vidalia still felt bad about Ruby, of course, but somehow the idea of five hundred euros all for herself made her feel pretty good, too.

After they'd eaten, Marco moved his chair closer to Vidalia's.

"Good trip, no?" he asked softly, putting his arm around her and looking out at the people walking down the street.

"Yes," she said, leaning into his shoulder.

"I like to go places with you," he said in her ear.

"Me, too," she said, a nervous thrill running down her spine.

"We should go more places together," he said.

"Definitely," said Vidalia, thinking of the money. Maybe she really could go away again now.

"Where you want to go?" he asked.

"Mmmm." Vidalia thought for a second and looked up at him. "Maybe Toulouse," she said. "Or the Pyrenees—it's supposed to be nice there."

"Yes," he said. "But more adventure. Why not Spain?"

"Spain could be nice," she said. She hadn't thought to suggest another country altogether. "Have you been?"

"I've been to Sevilla, Granada. It's very free there. The people are relaxed, not like France."

She imagined Spanish streets, a fountain where water splashed over a mosaic of tiny tiles. She imagined Marco walking along those streets with . . . who?

"Who did you go with?" she asked.

He shrugged. "An old girlfriend."

"Leila?" she asked, remembering the gallery assistant telling Marco to call her.

"No." He laughed, pulling back to look at her. "Why do you talk about her?"

"I don't know." She felt something ugly spring to life inside her chest. "It's just that she's the only one of your friends I've met."

"I told you," he said teasingly, touching the tip of her nose with one finger. "I don't have a lot of friends."

"No?" she asked, teasing back but with an urgency that she didn't quite understand. "I don't know if I believe you."

"What is it?" he asked. "What do you want to know?"

"What you're like with other people," she said. "What you do when we're not together. Where you lived when you were a kid. Just regular stuff." It was true, she didn't know anything about him.

"I thought we don't need these things," he said, pausing to light a cigarette in his cupped hand. "For me it's enough we are together right now. I don't care about all the details."

Vidalia felt her cheeks flush, sensing she'd disappointed him.

"Anyway, when I was a kid, it's not such a good story," he said. He sat up and exhaled smoke. Suddenly there was a distance between them.

"Why?" she asked. "What—"

"My parents were hippies," he said with a dismissive shrug. "We traveled around a lot, they took us a lot of places—communes in Germany, nude beaches on the Riviera, parties in Ibiza, things like that."

"It sounds . . . cool," she said, thinking that Marco had traveled more and seen more of the world than anyone she'd ever known. Sometimes she worried that he'd find out what a small-town girl she really was and lose interest in her altogether.

"No." He shook his head. "People like that don't know how to take care of children. Me and my brother saw a lot of things we didn't need to see. They took us out of school."

"Really?" she asked, surprised that a life like that could be bad. "When did you stop school?" It clicked all of a sudden that this wasn't what he'd told her before.

"I was twelve," he said, turning to look at her. His eyes were different, harder, like he was daring her somehow.

"Oh," she said, surprised and feeling intrusive. "I thought you'd stopped after high school."

"It's what I tell people," he said, shrugging. "No reason to tell the truth all the time."

"Well, you don't seem like you didn't go to school," she said. "I mean, no one would ever guess . . ." She trailed off. Somehow that hadn't come out right.

"I know," he said, grinding out his cigarette and looking up at her, one eyebrow raised.

"Right," she said, embarrassed. "I mean, obviously . . ."

Marco's expression was softer when he looked back at her.

"But maybe it would be better if I had more school, diplomas, all those things they want in the world," he said, leaning his head back against the seat and smiling at her, so that the tight thing in her chest released.

He laced his fingers through hers and leaned close again. The moment had passed. He was back with her now.

"What about you?" he asked. "You didn't travel with your mother? Searching for great art?" Vidalia looked out at the crowds of people on the sidewalk. Two women were laughing under a tree.

"Well, yeah," she said vaguely. "A little bit."

Vidalia wished she could tell him the truth the way she'd told Julien. But would he still believe that she belonged here with him if he knew that she'd barely stepped outside of East Hampton before this summer? That all she'd seen of the world had been in movies and books? If he knew how far her mother really was from being a sophisticated gallerist? No, she didn't want him to think she was desperate.

"So, another trip?" he asked after a minute.

Vidalia looked at him. His blue eyes were fixed on her, and his smile was playful.

"To Spain?" she asked.

She thought again of the old girlfriend he'd been there with. He looked at her like he knew what she was thinking.

"No," he said. "Italy. Rome."

"Rome could be nice," she said.

"After your art class is done?" His eyes were on hers.

"You mean . . ." She paused. "For real?"

"I don't want you to disappear back to America right away," he said. "I want a little Vidalia for me." He was smiling, but his voice and his eyes were serious.

"My last day of classes is Friday, August eighth," she said. "I'm supposed to fly home the Monday after that."

He leaned close to her ear and whispered, "Don't go home."

Vidalia thought of Heather going to the south of France with her parents for the second half of August. She thought of herself going home, spending the rest of the summer the way she'd spent her entire life, taking care of her mother.

"Maybe I could change my ticket," she said.

He was nodding, smiling, his eyes on hers.

"I . . ." She wondered if she was going to blow it by admitting this, but she knew she'd have to sooner or later. "I don't have any money."

Marco shrugged.

"Now you do," he said.

She was confused for a second before realizing that he meant the money from Ruby's painting.

"You think it will be enough?" she asked.

"You think we need more?" he asked.

She looked away again, into the street, but she could feel his eyes on her.

"Maybe," she said.

"We figure it out," he said, and he leaned in and kissed her on the mouth, smiling as he pulled away. "There are more galleries, more paintings, more rich people to buy them."

Vidalia's excitement caught in her throat.

"And then we go to Italy, two weeks just for you and me," he said.

"Okay," she said, not sure what she was agreeing to but wanting this so badly. "Let's go to Italy."

CHAPTER

⌐ **13** ⌐

VIDALIA AND MARCO WERE back in Paris at noon the next day, and by then they'd talked about their trip to Italy so much that it seemed it had always been a part of her summer plans.

"Let's go out on Friday and Saturday," Marco said as they were saying good-bye at the train station. "We'll go to galleries and talk about Roma."

Vidalia tried not to think about what he wanted to do at the galleries. She kissed him good-bye and walked home along the quiet Sunday streets. She'd talk to him about the galleries later, she thought. They'd find another way to pay for their trip later.

When she got to the apartment, Vidalia took a deep breath before going inside. She got ready to tell some vague lies about her weekend in Brittany. But when she opened the door, she could sense right away that nobody was home. Everything was dim and still without Madame Dubois there hustling Clara out of the house or dinner onto the table. Vidalia stood in the middle of the living room for a minute, breathing and thinking that no one in the world knew just where she was or what she was doing. On her way up to her room, she walked past the Dubois' bedroom. A briefcase lay open on the bed, its contents scattered around it. Aside from that, the room was immaculate.

Back in her little room, Vidalia put away her things and sat down at the desk. Picking up her sketchbook from the floor, she opened it and looked at a series of sketches of the girl with the unicorn. The positions were all wrong. She took her charcoal from the box on the floor and sketched the two figures, trying to make them more at ease with each other. But the girl still looked stiff and awkward. Vidalia chewed the inside of her cheek and tried to remember what the girl looked like in the painting. Maybe her knee crossed her leg a little higher? Then it hit her. Why not go to the museum and work for a while? It was open on Sunday, and even if the room with the easels was locked, she could sketch for a couple of hours. She threw her sketchbook and charcoals into her bag and jogged down the back staircase to the street.

The guard in his blue uniform sat in the ticket window at the Musée Apollinaire. It was the same guard who was always there, but she wasn't sure he'd recognize her without Monsieur Benoît and the rest of the class.

"Non non!" the guard said in French when Vidalia reached for her wallet. "Monsieur Benoît's students don't pay."

"Merci," Vidalia said, smiling. So he did recognize her. She started toward the hallway but he spoke again.

"Do you want your easel?" he asked. "I can unlock the room for you."

"Oui," she said. It would be even better to have all her work out. *"Oui, merci."*

She was surprised when he got her easel without her telling him which one it was.

"This one is my favorite," he said as he set it down in front of *La jeune fille à la licorne*. "I noticed you working on it." He smiled at her. "It is beautiful, no?"

"I love it," Vidalia said.

He nodded. "I am eager to see your version." He looked toward her easel.

"Oh, it probably won't be very . . ." She trailed off, self-conscious.

"*Non, non,*" he assured her. "I am sure it will be good." He looked at the painting and then at Vidalia and back at the painting. "She looks like you a little," he said. "Your name is Vidalia, yes?" he asked.

Vidalia nodded, surprised.

"It's hard not to notice a name like this," he said. "Mine is very boring, Jacques."

He smiled kindly at her before walking back to his booth at the front of the museum.

When Vidalia sat down at her easel, she felt like a puzzle piece fitting snugly back into place. She sketched the girl over and over, freely at first and then in more detail. Her ankles were crossed higher than Vidalia had originally drawn them, but her legs were swung farther to the left. Once the position looked a little more natural, Vidalia worked on making it look like the girl was really cradling the unicorn in her arms. As she drew, the forms started to work in a way they hadn't before. The girl's body looked more natural, more like she really was holding the unicorn in her lap.

Vidalia felt like she'd been there just a little while when the guard came up to her.

"We are closing now, mademoiselle," he said. "It is five o'clock."

She'd been working for three hours.

The next morning after taking the Métro to the museum, Vidalia set up her easel, propping the canvas on it. They were going to start painting today. Before they got started, she looked through the sketches she'd done the day before. The girl and the unicorn were better, but they still weren't exactly right. She was looking at them so intently that she didn't notice Monsieur Benoît until he was leaning over her shoulder. He reached one hand over and flipped through the stack, pausing at each sketch, and then returning to the one she'd done yesterday.

"This isn't what you did last week," he said.

"No, I, uh, came here yesterday," said Vidalia, surprised he'd noticed. "The guard let me in. I worked for a few hours just trying to get their positions. It's still kind of stiff, but it looks a little better than before. At least, I think—"

Monsieur Benoît cut her off.

"This is progress," he said.

"Oh, um, thanks," Vidalia said. Was *le Maître* actually complimenting her?

"But far from perfect," he said sharply, as if she'd been congratulating herself.

"No," she said quickly. "I know. It's still not right. . . ."

She raised her hand to the paper to show where the girl's shoulder bent too far.

"Sit on the floor." Monsieur Benoît interrupted her again.

"Now?" Vidalia asked.

"Yes," he said, standing and crossing his arms in front of her. "You must sit the way she sits."

Vidalia did as he said, looking at the other students over by the portraits as she sank down to the floor, bending her knees so that her feet were on one side of her body and her weight was on the other.

"Like this?" she asked.

"Look at her," he said. "How she is. She leans forward more, like this." He pushed her shoulders from behind. "She lifts herself toward the animal in her lap, and she pulls upward so she is like the cathedral behind her."

Self-consciously, Vidalia let him pull her shoulders into position.

"You have to be inside her body if you are going to paint her," he said.

Vidalia saw some of the other students glance over at them.

"Now, draw her," said Monsieur Benoît.

Vidalia got up and sat in front of her easel, still feeling Monsieur Benoît's hands on her back. She drew a few general outlines, to show how the girl was leaning.

"Yes," he said. "That's it."

She drew another line and made it harder, bringing the girl's hip and the side of her body into focus. Sketching quickly, she gave form to the side of the girl's lap where the unicorn's head lay. She could almost feel the way the girl held the unicorn's head on her knees, how she was protecting it by pulling it toward her.

"*C'est bien*," said Monsieur Benoît behind her. "*Très bien.*" For the first time, Vidalia heard a hint of enthusiasm in his voice. She finished outlining the girl and sat back and looked at the sketch. It was right this time. Vidalia looked up at Monsieur Benoît.

"This is much, much better," he said, nodding. It wasn't the highest praise Vidalia had ever received, but from him, it felt like it.

Monsieur Benoît walked away from her and clapped his hands together.

"Attention, class," he called. "Take out your paints."

That afternoon, when she met up with the institute group to go to Versailles, it turned out that Vidalia wasn't the only one who'd had an eventful weekend. Becky and Heather looked like they hadn't slept since she'd last seen them on Friday.

"We had a crazy weekend," Becky told her at the train station, smoothing her short flowered sundress. "I can't believe I even made it here." It was the first time Vidalia had seen Becky be anything less than totally cheerful and energetic. If it was possible, Heather looked even more distant than usual.

The two of them fell asleep almost as soon as they sat in their seats on the train. Vidalia noticed that Kenji was sitting with a bunch of other girls. Unlike his weekend traveling companions, he looked perfectly well rested and, Vidalia thought, seemed to be pointedly not looking Becky's way. Vidalia wondered if something had happened, before looking out the window and getting lost in thoughts of Marco, Rome, and art.

The castle was huge and sparkling. Madame Zafar led them through the rooms, pointing out mirrors and portraits and lecturing about Louis XIV.

"His court was the most decadent in history," she said. "The aristocrats who lived here had every luxury, and yet they did not have freedom. They were virtually imprisoned at the castle."

"Not a bad-looking jail," said Kenji, who was standing near Vidalia.

"Yeah," she agreed. "Lock me up, please."

They took a break to eat at two, since they'd met early, and Vidalia bought a sandwich for herself at the café—tuna and slices of boiled egg on a baguette. French sandwiches were weird but delicious. Then she walked out onto one of the vast, perfectly manicured lawns and sat down in the grass to eat. She glanced up to see Becky coming her way, Heather beside her, as usual.

"Oh my God, I don't think I'm going to make it through the afternoon," said Becky as she dropped onto the grass next to Vidalia.

"You look like you got run over by a truck," Vidalia commented.

"Thanks," Becky groaned, and lay back on the grass, throwing one arm over her eyes. Heather sat down next to her, carefully arranging her jacket on the grass so she wouldn't get her skirt dirty. Suddenly Vidalia felt fed up with talking only to Becky when Heather was sitting right there. It was ridiculous, and she wasn't going to play along with it anymore.

"What happened?" Vidalia asked Heather, pointedly meeting her eyes over Becky's prone body.

"A little too much fun," Heather said, looking back at her for a second before unwrapping her sandwich.

"Looks like you pissed off Prince Charming," Vidalia said, turning back to Becky. She'd just seen Kenji look at them and then go the other way to sit with his gaggle of prepsters.

"I don't remember," Becky said from under her arm.

Vidalia looked back at Heather and raised a questioning eyebrow.

"*What* doesn't she remember?" she asked.

Heather smiled and said in a singsong voice, "Well, it had something to do with a guy from Chicago . . ."

Becky groaned.

"And hooking up with this guy right in front of Kenji . . ."

Another groan.

"Kenji taking off . . ."

Silence this time, as if Becky were actually waiting to hear the end of the story.

"And Becky dancing and partying with this guy for the rest of the night."

"He was cute, I remember that," Becky said in a muffled but more cheerful voice.

"He wasn't bad," agreed Heather, taking a bite of her sandwich. "And I managed to get her home before she actually slept with him, which was kind of a challenge."

Heather raised an eyebrow at Vidalia, and Vidalia laughed and shook her head. It was funny—she felt a flash of connection to Heather that she hadn't felt in years.

"Good thing you were there," Vidalia said.

"Thank you, Heather," Becky said in a small voice. "What about you, V?" she asked, sitting up. "Another quiet weekend of art and culture?"

"Not exactly," Vidalia said in a bored voice. And then, drawing it out, she told them innocently, "I went to Cannes."

"You what?!" snapped Becky. She and Heather turned to her in surprise.

Vidalia looked off at the castle.

"I've been seeing this guy, Marco," she said casually. "We stayed at his friend's place."

"Marco?" asked Becky. "That's the bookstore guy?"

"No," said Vidalia. "That's Julien—he's just a friend. I met Marco through the Dubois."

Vidalia paused, realizing how much she'd been looking forward to telling them.

"It was nice to get some beach time in." She took a bite of her sandwich. It *had* been nice. It had maybe been the best weekend of her life, actually.

"I don't know what to make of you, Lady V," said Becky, shaking her head over her sandwich. "You're so full of surprises."

Vidalia laughed. "It's no big deal. Just a weekend away."

"A weekend in Cannes sounds like a big deal to me," Becky said dubiously.

"Yeah," agreed Heather.

"So, did you . . . ?" Becky smirked.

"Shut up," said Vidalia, laughing. "None of your business."

Heather was still looking at her with a surprised and curious expression.

Vidalia blushed, remembering how close she'd felt to Marco all weekend. She laughed again as she saw Becky and Heather still watching her.

"Someone's in love," said Becky in a knowing voice.

CHAPTER
◄ **14** ►

THE NEXT DAY, AFTER class at the Musée Apollinaire, Vidalia walked to the Métro with Caroline and another girl.

"Laurent m'a vraiment découragée ce matin"—*Laurent made me feel so discouraged this morning*—said the girl, whose name was Jeanne.

"Qu'est-ce qu'il t'a dit?" asked Caroline. *What did he say?*

"He told me I haven't made progress on shading since I started studying with him, that if I can't learn that, then I shouldn't expect to get into the Beaux-Arts."

Jeanne sounded like she was about to start crying. Vidalia glanced over, feeling bad for her, but also a little relieved to hear that she wasn't the only one Monsieur Benoît was mean to. Caroline made a sympathetic noise.

"And of course everything Bruno does is perfect." Jeanne sighed.

"Vidalia, tu as de la chance"—*You're lucky*—said Caroline. "You're not in competition the way the rest of us are. You can enjoy yourself."

"I guess you're right," said Vidalia. And it was true, she realized, that there was something nice about being the outsider here, even though she felt so far behind the others in her work. It hadn't been like that in Mrs. Greenberg's class. Ellie and some of the others were really good, but they weren't classically trained or anything. And several of them had gotten into art schools for the fall. Ellie was going to Cooper Union.

Vidalia took the train to Saint-Michel and Shakespeare and Company, figuring she'd stop in to say hi to Julien before heading over to the institute for art history. He was behind the register when she walked in, deep in conversation with a willowy girl in a blue sundress. Her blonde hair was pulled back in a bun at the top of her long neck. Julien didn't look up when Vidalia came in. She hesitated for a second, and then walked toward him, letting the door jangle shut. Julien's eyes widened when he saw her, and he raised his hand to wave her toward them.

"Vidalia!" he said as she approached. He turned to the girl. "This is Vidalia," he said to her, and then, to Vidalia, "This is Katarina. She's a student, too, from Italy."

"Hi there," Vidalia said, feeling a funny tension, like this girl wasn't too happy she'd appeared.

Katarina nodded coldly and turned back to Julien.

"I will see you next week, then," she said in accented French. "For the reading?" Julien nodded.

As they turned to each other after Katarina was gone, he smiled his warm Julien smile.

"Inviting her to a reading, huh?" Vidalia teased. "Now I know for sure you do that with all the girls."

He shook his head, laughing and looking a little embarrassed.

"It's my job!" he said, throwing his hands up. "What do you want me to do?"

Vidalia was shaking her head and making a *tsk-tsk* sound when Margie appeared behind Julien.

"Hey, Vidalia," she said. She was holding a stack of books and peering over them, her eyes bright and happy. "Are you coming?"

"Coming?" Vidalia asked, turning to Julien. "Coming where?"

"To Julien's!" she said, turning her back to them, so that she was facing the wall of books. She carefully removed one from the top of her stack and fit it into a space on a shelf. "It's gonna be great!"

"I didn't ask her yet," Julien said, still grinning at Vidalia.

"Well, hurry up then," said Margie, standing on her toes to slide another book onto a shelf. "I don't want to be the only girl along. Your parents will think I'm their new daughter-in-law."

"What are you guys talking about?" Vidalia asked, sitting in the chair next to the register.

"I was going to ask you," Julien said, "if you want to go to the country this weekend. Margie's coming and maybe Andy."

"Nope," Margie said. "Andy can't. His mum's coming into town on Saturday."

"Really?" Julien turned to her. "That's too bad." He turned back to Vidalia. "We're going to my parents' house in the south, a region called the Périgord."

"Yeah," said Margie. "I was there last month and it's gorgeous. Now that it's hot out, we can swim and everything."

Margie had finished unloading her books now, and she turned to Vidalia. She and Julien were both looking expectantly, waiting for her to say yes.

She almost did say yes—she wanted to go with them; it sounded like so much fun. But she was going out with Marco this weekend—Friday and Saturday, galleries, and making plans for Rome. The thought of it made her nervous because she was pretty sure that what Marco meant was that they would steal again, to pay for the trip, and she didn't want to do that. She did want to see him, though, and she wanted to go to Italy. Two weeks in Rome with Marco were worth a missed trip to the countryside. She shook her head and tried to look disappointed.

"I can't," she said. "I have a thing with the Dubois. I told them I'd go to . . . their friends' house with them."

"Oh." Julien looked disappointed.

So did Margie.

"You couldn't tell them this was more important?" she asked plaintively. "You've got to get out of Paris at least once this summer."

They didn't know about Cannes. Vidalia felt ashamed for hiding it.

"I can't," she said, looking down at her feet. "I already told them."

"Okay," said Julien with a sigh. "Maybe we'll go again before you leave."

"Yeah," Vidalia said. "I'll go another time. It sounds really nice."

᠅   ᠅   ᠅

When Vidalia got home on Wednesday night, Madame Dubois was setting the table while Clara did a puzzle in the living room.

"Oh, good, Vidalia," Madame Dubois said. "You'll eat with us. We've hardly had a chance to talk since you've been here. I am very busy with my private students in the summer and Clara has so many activities. Here, please carry this."

"Oh, don't worry," said Vidalia, taking the bowl of boiled carrots and cauliflower Madame Dubois handed her. It didn't seem that her host mother was apologizing, exactly, though.

"I'm sure you're very busy with your classes as well," Madame Dubois said.

Vidalia watched her pull a tray of what looked like frozen fish fillets from the oven. Since her first meal, they'd eaten quickly prepared dishes like this one. It wasn't what Vidalia's mother had led her to expect from the French, who she swore spent a lot more time cooking and enjoying food than Americans. Vidalia's mom, who'd been cooking from her tattered copy of Julia Child's *Mastering the Art of French Cooking* for as long as Vidalia could remember, was more of a gourmet than the Dubois were proving to be.

As the three of them sat down to eat, Madame Dubois said, "I never asked you, where did you get this interesting name?"

"My name?"

"Yes, 'Vidalia.' Is it a family name?" asked Madame Dubois.

Clara looked at Vidalia like she was waiting for the answer.

"No," Vidalia said. "My mother just liked it. She made it

up for me. It's, you know, a kind of onion. My mom says she always thought it was the most beautiful word in the English language."

Vidalia smiled, hoping Madame Dubois would find this charming.

"Ah, how . . . interesting," said her host mother in a pinched way, not amused at all.

Clara was more direct.

"In France, we don't make up names," she said disapprovingly.

"Oh," said Vidalia, glancing at Madame Dubois, expecting the scolding *Clara!* that she heard so often around the house.

But Madame Dubois just smiled tightly. The disapproval was unanimous, it seemed.

"Where is Monsieur Dubois?" Vidalia asked as she served herself fish.

"Away on business," said Madame Dubois, putting fish on Clara's plate.

"He travels a lot," said Vidalia. "What does he do again?"

Clara spoke up, though not to answer Vidalia's question.

"He doesn't have to go away so much," she said. "He just doesn't like being with us."

"Clara!" said her mother.

Ah, there it was. Madame Dubois glared at her daughter for a long moment before turning away.

Clara was looking down at her plate, and though she couldn't be sure, Vidalia thought she saw the little girl's eyes fill with tears.

❧ ❧ ❧

Vidalia had talked to Marco a few times since they'd gotten back from Cannes on Sunday, but he'd been busy at night, and she hadn't seen him. They'd planned to meet later tonight, and she was impatient for his call all through dinner. Her phone finally buzzed while she was clearing the table with Clara.

"Hi," she said, walking down the hall toward Clara's dark bedroom. "Are you ready?"

"Yes," he said. "Can you meet me on the boulevard outside your place?"

"Sure," she said, her heart speeding up. "When?"

"I'll come now. In twenty minutes maybe."

"Okay, I'll see you there," she said.

Vidalia hummed as she and Clara put away dishes. Clara glared at her for it, but Vidalia didn't care. She'd hum whether this grumpy nine-year-old liked it or not. She excused herself to Madame Dubois after that, telling her she was going to do some reading for school in her room. Then she took the back stairway down to the lobby and stepped out onto the street.

Out on the grassy median under the trees, Vidalia waited impatiently for Marco. When he appeared, walking out of the soft darkness toward her, he held a leather travel bag in one hand and something under his other arm. She stood up and walked toward him. Without saying anything, they smiled at each other in the light from the moon and the streetlamps. Just like always, everything felt right as soon as they were together.

"*Ça va?*" he asked.

"I'm good," she said. "You?"

"Yes," he said. "Good, too." He sat down on the bench, pulling her with him. It was a package he was holding under his other arm.

"But something comes up." He sighed and ran his hand through his hair, giving her an apologetic look. "I go away again tomorrow," he said. "Five days."

"You're going away?" Vidalia was alarmed. "But what about the galleries this weekend?" For a second she felt like Clara whining about her father's business trips. She even forgot how nervous she'd been at the thought of going to the galleries and what Marco might expect of her there.

"I know," he said. "It isn't my choice." He stroked her hair away from her face. "Business."

"Okay." She looked down, trying to hide her disappointment.

"The Dubois are home tonight?" he asked softly, bending his head to see her face.

"Not Monsieur Dubois," she said, looking up. "Madame and Clara are up there, though." She sighed, thinking of their tense dinner together.

"*Ah, oui,*" he said, nodding. "Vidalia," he said in a different tone of voice. "Can you keep this for me while I'm gone? Just put it in your room?"

He handed her the package. It was thin and no more than a foot and a half long, and it was wrapped in brown paper.

"Okay," she said, taking it from him. "What is it?"

"Just something I don't want to take with me. I've got to make the train tonight."

Vidalia nodded and looked at him, trying to get used to the idea of not seeing him for the next five days.

"And this is for you," he said, taking something from his pocket and putting it in her hand, closing her fingers around it. She started to open her hand and saw a smooth roll of bills.

"No, don't look now," he said, pushing her hand back down. "You see later."

She dropped her hand by her side.

"We'll go to the galleries next week, okay? We will do our plan. It will all be like we said."

"Okay," she said, nodding and trying to look like she was taking all this in stride. Really, she was shocked to see that actual money had come from Ruby's painting. It hadn't seemed quite real when Marco had said it in Cannes. Could it be as much as he'd promised?

"When will you be back?" she asked.

"Probably Monday." He gave her a regretful look. "I'm sorry, I have to go now. The train leaves soon from Montparnasse."

"Okay," she said, and swallowed as she raised her head and smiled at him.

He took her face in his hands and leaned in to look into her eyes.

"You will be here when I come back?" he asked.

"Of course," she said. "I've got almost four weeks left."

He nodded.

"And then our two weeks together," he said. "This is what I'm waiting for."

Vidalia walked back to the Dubois' with the package under her arm. Upstairs, she tucked the package under her bed and opened her hand with the money in it. She counted five hundred euros, just like Marco had promised. They were really going to Rome, she thought. This proved it.

When Vidalia came outside after art history the next day, the girls had gathered around a table in the courtyard.

"So where are you off to this weekend?" Vidalia asked.

"Staying here," said Becky. "Last weekend sort of did me in. Maybe I'll try to do like you and absorb a little of the local culture. Do you want to go out Saturday night?"

"I can't," Vidalia said. "I'm going away, actually."

She had called Julien the night before to tell him she could go down south after all. He'd been happy, and Vidalia was looking forward to the weekend with him and Margie.

"Again? You are such a hypocrite," whined Becky. "Where to?"

"My friend Julien, the guy from the bookstore, asked me to go to the country," she said. "To his parents' house."

"Wow, meeting the family," she said. "What does Marco think of this?"

"Julien and I are just friends," Vidalia said. "A bunch of people are going. Besides, Marco's away this week, doing some work stuff."

"What does he do, anyway?" asked Becky. "He doesn't look that old."

"He's nineteen," Vidalia said. "He dropped out of college to work in the art business. He's trying to start a gallery." Vidalia hardly noticed that she was repeating Marco's lie even though she knew the truth now.

"Huh," said Becky, looking at her for a long moment. "Well, Heather, do *you* want to go out on Saturday?"

Heather shrugged, her shoulders deeply tanned under her white tank top. She must have been lying out, Vidalia thought. She herself had never tanned. Her hair might be dark, but her skin was pale as milk.

"Sure," Heather said. "What do you want to do?"

"I don't know, go dancing?" said Becky. She looked across the courtyard at Kenji, who was sitting alone. "Kenji will come!" she said brightly.

"You haven't spoken to him since Brittany, have you?" asked Heather, giving Becky a skeptical look.

"Well, no, but . . ." Becky paused and then turned firmly to Heather. "You're right. It's time to make up for my sins."

She stood up and walked over to him.

Vidalia watched Becky position herself in front of Kenji, her hand on her hip, a sorrowful expression on her face. He looked up at her, squinting and suspicious.

"She'll probably get him back, too," Vidalia said. Becky amazed her with a totally unabashed determination to go after what she wanted. She waited for a reaction from Heather. They hadn't talked since their moment at Versailles on Monday, but Becky's behavior seemed like a safe subject.

Heather didn't answer, though. Vidalia turned to her and saw that she'd leaned her head in her arms on the table in front of her.

"What's up, Heather?" she asked. "Are you okay?"

Heather looked up at her, a blank expression on her face.

"I'm just . . . I don't know," she said, shaking her head. Tears came into her eyes. "I guess I'm not having such a great time here."

"Why not?" Vidalia asked, surprised. "Don't you like your family?" She remembered the happy-looking young couple who'd picked her up at the airport. They had to be more fun than the Dubois.

"Yeah." She rubbed her eyes. "I don't know. I mean, they're fine. I feel like crap, though." She sighed. "There's no real reason."

"Maybe you're just tired?" Vidalia offered.

"I'm always tired," Heather said, slumping forward again. "All I ever do is sleep."

How had it happened that shiny perfect Heather was miserable and exhausted and Vidalia was having the most social summer of her life? Funny how quickly things could change. But Vidalia was surprised to find that the comparison didn't make her feel good at all.

"I'll be okay," Heather said, meeting Vidalia's eyes for a second and then looking away as she stood up and pulled her bag over her shoulder. "See you later," she said, obviously forcing herself to sound cheerful. Vidalia watched her walk slowly out of the courtyard.

It was strange. Vidalia had a natural impulse to help her, just like when they were kids. She remembered the times Heather had gotten upset over the way somebody had treated her at school, or maybe a boy she liked who didn't like her back. Vidalia had been the strong one then, comforting her and telling her she didn't need those people anyway. That was part of what had been such a shock when Heather had ditched her. Vidalia had always felt like she was more in control in their friendship. After that had happened, Vidalia had hung out with kids at school, but she'd never allowed herself to get that close to another girl. Even Ellie hadn't been the kind of best friend that Heather had been once. Now Heather was on her own, just like Vidalia had been for the past three years.

CHAPTER
15

"ALLO?" VIDALIA SAID, ANSWERING her cell phone.

"You're ready to go?" It was Julien.

"Uh, yeah," she said. "I mean, I have to pack my stuff, but don't we have, like, an hour and a half?"

"Yes," he said. "I'm just making sure you're still coming."

It was Friday, and they were all meeting at the train station at six. Vidalia smiled at Julien's enthusiasm. She was looking forward to the weekend, too.

"I'm coming, I'm coming," she said. "I'll see you guys at Montparnasse."

"Okay, don't forget your swimming suit!"

"I won't," she promised.

Monsieur Dubois had been away most of the week, but when Vidalia jogged down the stairs to the dining room, she found him sitting at the table like he'd never left.

"Vidalia," he said, his same old jolly self.

"Hi," she said, surprised. "You're home."

"Yes," he said, chuckling. He was wearing a suit like always. "But I go away again right away. More business." He shook his head in a woeful way and took a dainty sip from his espresso cup.

"Are you enjoying Paris?" he asked, smiling in that serenely friendly way of his. It was funny, he still seemed like the nicest member of the Dubois family, but he was also the one Vidalia felt she knew the least.

"I am," she said. "It's great." She stopped, unsure of what else to say. "There's so much wonderful art here."

"Yes." He seemed delighted to hear this. "A lot for you to talk about with your mother, I suppose."

"Right." She paused. Why did everything always have to come back to her mother? "I've already been to the Louvre, the Musée d'Orsay . . ."

"Ah, yes," he said, nodding and smiling. "I will be to New York soon," he said then, looking at her. "Perhaps I could go to see your mother's collection while I am there."

"Oh, yeah," Vidalia said, trying to keep from looking horrified. "But she's not in the city, you know. Her gallery is way out on Long Island, pretty far away. And, actually, she closes up for part of the summer so she can travel." She coughed. Monsieur Dubois just gazed calmly at her. "She might not even be there."

"Well." Monsieur Dubois seemed to dismiss the topic with the word. "We will see. I will tell you before I go."

"Okay," Vidalia said. "Have a good weekend. I'm going to the Périgord with friends for the weekend."

Once again, Madame Dubois had barely seemed to notice and certainly hadn't objected when Vidalia had informed her of her plans.

"Enjoy yourself," Monsieur Dubois said, nodding and picking up his newspaper. "We will meet next week."

Vidalia exhaled with a combination of relief and irritation as she left the apartment. She hoped she hadn't gotten herself into trouble with the art gallery story. She thought of how unlikely it was that an East Hampton art dealer would leave town during summer, the busy tourist season. Oh well, she thought, starting down the stairs, nothing to do but hope Monsieur Dubois didn't know that.

"Vidalia!" That was Julien's voice.

She looked around and saw him and Margie waving to her from the other side of the station.

"The train is here!" cried Julien. "Come on, we have to get good seats!"

Vidalia hurried over to them and they rushed down the long platform to Julien's preferred car at the front of the train.

"This is the best one," he told them as they put their bags overhead. "Because when we get off, it will put us just where my mother comes to pick us up."

"I'm glad you've got it all figured out," said Vidalia, sitting down.

"Julien is organized in all things," said Margie. She was wearing a long flowered skirt, and her blonde hair was tied into several little pigtails. "I wish Michel could have come this weekend." She sighed.

"Why didn't he?" asked Vidalia.

"He's preparing for a big exam in the fall. All he does is study. It's getting quite depressing, actually." Margie looked glum.

Julien sat down and looked at them with a pleased expression. He was happy to be going home, thought Vidalia.

When they got off the train, it was dark out, and they were at a tiny station in the middle of nowhere, with trees all around. They walked across the empty platform to a little bench on a crumbling road. A moment later, a tiny car screeched to a stop in front of them.

"That's my mother," Julien said, smiling. A small woman leapt out of the front seat.

"Julien!" she cried.

"*Salut, Maman,*" he said, hugging her. Julien wasn't all that tall, but his mother was tiny. She disappeared into his hug for a second before firecrackering back out of it.

"*Marguerite!*" she cried, rushing toward Margie.

"*Bonjour, Madame!*" cried Margie, dropping her bag on the cracked cement and hugging her back.

"*Et Vidalia!*" she said, turning to her. She grabbed Vidalia by the arms and kissed her on each cheek before picking up her bag and hoisting it into the back of the little car. Julien waved Vidalia into the front seat and climbed into the back with Margie. In seconds they were flying off down a country road through dark, sweet-smelling trees.

"You are hungry?" Julien's mother asked in French, and they all said *oui, oui,* they were starving in spite of the chocolate they'd eaten on the train.

"Good!" She turned back to the road and gave the wheel a satisfied smack. "We have good lamb and wonderful bread. Oh, and I found such a delicious *chèvre* at the market to-day—very soft, perfect!"

She took a hairpin turn fast into a sloping driveway.

"Julien, you take Vidalia and Marguerite up to their room. I must check the dinner!" And she was gone.

Julien led them through a small door between flowering bushes and into the house. The ceilings were low and the living room and dining room and kitchen all opened onto each other, with a big wooden table in the kitchen and soft old couches gathered around a small table in the living room. Julien's mother was moving quickly around the kitchen, and delicious smells came from that direction. Margie and Vidalia followed Julien up the creaky stairs to the second floor, where it smelled piney and summery, like Vidalia imagined camp would smell.

"That's my bedroom," said Julien, gesturing. Vidalia looked in at a little boy's room with blue curtains with sailboats on them and board games stacked in a corner. Julien smiled shyly. "Yours is upstairs," he said. He walked up the narrow stairs and Vidalia and Margie followed him. It was a small room with slanted ceilings and it was full of old books.

"This is the library," Julien said, and they laughed.

Margie sat down on the neatly made queen-size bed and bounced on the mattress.

"You're both in here. I hope that's okay," he told them.

"Fine with me," said Margie. "I sleep like a log anyway. How about you, Vidalia?"

"No problem," said Vidalia. She hadn't slept in a bed with a girlfriend for years, she thought, though she and Heather used to do it all the time.

"Julien! It's ready!" his mother yelled.

All three of them hurried downstairs.

At dinner, big plates of lamb and potatoes and salad went around. Julien's father was as friendly and enthusiastic as his wife.

After dinner, Julien's father made them taste each one of the cheeses on the heavy board that he passed around. The chèvre was the last one Vidalia tried, and it was her favorite, delicious and creamy on the crusty bread.

"It is good, *non*?" said Julien's father, overjoyed at her reaction. "I told you," he said triumphantly.

"Very, very good," Vidalia said, sinking her teeth into another creamy, crusty bite. "It's nothing like the goat cheese we get at home."

After dinner, they ate plums outside in the garden, sitting around a metal table.

"The air is sweet here," said Julien's father. "You smell it, girls? It's the hay from the farm next door." He inhaled deeply through his nose, filling up his chest. "My wife grew up in this house. She's a real farm girl, right, Marie?"

"Georges, you talk too much," said his wife playfully. "Vidalia, how is it at your home?" Vidalia felt Julien glance at her like he was telling her that she didn't have to talk about it. She didn't mind, though.

"We live in an old house, too," she said. "My great-grandparents built it. It's kind of falling apart now, but it's full of old stuff, furniture and books and clothes."

"An American with history," Julien's father said approvingly. "It's very rare."

"Yeah," Vidalia said with a laugh. "I don't know what good it does us but we do have history."

Julien's mother got up and announced that she was going to do the dishes.

"I'll help you, *Maman*," said Julien.

"My boy," she said, putting her arm around him briefly. "He is so good!"

Julien rolled his eyes before following her inside.

When the dishes were done and his parents had wished them all good night and walked up to the house, Julien sat down at the table with Vidalia and Margie.

"They are a little crazy, no?" he said.

"They're so nice," Vidalia said. "They seem like they really like having people around."

"I know," he said. "They always wanted me to have my friends at the house when I was growing up. Everyone loved them. They had their problems, too, though."

"Oh, yeah?" Vidalia asked. "Like what?" She found it hard to believe.

"My father used to drink a lot," Julien said. "It was really bad for a while when I was in high school. He was never violent or anything, but he stayed out so late every night, and sometimes he didn't come home on the weekends. My mother got scared wondering where he was, but he would just yell if she asked him."

"Really?" Vidalia asked, shocked that such a perfect pair of parents could have such serious problems.

"Yeah, I can't picture it," said Margie.

"Only one time I got angry at him. I couldn't stand that

he made my mother so upset. I pushed him against the wall and I screamed at him. It was terrible." He shook his head and looked toward the house.

"I guess that's why there was no wine at dinner," Vidalia said.

"Yes, a couple of months after that fight, he just stopped. He said it was over. I don't think he's had a drink since."

"They seem happy together now," Margie said.

"Yes," he said. "I think now they are."

He smiled at Vidalia and she smiled back, feeling sad for him. If anyone deserved to have things go well, she thought, it was Julien.

That night, lying in bed next to Margie in the attic room, Vidalia felt the summer breeze wash over her and listened to the crickets and frogs outside the window. This wasn't like the gorgeous happiness and sense of possibility that she felt when she was with Marco, but it was nice. She felt safe here.

CHAPTER
16

"COU COU," JULIEN SAID, waking Vidalia with a French greeting.

She rolled over and, behind her closed eyes, felt the world come into focus. Sun, crisp sheets, the smell of hay and flowers. She opened her eyes. The door, made of uneven planks of wood, was half open, and Julien was peering in around it. She was alone in bed. Margie must have already gone downstairs.

"Awake?" he asked.

"Mmmm," she said. "Almost."

"I wouldn't bother you, but my mother's going to the market soon and I thought maybe you'd want to go." He smiled.

"I want to go," she said, stretching in the white sheets.

"There's coffee ready," he said, and he disappeared behind the closing door.

"The artichokes are very good right now," Julien's mother was saying when Vidalia came down to the kitchen. "I tried them last week from a woman at the market. She said they're good everywhere but I tried others that the Maréchals had at dinner two days ago, and they were nice but not as sweet."

"And the tomatoes?" asked Julien. "We could have tomato

salad with salt and vinegar and maybe some sweet onions."

"*Bonjour,*" Vidalia said. They both turned to her.

"*Vidalia, bonjour!*" said Julien's mom. "You're coming to the market with us?"

Julien was leaning against the counter in jeans and a worn blue T-shirt. Margie was at the table nursing a big bowl of milky coffee. She raised her hand limply to Vidalia.

"Yes," Vidalia said.

"Sit," said Julien. "I'll get coffee for you. There's bread there in the basket." He waved to the wooden table as he turned to pour coffee from a small espresso pot into a pan and switched on the burner beneath it. "And butter and jam." He leaned over to hand her a knife before she sat down.

"And you, Marguerite?" asked Julien's mother. "Will you come to the market?"

"I think I'll stay here," said Margie, smiling weakly over her coffee. "I'll just lie around in the yard for a little while, work on my tan."

Vidalia, Julien, and Julien's mother all looked skeptically at Margie's pale arms.

She waved them off.

"You know what I mean," she said.

The market was a buzz of color and noise in the square of a little town, an old stone church standing over it all. Julien's mother took three big baskets from the trunk of the car and handed one each to Vidalia and Julien. They went from stand to stand, making their way through the clusters of people shouting back and forth. *"Madame!"* a vendor would shout when he or she was ready for the next customer. Julien's mother joined the fray, pushing her way between people and reaching for heads of lettuce and artichokes, calling out questions to the vendors. Vidalia and Julien stood back and watched her go. When she emerged from the crowd, she called, "Julien! Go get bread from the baker all the way over by the church. Get three of the long ones, the country loaves!"

"Oui, Maman," said Julien, and he took Vidalia's arm and led her toward the church through the crowds. She kept making him stop to look at things, the pink fish laid out googly-eyed in beds of crushed ice, the meat stand where cow tongues sat next to sliced ham.

They bought the bread his mother wanted, plus a couple of fruit tarts, which they sat down on a bench to eat. Julien's mother came over to them.

"Here," she said. "I'll leave this with you while I go get the meat and the cheese."

She put down her big basket, which was overflowing with fruits and leafy green vegetables, and took Vidalia's empty one before rushing off again.

"You're a country girl, really," Julien said, watching her dig through the baskets to pull out a plum.

"I am not," Vidalia said. "East Hampton is very sophisticated."

Julien laughed.

"I would love to visit New York City," he said. "There must be so much energy there."

"Yeah," Vidalia agreed. "The city's fun." She went in on the weekend sometimes, with Ellie, to go thrift-shopping or to museums.

"Do you think you'll go to university there?" he asked.

"I don't know," she said. "There's an art school that I like, Cooper Union, but it's hard to get into." Vidalia finished the plum she'd found in the basket and tossed the pit into the gutter with the leaves of spinach and tomato stems that had been swept there.

"School is expensive in the States," Julien said matter-of-factly.

"Yeah," she said, thinking of her mother so helpless at home for just six weeks. How would Vidalia ever leave her to go to college? "Cooper Union's free if you get in, but who knows? Maybe it's not even necessary."

Julien raised an eyebrow at her.

"What do you mean?" he asked.

"Well," she said, "I've always thought of school as my way of getting to the city and everything, but the reality is, if I'm going to be an artist, what do I need it for?" She felt defiant all of a sudden. "Some of the best artists never went to school for it. I mean, maybe I'd learn more by traveling or something anyway." She looked around the marketplace at all the people. Suddenly, the crowd was too hectic, the noise unpleasant. She felt prickly.

"I suppose," Julien said. "But education is a good thing. If you go to art school or any kind of school, then you're meeting people who can teach you things. You won't necessarily meet those people if you're just traveling."

Vidalia shrugged. She thought of Marco, who hadn't even finished junior high.

"If you're smart then you don't need it," she said. "I'm really starting to believe that."

Julien, who she knew was eager to start college in September, looked a little offended, but before he could answer, his mother was back with a basket of packages wrapped in paper, the cheese and the meat and the fish she'd bought.

"*Allons-y*," she said. *Let's go.*

Vidalia and Julien walked to the car in silence.

That afternoon, after getting back to the house and unpacking the bags of groceries, Julien and Margie and Vidalia all rode bikes to a river nearby. They spent several hours jumping into the cold water, swimming, and then lying around on the shore. Whatever tension there had been between Vidalia and Julien had disappeared by the time they biked back to his house.

When Vidalia went up to the attic room before dinner that night, she saw that there were messages on her phone. She listened and heard her mother's voice. It was cheerful, but Vidalia wondered if there was a layer of desperation lurking beneath the cheer.

"Baby," she said, "could you please call me? I'd just like to have a chat."

Ever since the conversation at Luxembourg Gardens, the day of Ruby's painting, her mother seemed to have realized she'd gone too far in trying to get her to come home. She hadn't mentioned it again, instead making a big show of how great everything was—the weather, the produce from Fresh Direct, the working electricity. Vidalia had gritted her teeth as she listened to the charade. All she heard in her mother's descriptions of her wonderful days was that she wasn't leaving the house. She pressed her finger hard on the erase button and listened to the next message. It was from Marco.

"Vidalia," he said. "I just want to say hello, to hear your voice. I'm coming back a little early, tomorrow night, and I want to see you. I've had an idea, that maybe we could do something like we did the last time, at the gallery." She could hear the excitement in his voice. "I have . . . interest . . . from a buyer." He paused. "In any case. I will call you tomorrow night, about eleven, when I arrive in Paris, and then maybe we can meet?"

Vidalia had forgotten how smooth and elastic his voice was, like caramel. Even so, the words he actually said made her feel awful. She didn't want to steal anything else, but she didn't want to give up their trip, either. Maybe the return call could wait until tomorrow.

She called her mother instead, and was glad to find that nothing urgent was going on.

"It sounds lovely!" her mother said when Vidalia told her about Julien's family and the house in the Périgord.

"It is," said Vidalia. "And you would have loved the market. There were so many kinds of meat and fish and cheese."

"I long for a French market," sighed her mother. "Well, remember it, darling, and you can draw it all for me later. That's just about as good as the real thing."

"It's not really the same thing," said Vidalia.

"But I like it just the same, that's what I mean," said her mother decisively.

They had another long dinner with Julien and his family, talking about the country and the food, and about art and museums.

"We have an artist in the neighborhood," said Julien's father. "A real eccentric who builds sculptures in his yard. Julien, you should take the girls to see!"

After dinner, Julien asked if Vidalia and Margie wanted to go for a walk.

"Not me," said Margie. "I'm staying here with my coffee."

"She just likes talking with me," said Julien's father. Margie and he had been kidding around throughout dinner. "I know the effect I have on young girls." He laughed heartily.

"Oh, Georges." Julien's mother faked disgust and swatted him with her napkin.

"I'll go," said Vidalia.

She followed Julien across the field behind his house. Everything was bright and clear in the light from the full moon.

"Are you cold?" Julien asked.

"No," she said. Her mind was still on Marco and the galleries. On her mother shut inside the house. "I'm fine." She smiled and tried not to look too distant.

"Come on," he said. "I want to show you something."

Vidalia followed him past the edge of the hayfield and around what looked like the backyard of another house, where he stopped.

"Look through here," he said. He peered through an

opening in the wooden fence that lined the property. Vidalia leaned in next to him. The yard was filled with whirling, turning metal propellers and moving parts of all different colors and sizes.

"What is it?" Vidalia asked, trying to get a better look.

"The guy next door, remember my father told you he's an artist?"

"It's amazing," Vidalia said, looking at a little black metal fountain where water fell from one level to another, turning windmill pieces as it went.

"I thought you'd like it," Julien said.

"It's like a little fantasy land," said Vidalia.

"He makes it all out of garbage," said Julien.

"Magical garbage," said Vidalia, and Julien laughed.

They both bent forward again and looked through the hole in the fence, and as they did, Julien rested his arm against Vidalia's. She felt a sudden shock of alarm. She hadn't really seriously considered the possibility that Julien was interested in being more than her friend. But now, suddenly, it seemed like maybe that's what had been going on all along.

They stood up and walked toward the edge of the trees. What if he'd brought her out here to make out or something? But, no, he'd invited Margie, too. Still, Vidalia thought, this would be a good time to set things straight, just so there was no confusion about it. Julien was walking ahead of her, and he sat down on a big rock and gestured for her to sit next to him.

"Look." He pointed up at the sky. "You can see the moon."

Vidalia glanced briefly where he indicated, but she was intent on starting this conversation.

"Julien," she said. It came out abruptly.

"Yes?" He looked at her, startled.

"I just want . . . It's been really nice to be here."

"Oh." He looked puzzled. "I'm glad you came."

"Listen, I just wanted to tell you that I'm really glad we're friends."

Julien looked a little more ill at ease than before.

"I mean, I just want to be clear because I like being friends so much and I don't want anything to, like, get in the way." She looked down at her hands.

There was a pause before Julien said anything.

"Okay," he said, like he was waiting for more.

"I mean, in case . . ." Vidalia paused and gave him a worried look and forced the rest out in a rush. "I didn't want you to think we were going to, like, get involved, because I just really see this as a really great friendship."

There, she'd said it.

Julien looked at her.

"I just didn't want you to think . . ." she said.

"I don't think anything," he said. "I like being your friend, too."

He looked really uncomfortable.

"Oh, okay," she said. So she hadn't needed to say any of this after all.

"Why do you feel like you have to say this now?" he asked. "Did I do something?"

"No! I just thought, well, I've been seeing this guy, so I just wanted things to be clear."

"Oh," said Julien. He looked up at the moon.

"I'm sorry," Vidalia said. "I didn't mean for that to sound weird."

Julien turned to her, and Vidalia thought his smile was more distant than usual.

"Let's go back to the house," he said. "We have to get the train tomorrow morning, and I want to go swimming before we leave."

"Okay," she said.

Julien put his hands in his pockets and started walking. Vidalia followed a few feet behind him. She felt awful. She knew someone had just been rejected, but she wasn't sure if it was Julien or if it was her.

CHAPTER

⌐ **17** ⌐

THEY WERE ALL QUIET on the train ride back to Paris, not like on the ride down. Julien had announced as soon as they got on that he was planning on using the trip home to catch up on his sleep before he went back to work that night, and he'd stretched out across a bank of seats. Margie sat down in the seat next to Vidalia and opened the magazine she'd bought at the station.

Vidalia tried to forget about her conversation with Julien the night before, which she still felt bad about. She sketched absentmindedly as she looked out the window at the fields and the houses. The block of a stone church, the twisting rows of grapevines on the curve of a hill, two people walking along the train tracks, all appeared in faint pencil lines in the sketchbook she had propped up on her knee. Next to her, Margie flipped the pages of her magazine with a kind of disdainful satisfaction, scoffing out loud every once in a while.

"What are you reading?" Vidalia finally asked her, when an especially loud snort jerked her out of her reverie.

"Trash, really," said Margie, but she kept staring intently down at the open page in front of her.

Vidalia leaned farther over, and Margie briefly flipped the cover closed for her to see.

"Paris Match," Vidalia read out loud.

The title hovered over a photograph of a youngish woman sitting in a white chair. Her long brown hair was neatly brushed and she was tastefully dressed in white and beige, with some even more tasteful gold jewelry at her neck and ears and wrists. Her smile was bland and, Vidalia thought, insincere. An older, gray-haired man stood behind the chair, gazing fondly down at her. It looked like an elaborate stage set, hardly like anybody's real life. *"Les jeunes maries,"* the caption read. *The Newlyweds.*

"Isn't she kind of young to be married to that guy?" Vidalia asked as Margie snapped the magazine open so that Vidalia could no longer see the cover.

"Dunno," said Margie. "Haven't gotten to them yet."

"So you're into celebrity gossip?" asked Vidalia, leaning back in her seat and looking sideways at Margie's tight shoulders hunched over her magazine. "I'd never have pictured you drooling over movie stars' love lives."

Margie gave a sharp laugh. "Me being so literary and all," she agreed. "Only it's not actually movie stars. It's more millionaire playboys, political families, the rotten remains of the European aristocracy. I like to think of it as kind of an anthropological interest."

"Sounds stimulating," Vidalia said, yawning.

"I don't know what to tell you, it just turns me on." Margie shrugged and turned the page. "Like, here." She held out the magazine for Vidalia. "Aphrodite Niarchos, the richest little girl in the world."

Vidalia looked down at a photograph of a girl in sunglasses getting out of a sleek black car, her head turned to look at something above and to the left of the camera.

"She's exactly my age, eighteen. I've been reading about her forever." Margie snapped her gum and straightened up in her seat. "She's gone to all the best schools, plays polo, lives in a castle. And she's the heir to the biggest fortune in the world. She'll start collecting when she turns twenty-five."

Vidalia looked at the girl, strange and unknowable behind her dark glasses.

"Must be nice not having any problems," she said, trying to sound blasé so Margie wouldn't hear the jealousy in her voice.

Margie snorted.

"She's got more problems than you do, love," she said.

Vidalia raised her eyebrow skeptically. Margie had no idea.

"Like for example?"

"Like having to worry that every guy she ever dates is after her money, for one. What do you think I'm reading about? The desperate loneliness of Aphrodite, goddess of love, poor thing." Margie laughed, but it was a sorry laugh, not cruel, which was how Vidalia felt looking at that girl pinned in the middle of her perfect world.

"Well, I guess *that's* not a problem I've got," admitted Vidalia, still pretty sure that Aphrodite Niarchos wouldn't trade lives with her if she had the chance.

"People never are what they want you to think," Margie said. She tapped Vidalia's knee with the magazine, which she'd folded in half.

Vidalia rolled her eyes. "The infinite wisdom," she said with a sigh, "is, like, so original."

"It's not original but it's true," said Margie with certainty. "It's the lesson of the gossip world. Happily married? Turns out the guy goes cruising for teenage hookers on Saturday nights. Kids smiling pretty for the camera? Mum beats 'em with a hairbrush every night before bed."

"I think I saw that movie," said Vidalia.

"Tabloids are a crucible of truth," said Margie. "I'm just waiting for the other shoe to drop on Aphrodite. Nobody grows up all healthy and happy with everything she's got."

"I don't know," said Vidalia, thinking of the summer people in East Hampton, driving through town in their brand-new cars, money dripping from their tanned, jeweled hands. "Maybe some people just get lucky."

"You're a hopeless romantic, love," said Margie. "It's what Julien adores about you." She dropped the magazine into Vidalia's lap while Vidalia cringed at the mention of Julien adoring her. "Read and learn. I'm going to get some beauty rest, too." Margie yawned and closed her eyes.

Vidalia looked at her for a second, still a little surprised by the Julien comment. He must not have told Margie about their awkward little tête-à-tête the night before. She looked around Margie at Julien's boot hanging over the edge of the seat.

Vidalia opened the magazine, looking for something else to think about. At first, all she saw were blurry photographs of people on the beach. Then, farther in, there were more posed pictures of the couple from the cover. There was the

woman—her name was Marie Cartier, according to the cap-
tions—in full riding gear on a horse in front of an endless
manicured lawn. From what Vidalia picked up in a quick scan
of the article, this woman's father had died in a boating ac-
cident in the spring. Now Marie had just married her dad's
best friend, who'd been there in her time of need. There was
another picture of Marie and her new husband, lying on a
fuzzy white rug, his arms wrapped protectively around her,
her head nestled into his shoulder. This scandalous love af-
fair had ended in a fairy-tale wedding, the article informed
Vidalia, though some unnamed sources continued to say that
it was disrespectful to Marie's father.

Vidalia was interested now. Had they been involved before
her father got killed? Maybe he'd been against the marriage
and so they'd killed him and made it look like a boating ac-
cident. That would explain the quick wedding after his death.
She turned the page. At the top of the left-hand spread there
was an old snapshot of a man with shaggy, streaky brown hair
and sunglasses standing on the deck of a boat. He was smiling and he had one tanned arm wrapped around a little girl's
shoulders. Her hair was flying around her face and she was
laughing and looking up at him. It was Marie and her father.
Funny, she'd looked like a real person when she was a kid.

A bigger picture filled most of the next page. It showed the
adult Marie sitting in a window seat gazing out. It was raining
outside and her expression was mournful, her forehead lightly
touching the glass. God, Vidalia thought, it was so obvious
that the picture was set up to show "Marie feeling sad about
her father's death." Next to the old photograph, it was almost

obscene. I mean, the guy was dead, why not show some respect?

Scanning the article, she read that Marie and her new/old husband were planning a party at their Paris residence, which they were about to reopen after three months of renovations. *"'It was my father's favorite place in the world, right in the middle of Paris,' says Marie."*

How did Margie read this stuff? She was about to close the magazine when something caught her eye. It was a framed painting hanging next to the big window seat, its canvas half in darkness, half lit by the gray daylight. She leaned close to the magazine to see it. Swirling shapes floated on white canvas, a star hung in one corner, and stretching across the bottom was a hallucinatory landscape of black lines dotted with slivered moons of color. It looked vaguely familiar, like one of the paintings they'd looked at in Madame Zafar's class the week before. Maybe if her mother really was an art dealer, Vidalia thought, they'd have things like this on their walls too, paintings by people who were famous, and dead.

A strange thought occurred to her. Vidalia couldn't steal from people like Ruby, from artists who were trying to make a living. But behind this canvas, there was no living artist, Vidalia was sure. There were just a bunch of people with too much of everything who offered up their deepest secrets to tabloids and TV, either for money or just to get even more attention from the world than they already had.

Marco's face as he'd looked in the kitchen in Cannes the week before flashed in Vidalia's mind. *Who are we hurting?*

he'd asked. *What's wrong with taking just a little bit of what they've got?* Vidalia hadn't known what to say at the time but now she did.

No one, she thought. *Nothing.*

Madame Dubois was on the phone in the entryway, yelling at someone, when Vidalia let herself into the apartment that night. She hurried past her host mother, who was crying, *"Ah, non! Mais ce n'est pas possible, tout ça!"* Vidalia stuck her head into the living room and saw Clara watching TV with a blank look, the weird bluish light reflecting on her face.

"Bonsoir," Vidalia said.

Clara glanced up quickly, almost eagerly, Vidalia thought.

"What are you watching?" she asked, stepping through the glass doors.

"Oh, it's you," said Clara in a bored voice that contradicted the look she'd just given.

"Yup, just me," said Vidalia. Clara was already looking back at the TV.

"Hello, Vidalia," called Madame Dubois, walking into the room, having finished her argument and hung up the phone. "Did you have a nice weekend in the south?"

"Oh, yeah, it was great," said Vidalia. "Just total country vacation." She smiled.

"Good," Madame Dubois said. "We will eat dinner very soon."

"I'll just go up and put my stuff away," Vidalia said, walking to the stairs.

But Madame Dubois stopped her.

"Vidalia," she said, and Vidalia turned to see her standing in the doorway, giving her a strange look.

"Yes?" Madame Dubois couldn't have found out about Ruby's painting, could she? Vidalia stopped breathing and waited.

"I left some clean sheets for you. They are on your bed."

That was it? Vidalia exhaled.

"Oh, okay, thanks," she said in a forced cheery voice.

Madame Dubois spun around and hurried back to the kitchen. When Vidalia glanced over at Clara, she was giving the empty doorway where her mother had just been standing a puzzled look. Clara saw Vidalia looking at her and rolled her eyes.

"*Elle est complètement folle*"—*She's completely crazy*—she said, and turned back to the television.

Vidalia smiled. Clara didn't know from crazy.

Upstairs, as Vidalia took her key from her bag, it hit her. Marco's package. Had Madame Dubois seen it? Was that what that look meant? Had she *taken* it? Vidalia unlocked the door in a hurry and, pushing it closed again, dropped to her knees next to the bed. The package was right where she'd left it. She took it and turned it over in her hands. The brown paper was neatly folded and taped, but one of the pieces was loose, as if it had been opened. She froze for a second, not sure why it made her feel so panicked to think of Madame Dubois up here in her room, looking around under her bed, opening this package. Gently, she unfolded the paper and gripped the rough edge of the frame. She pulled it out, careful not to tear the paper.

The painting was small and dark with age. It was a country scene with cows chewing grass and a milkmaid walking toward them from a barn.

She stared at it for a minute longer. Whatever. If Madame Dubois ever asked her about it, she'd just say she'd bought it at a flea market or something. There was nothing incriminating about having some old painting under her bed.

Vidalia slid the painting back into the paper and closed it up the way it had been, pressing the piece of tape down so that, when she took her thumb away, it stuck.

It was almost midnight when Marco called. Vidalia was lying on her bed, using pastels to sketch what she remembered of the market down south. There were the fruits and vegetables and fish, and the people in patches of color. She dropped the purple pastel as she grabbed the phone from the floor.

"Hi," she said, trying not to sound nervous, her heart beating unevenly.

"Sorry to be late," he said, out of breath. "Can you meet me on the boulevard? The same bench as before?"

"Sure," she said.

"I'll be there in fifteen minutes. And could you bring this package I gave to you?"

"Okay," she said. "I have to finish something, though, so it might take me a little longer than that." That was a lie. It would take her less than five minutes to get to the bench down the street, but she didn't want him to think she'd just been waiting for him, and she felt a little put off by how rushed he sounded. Was he excited to see her or not?

"Okay," he said. *"Eh, Vidalia?"*

"Yeah?" she answered quickly.

There was a pause, and when he spoke again, his voice was slower, calmer.

"Tu m'as manquée," he said.

Vidalia smiled up at the night sky through her window.

"I missed you, too," she said.

The bench was empty when she got there, so Vidalia sat and leaned her head back. She closed her eyes, not wanting to see anything until she saw Marco.

After a minute or so, she heard steps and then felt movement close by. A nervous thrill ran through her, but she kept her eyes closed.

"Bonsoir, ma belle," he said, and she felt his warm breath and lips on her neck. She turned her head slowly toward him and smiled, then opened her eyes.

"And if it wasn't me?" he said, teasing, his eyes bright and close to hers.

"I knew it was you." She smiled.

"You're lucky," he said.

"Yeah," she said tauntingly. "So are you."

"This is true," he whispered, and he kissed her mouth. She closed her eyes, so glad to be with him again.

"Did anyone see you with that?" Marco nodded at the

package in her lap. She thought of Madame Dubois in her room and turned away uneasily to look down the boulevard.

"No," she said, not wanting to talk about Madame Dubois after their weird interaction. "What is it anyway?"

"One of those country things I told you about," he said, tossing a match to the ground. "From the estate sale in Switzerland. You want to see it?"

"Sure," she said, realizing as she said it that she was pretending not to have looked already. It didn't really matter, but it was too late to tell the truth now.

Marco held his cigarette between his lips and took the package, pulling it open at the end, just like Vidalia had earlier. He slid it out a little more roughly than she had, and they both looked down at it.

"I had an appointment to sell it last week before I left, but the guy doesn't appear. This is why I gave it to you to hold instead."

"It's nice," she said.

"Not too exciting," he said. "But people pay a lot for something like this." He folded the paper back up and put his arm around her.

"Did you have a good weekend?" he asked.

"Yeah," she said. "I went down south with Julien and Margie to Julien's parents' house."

He raised his eyebrows.

"I should be jealous?" he asked, smiling.

"No," she said, feeling like she was a little too eager to reassure him but going ahead anyway. "There were a bunch of us there. Nothing to be jealous about." She smiled and felt lame. He hadn't really been jealous, he was just teasing her, but all of a sudden she wanted him to be.

"So, where'd *you* go?" she asked.

"I was traveling, too," he said. "To Zurich. I sold something."

"That's great," she said.

There was a pause, and then they both spoke at the same time.

"Listen," she said.

"Vidalia," he said.

They both stopped, and laughed nervously.

"Go ahead," he said.

"I just . . . I got your message, and I wanted to tell you, before we make any plans, that I just don't want to steal from galleries like that anymore." She looked up but his face was unreadable. "I can't do it. I felt too bad about Ruby. I still feel bad."

She looked down at her hands, afraid to see his reaction.

"Well," he said softly. "Then I won't say what I was going to." He looked up at her with an accepting smile, like he *was* disappointed, but he wasn't going to push her.

"But . . ." she said, eager to feel close to him again. "I have another idea."

He looked at her, waiting.

And she told him.

THE NEXT DAY SHE was at the museum a little early. Jacques, the guard, was happy to see her, and he let her into the closet to get her easel and canvas.

"It's coming along, isn't it?" Jacques asked as he lifted the easel for her. "It will be just like the real one when you're done."

"It's starting to," Vidalia said. She wasn't as confident as Jacques was about her ultimate success, but she'd been painting for a week now, and at least her colors had stopped bleeding into each other.

As she and Jacques stood there looking at her painting, which he'd set down in front of the real one, Monsieur Benoît entered the museum from the front.

"*Bonjour, les enfants!*" he called. *Hello, children!*

Jacques and Vidalia turned to him, Jacques raising a hand in greeting.

"Ah, these Americans!" Monsieur Benoît cried to Jacques as he walked across the room. "They start early in the morning, don't they?"

"*Mais oui, mais oui,*" said Jacques sagely.

Monsieur Benoît planted himself in front of Vidalia's painting.

"And what do you think of her masterpiece?" he asked Jacques.

"I tell her every day that it's my favorite," said Jacques.

Vidalia held her wrist behind her back and chewed the inside of her cheek.

"Oh, she's still got quite a bit of work to do," said Monsieur Benoît. "Right, Vidalia?"

"Oui," mumbled Vidalia. *"Beaucoup."*

"You see?" said Monsieur Benoît to Jacques, his arms folded in front of him.

"Yes," said Jacques. "But she's going to surprise us, you'll see." And he winked at Vidalia as he turned to go back to the front of the museum.

Vidalia smiled at Jacques and then looked back at her painting. Monsieur Benoît was still standing in front of it with his arms crossed.

"I'm not saying you don't have potential," he said thoughtfully. "But it's raw, it's very raw." He turned to her. "Put it in the oven and cook it a little, that's my advice." He turned to go to the supply room and began taking out the other students' easels and setting them up in front of their portraits.

Put it in the oven and cook it, Vidalia thought. What kind of advice was that? She shook her head and sat down at her easel. A little while later, the other students began drifting in and going to their easels.

"Ah, voilà!" Monsieur Benoît cried. "Vidalia and I thought

it was some French holiday that we forgot! Here are my students, arriving only a little quarter of an hour late."

She turned to see Caroline walking in with another girl. Caroline winked at Vidalia, pointing to Monsieur Benoît's back. Vidalia understood that Caroline was saying that Monsieur Benoît was being nice to her for once. She rolled her eyes and gave an exaggerated shrug before turning back to her easel. Who knew what went on in *le Maître*'s head? One day he hated her, the next he didn't. Vidalia had given up trying to understand.

"Hand your papers in to me before you go," Madame Zafar said as the lights went back on.

Vidalia realized that she'd forgotten all about the assignment that was due today. She stood up and tried to slip out the door to the courtyard among the other students.

"Vidalia?"

She stopped on the threshold.

"Please wait, I'd like to talk to you for a moment."

Madame Zafar was still collecting homework from people. Vidalia leaned against the wall next to the door to wait. A minute later the room had emptied out, and Vidalia approached Madame Zafar, who stood straightening the papers on her table at the front of the room.

"I'm, uh, sorry about the paper," Vidalia said. She hadn't worked out an excuse. "I'm almost done but . . ."

"Yes, all right," Madame Zafar said sharply. "Give it to me by the end of the week, no later." She dropped the papers into a droopy cloth bag with a long, wide strap that she slung across her chest. "That's not what I want to talk to you about, though. Please, sit."

Madame Zafar sat in one of the chairs with its half-desk armrest and Vidalia sat, too.

"What is it?" she asked.

"You and Heather know one another from home," Madame Zafar said. It wasn't a question: it was a statement of fact. Vidalia exhaled, relieved that she wasn't in trouble.

"I wonder if you have spoken with her recently," Madame Zafar continued.

"Not really," said Vidalia, realizing she hadn't seen Heather today. When had they had that conversation in the courtyard? A week ago? "We're not that . . . Becky might have talked to her."

Madame Zafar pursed her lips and nodded, seeming to think about this.

"She's okay, isn't she?" asked Vidalia.

"Yes," said Madame Zafar, turning to her with brusque reassurance. "Nothing's happened. I just wonder, how is she doing here in Paris?"

"I don't really know." Vidalia thought of how sad Heather had been last week. "The last time I talked to her, she did say she wasn't having such a great time."

"Yes, well, I am a little worried about her," Madame Zafar said. "In confidence, I would like to ask you to try to see how she is, if she seems very unhappy or just a little sad. You don't have to tell me what she says to you, but I would feel better if someone who knows her a bit better than the others were keeping an eye on her."

"I guess," Vidalia said. "Like I said, we're not that close. Maybe if you ask Becky . . ."

"I would appreciate that," Madame Zafar said, ignoring Vidalia's suggestion as she stood and adjusted the strap of her bag across her chest. "Thank you."

"No problem," said Vidalia, standing and following Madame Zafar to the door.

"And, Vidalia," Madame Zafar said, turning.

"Yes?" Vidalia answered.

"Your paper."

"Right," said Vidalia hurriedly. "I'll get it to you."

Madame Zafar nodded and walked out into the courtyard.

Vidalia didn't get a chance to do Madame Zafar's detective work for the next few days. Either Heather was with big groups of people, or Vidalia was rushing to meet Marco. But on Thursday before art history, as she walked into the courtyard with a sandwich and her sketchbook under her arm, she saw Heather sitting at a table alone. Becky was at another table with Kenji. They'd been spending all their time together since they'd kissed and made up. Vidalia hesitated. At home, she never would have gone over to sit with Heather, but she'd promised Madame Zafar, and, in fact, she saw Madame Zafar glance over at her from where she stood talking to a student on the other side of the courtyard. So Vidalia swallowed her pride and walked over to Heather's table.

"Hey, can I sit here?" she asked.

Heather looked up from the sandwich she had open in front of her. She seemed to be scraping the mayo off her bread.

"Yeah," she said. "Go ahead." She went back to what she was doing with her sandwich as Vidalia sat and placed her sketchbook on the chair next to her. "I hate mayonnaise," Heather said. "It's so disgusting and they put it on everything here. I forgot to ask them to hold it today. Not that they understand me when I do ask." She shook her head, making her silver earrings swing on either side of her face. One of them caught in her hair. "My French still sucks. These classes haven't helped at all."

"Really?" Vidalia said mildly, opening the white paper bag to take out her tuna-and-egg sandwich.

"Yeah." Heather slapped the top of her baguette back onto her now mayonnaise-free sandwich. "You don't even have to take language class, right?" She glared up at Vidalia.

Vidalia shrugged, thinking that this project was doomed and wondering why she'd even bothered trying. After all, she knew what her relationship with Heather was like and Madame Zafar didn't.

"No, but my French has still gotten better, I think," Vidalia said.

"Yeah, but you've got the French boyfriend and everything. That probably helps."

Heather glanced quickly up at her in a way that Vidalia couldn't quite read. Was it possible that Heather was *jealous* of her? Even if things between them had changed a little since they'd gotten here, that seemed impossible. Heather was the queen of the school, the popular blonde. And, in Heather's own words, Vidalia was *just so weird*.

"I guess." Vidalia shrugged again. "So, how are you doing?" She figured she'd better get this over with so she could report back to Madame Zafar.

"All right."

Heather might be sullen, but she didn't seem surprised Vidalia was asking.

"'Cause I know you were kind of upset last week. . . ."

"Yeah, well, I'm fine," Heather said, a little defensively. "I was just homesick or whatever. I mean, I didn't really want to come here, and now it feels like it's going on forever and I'm just sick of it. I want to hang out on the beach at home with my friends, that's all. It's no biggie."

"Yeah, okay," said Vidalia. "If you ever . . . I mean, if things aren't going well, you can, you know, call me or whatever." She looked over at the other table of kids and kind of squinted as she spoke. She felt Madame Zafar watching her from the doorway. "Uh, I'll give you my number," she said, reaching into her bag for a pen. She tore out a sketchbook page, wrote her cell phone number on it, and pushed it across the table to Heather. She felt ridiculous. Heather had decided a long time ago that she didn't want to call her anymore. Heather picked up the piece of paper, though, suddenly seeming just as uncomfortable as Vidalia felt.

"Thanks," she said. "I mean, I'm okay. Don't worry about me or anything." She slid the paper with Vidalia's number on it into her notebook.

"No," said Vidalia, and tried to smile through her discomfort. "Just in case you're having trouble with your family, or if you . . ." She paused, uncomfortable again. "You know, want to get together or something."

Heather nodded and mumbled, "Thanks, cool," before picking up her bag. "I'll see you later."

"Yeah," said Vidalia. "See you."

Heather walked away, Ugg boots dragging a little on the ground, and Vidalia gritted her teeth. Heather must think she was desperate and still pining over their lost friendship.

Oh well, at least she'd done what Madame Zafar had asked. Heather wouldn't call her—she was pretty sure about that—but nobody could say she hadn't tried.

Marco was waiting for her when she came out of class.

"Hey," Vidalia said, watching Heather leave with a group of people. She was fine, Vidalia thought. Madame Zafar didn't know what she was talking about.

"Let's go," Marco said, standing. "We have things to do." He smiled mysteriously.

As they walked down the street toward Montparnasse, Marco said, "You had a very good idea, you know." He glanced at her and Vidalia felt warm all the way through, just like she had the night before when she'd watched the understanding slowly dawn on his face as she'd told him her plan. She'd impressed him.

"I think I get us into this party you told me about," he said as they pushed through a crowd coming out of a movie theater.

"You can?" asked Vidalia. "The Cartiers' party? The one tomorrow night?"

"Yes," he said. "I got an invitation."

"A real one? How?" Vidalia had thought they might be able to find some way in but this was much easier than she'd expected.

"It doesn't matter," he said. "I got it." They started down the steps into the Montparnasse Métro station.

She'd gotten used to his mysterious evasions. "So, you think we can really do it?"

"Yes." His eyes were full of that excitement that she loved.

"Where are we going?" Vidalia asked as they stepped through the turnstiles into the Métro station.

"To the Marais," he said. "To get you dressed for this party."

A little while later, Vidalia stepped out of a dressing room in a boutique hidden away on a narrow cobblestone street. Together, she and Marco had picked out three dresses for her to try on. This one—a shimmering purple sheath that came to just above her knees—was the third. Marco whistled between his teeth as she stepped in front of the oval-shaped mirror. When she looked, she saw why he'd reacted differently to this one than to the others. The simple cut made her look graceful instead of gawky, slender instead of skinny, and the color made her dark eyes shine with a deep purplish tint. The saleswoman zipped Vidalia up, then stood back and eyed her approvingly. Vidalia turned to Marco.

"It's nice," she said.

Marco and the saleswoman both laughed.

"You look very beautiful," Marco said, smiling at her. The woman said something quick to him in French that Vidalia didn't catch, and he nodded.

"What?" Vidalia asked, turning to look at herself again.

"She said it would be better with your hair up, so it's lighter around your face." He pulled back her thick hair. "You see your long neck this way," he said, running a finger over her collarbone. He kissed her ear before turning back to the woman.

"We'll take it," he said to her in French, and the woman nodded crisply and walked toward her desk at the front of the store.

"Um, Marco," Vidalia said, calling him back to the mirror where she stood.

"Yes?" He leaned close to her.

"I can't afford this," she said, holding up the price tag, which said 480 euros.

He smiled and kissed her quickly.

"Don't worry," he said. "I sold another painting today." He followed the saleswoman to the front of the store and took out his wallet.

Vidalia pulled the curtain in the dressing room closed and just stood there for a few seconds. She suddenly remembered her mother telling her never to accept expensive gifts from men. At the time she'd just laughed. What man was trying to buy *her* expensive gifts? She looked at herself in the small mirror. The dress really did look great. And, after all, this whole thing was her idea. She pulled off the dress and changed back into her black miniskirt and Nirvana T-shirt.

Out on the street, Marco leaned back and looked at her.

"Your hair," he said. "I think we cut it."

Vidalia stepped away from him, like he was going to go at it with scissors right there.

"Just a little," he said with a smile. "Come on."

She followed him down a narrow street to a door with a sign that said COIFFEUR outside. Three small women turned politely as Vidalia and Marco entered.

"Can I help you?" asked one of them in French.

Marco spoke to her, gesturing back at Vidalia. She felt a little silly, like she was being dragged from store to store by a parent. Not that she was complaining.

"Of course," said a small dark-haired woman, and she motioned for her to come back to one of the seats. Marco went to the front to wait for her. Vidalia tried to relax as the woman massaged orange-scented shampoo into her scalp.

"What you want to do?" the hairdresser asked once Vidalia was seated in front of a mirror, her damp hair combed straight around her face.

"Just make it a little shorter," Vidalia said. "Not too different."

The hairdresser looked at her in the mirror, turning her chin one way and then the other. Then she leaned to take a book from the next chair over and handed it to her.

"You can tell me what you like," she said.

Vidalia flipped through the book, which was full of photos cut from magazines and hairdressers' catalogues. There were women with short bangs, dramatic twists, long romantic tresses, severe spikes. Vidalia didn't see anything that looked remotely like hair she'd have. It was all so *hairstyley*. She'd had long witchy locks that she'd cut herself since middle school. But then she turned the page and saw a girl with a small, pointed face looking up at her. Her hair was really short, maybe an inch long or even less. She looked big-eyed and pixieish. The hairdresser leaned over her shoulder.

"*Oo-la-la*," she said. "That's a bit dramatic. But . . ." She leaned back and looked at her. "On you it would be nice." She lifted Vidalia's chin with one hand. "Yes. You have the face for a *gamine*."

"*Gamine?*" Vidalia asked.

"A girl with hair like a little boy."

Vidalia shut the book. She twisted to look for Marco at the front of the store but didn't see him. She met the woman's eyes in the mirror.

"Okay," she said. "I want the *gamine*."

The woman lifted her scissors. Vidalia squeezed her eyes shut and kept them closed the whole time.

After what felt like hours of snipping around her face and ears, feathery hair falling onto her cheeks and her neck, the woman stopped.

"*Voilà*," she said.

Vidalia opened her eyes.

She was a different person. She was long-necked, big-eyed like the girl in the picture, and her thick black hair was gone. She moved her head tentatively from one side to the other. It felt like it might float up off her shoulders.

Marco walked over.

"Wow," he said. "This is more than I thought."

"Do you like it?" she asked him. Marco took her chin in his hand and tilted her face up to him while the woman brushed off the back of her neck.

"It is perfect," he said, and Vidalia smiled. He was right.

It was only when she got home that night, going straight up to her room without seeing the Dubois, that she remembered she'd had plans with Julien that day. They'd talked—only somewhat awkwardly—on Monday and planned to meet at the bookstore and then have coffee together. It was going to be the first step in their new friendship, the one that followed her bumbling proclamation in the country that night. And she'd forgotten all about it when Marco had appeared in the courtyard after class. She took out her phone for the first time all afternoon. Yup, there was one *appel manqué*—missed call—from Julien. No message. Vidalia thought about calling him but then decided it could wait until tomorrow. She didn't know how to explain standing him up, and she was too tired to think of an excuse right now.

CHAPTER

⌐ **19** ⌐

THE NEXT MORNING, VIDALIA found a note from Madame Dubois in the kitchen, saying she and Clara would be in the country until Monday. That was okay with Vidalia—she didn't want to explain anything about her evening plans. She spent all day fielding startled responses to her haircut and trying not to think about the party that night. She was so dazed in Monsieur Benoît's class that he snapped at her like he hadn't done since the first day, and she hardly heard a word in art history in the afternoon.

After class, she saw Heather sitting in the courtyard with a group of girls who were all talking and laughing. But in the middle of them all, Heather looked still and distant. It made Vidalia think of a time when they were little, maybe six or seven years old, when Heather had been playing at her house. Heather had been there all afternoon, and they'd been outside until it started raining. When they came in, Heather had called her mother but there hadn't been any answer. Vidalia had barely noticed and had run upstairs to her room with Heather behind her. They'd set up her dollhouse and played with it, Vidalia leading the redecoration of several of the rooms before they actually put the dolls inside the house. Heather had played along, handing her things, doing what she asked, but Vidalia remembered feeling like Heather was somehow disappearing at the same time. It had made her play harder, get bossier, try to pull Heather into the game. But Heather had just gotten further and further away, stiller and stiller until Vidalia felt like she was alone. And then, out of nowhere, Heather had started crying. She didn't answer when Vidalia asked what was wrong, and by the time she'd brought her mother upstairs, Heather couldn't speak because she was choking on tears.

It had turned out that she was worried about her mother. Something about the rain and the unanswered phone had terrified her—Vidalia never completely understood why—and she'd been pretending everything was okay until she just couldn't anymore. Looking at her now, Vidalia wondered if that was what was going on, if some obscure fear or sadness was welling up underneath her smooth surface.

But what could she do? Vidalia had enough to think about with the party tonight.

A couple of hours later, after buying an array of makeup at a department store and spending even more time trying on clothes that she wasn't going to buy, Vidalia was walking home to the Dubois' when her phone rang. There was an unfamiliar number on the screen.

"Hello?" she said.

There was silence on her cell phone, then a sharp, choking breath.

"Hello?" she said again, and suddenly worried, she said, "Mom?"

"No," the voice on the phone said, and Vidalia realized with relief that of course it couldn't be her mother—the number had been from Paris. "It's Heather."

Vidalia paused, surprised. Heather's voice was cracked and small.

"Hi," Vidalia said. "Are you . . . ? What's up?" She had stopped walking and was standing on the sidewalk, listening to Heather's jagged breath.

"I was just wondering . . ." Heather's voice broke again, and she tried to laugh to get herself out of the sob. "If you could meet me," she said. "I mean, if you're free."

Vidalia paused again. So Heather was taking her up on her offer.

"Sure," she said. "You mean right now?"

"Well, if you can," said Heather. "If not, it's okay, though. I mean, I just thought . . ."

"No," said Vidalia, calculating that she had a few hours before meeting Marco. "It's fine. Where are you?"

"Not far from school." Vidalia thought Heather sounded relieved. "I'm at a café on Raspail just, like, a block up from Montparnasse."

"Okay," said Vidalia. "I'll come meet you. Raspail and what?"

And ten minutes later, Vidalia walked up to the café where her former friend sat at an outdoor table. Heather was dressed like she had been earlier that day, in boots and a purple baby-doll dress, but she was slumped down in her chair. Vidalia could see long before reaching the table that her eyes were red behind her sunglasses and her face was blotchy. Vidalia made her way over and sat carefully next to Heather, who looked up at her briefly and then back down.

"Thanks for coming," Heather said, and her voice broke with a sob. Vidalia had been so angry at Heather for so long, but that all disappeared when she saw her crying. She reached her hand over to Heather's arm. It shook under her palm.

"Hey," she said gently. "Hey, it's all right." She rubbed Heather's arm. Heather leaned forward, wrapping her arms around herself and shaking with sobs.

"What's wrong?" Vidalia asked, still not sure how much help Heather would really want from her. "What happened?"

"N-nothing," Heather choked. "That's what's weird."

While Heather tried to catch her breath, a waiter approached.

"What do you mean?" Vidalia asked after the waiter left to get her *citron pressé*.

Heather leaned back and wiped her eyes with her sleeve.

"I mean nothing's wrong," she said almost angrily. "Nothing happened. I don't know what my problem is." Vidalia looked at her and chewed the inside of her cheek, waiting a minute before saying anything else.

"Have you been crying for long?" she finally asked.

"Yeah, I've just been wandering around. I mean, I should probably go home—it's getting late—but I can't really get it together." Heather rubbed her nose with her sleeve. "I don't want to freak out my host family too bad." She looked up at Vidalia and gave a short laugh. The waiter came and put Vidalia's *citron pressé* on the table.

Heather sighed and then choked a little as she took a sip of water.

"I know you probably didn't really expect me to call when you gave me your number yesterday," she said when she'd put her glass down.

Heather squinted up the street like she was embarrassed.

"Not really," said Vidalia. "But it's cool that you did. I wasn't doing anything anyway."

Heather nodded and wiped her nose.

"But what's up?" asked Vidalia again. "I mean, you're just tired of being here, or is there something else?"

She took a sip of her *citron pressé*, a lemon drink that came unsweetened, and winced at how sour it was. She poured some sugar in.

"No, I'm . . ." Heather was crying again. "I'm just fucking miserable, I don't know. I really don't know why."

Vidalia nodded and stirred the sugar into her glass with a long spoon.

"I've been feeling pretty shitty the whole time we've been here, and it just got worse in the past week or so, like I don't want to get out of bed and I can't stand doing all these things that everyone says are so great about Paris, like the clubs and the museums and everything." She paused. "I guess you're into the art, though."

"Yeah," said Vidalia. "I've been pretty into that part of it."

That was more true than Heather could possibly know. "Is your host family worried about you?"

"I don't know," said Heather. "Probably. Mostly they just think I'm a total bitch, I guess." She laughed again.

They sat in silence for a few moments and then Heather asked, "How's your family?"

"They're fine," Vidalia said. "I mean, they don't seem to care at all whether I'm around or not. I don't really get why they bothered hosting me, but it's okay."

"Well, they get paid," said Heather. "Maybe that's why?"

"You think?" Vidalia hadn't thought of that. "They seem to have plenty of money, though. Anyway, I don't know, it's fine."

Heather looked a little calmer, so Vidalia thought she'd keep talking about normal stuff.

"How's your European history class going?" she asked.

"It's okay," Heather said. "I mean, I'm interested in that stuff, but I haven't been doing all that much of the work."

They talked about papers and classes for a while. Heather calmed down as Vidalia made conversation, complaining about schoolwork and asking Heather about her French class with Madame Geen. As the conversation slowed, Heather seemed to get depressed again.

"I should probably go," she said finally.

"Okay," Vidalia said. She was worried, though.

"Thanks for coming," Heather said again, looking down at her hands. "I was thinking someone might call the police or something if I just sat here crying by myself."

"No problem," said Vidalia.

"I'll be okay," Heather said, looking up the street with a lost expression.

"What about your parents?" asked Vidalia. "When are they coming?"

"At the end," said Heather. "In two weeks. Is your mom coming?"

"No," said Vidalia casually. "Marco and I might go to Italy after classes end, though."

"That sounds cool," said Heather.

"Maybe I'll give you a call this weekend," said Vidalia as they stood. "Are you doing anything?"

Heather shrugged. "Not really. Some stuff with the family, that's all."

"Okay, well, let's talk?" Vidalia asked.

"Yeah, that'd be cool," said Heather. "See you."

Vidalia raised a hand to wave back to her as she headed down the street toward home. She felt sort of churned up after seeing Heather so sad. Soon, though, she started thinking about the party that night, and she forgot about Heather's problems and their strange nonfriendship.

It was time to get ready. Vidalia slid on the purple dress, and stepped into her new heels. She put a pair of dangly silver earrings in her ears and clasped a necklace at the bare nape of her neck. Then she sat at her desk and spread out her new makeup. She approached this like an art project, starting with the background, spreading a thin layer of foundation over her face and neck with a foam cube. Then she did her lips, lining them so they were a little fuller than usual and carefully filling them in. When she got to her eyes, she stroked pale purple shadow over the lids and then used silvery white to reach out in a point to her eyebrows before brushing on some mascara. Vidalia leaned back and looked at herself. It was good—kind of shimmery and ethereal, which was what she'd been going for—but something was missing. She searched through her makeup bag and pulled out a bottle of liquid eyeliner. The small brush ran a line over the edge of one lid and out at the corner. Yes. She did the other eye and *voilà*—perfect, swooping sixties eyes. She ran her hand through her short hair, ruffling it up a little and turned her head from side to side. She was ready.

She looked at her cell phone. Eight o'clock. Her date with Marco wasn't until nine, and it wouldn't take even a half hour to get to the Pont des Arts. She sighed and sat down on her bed. It had been a couple of days since her last conversation with her mother. She picked up the phone.

"Hello?" Her mother sounded out of breath.

"Hi, Mom." Vidalia crossed her legs at the ankles and smoothed her dress over her thighs.

"Vidalia, I'm so glad it's you! I was just thinking about moving those rosebushes in the yard, and I was wishing I could ask your opinion."

Vidalia relaxed. Her mother sounded like she was in a genuinely good mood.

"Where to?" Vidalia asked.

"Over to the back," she said. "So that they're lining the edges of the property. I want to open up the center of the yard to make room for a bigger garden."

"So you'd put the bushes against the hedge? That sounds kind of weird."

"Well, not exactly against it, closer to the birdbath. I think it would make for a romantic little corner."

"What kind of garden are you putting in?"

"I'm picturing something big and colorful for next spring. I've been wanting to get some wildflowers in here. Everything just looks so tame in the back."

"Yeah," Vidalia said, looking up at the dimming sky through the window. "I like those gardens where it looks like they just throw seed everywhere and all different wildflowers come up. You should do the whole yard like that."

Her mother laughed her most genteel laugh.

"Lovely," she said. "I might just do that. And how about you, darling? I'm surprised to hear from you on a Friday night. Don't you have plans?"

"I do, actually," Vidalia said, and suddenly she knew that this was why she'd called. "I'm going to a party."

"Oh, whose?" her mother asked, echoing and amplifying the excitement Vidalia felt about the evening.

"It's this lady, Marie Cartier, who's holding it at her house. It's a huge mansion, a *hôtel particulier* on the Seine."

"Oh, darling, how exciting. What will you wear?" It had been a long time since she and her mother had shared this kind of girly excitement. They used to do it a lot when Vidalia was younger. Her mother had fully approved of her eccentric middle-school style choices. Vidalia described her dress and jewelry, and then she said, "Oh and I got my hair cut in a *gamine* style."

"Oh, just like Jean Seberg!" cried her mother. Vidalia should have known she'd know exactly what kind of haircut it was. "I'll bet you're ravishing." She sighed. "But who's going with you to this party?"

"I've been seeing this guy, Marco." Vidalia paused, trying to calculate how much to tell her. "You'd like him, Mom—he's really smart and he's an art dealer. He travels all over the place buying art from estates and then he sells it to collectors."

"An art dealer," her mother said slowly, sounding impressed and maybe a little worried. "Is he much older than you?"

"No—I mean, a little. He's nineteen. He decided to do this instead of going to college."

"Oh, well," Her mother said, the worry gone from her voice. "That can be the best decision for some people."

Vidalia paused and felt the easy connection with her mother that had been so absent since she'd gotten to Paris. This was probably a good time to ask about the hard stuff.

"Mom, are things okay with the bills and everything? I mean, are the lights still on?" She tried to say it lightly, like it was a joke.

But when her mother answered, her voice was constricted.

"Oh, I'm all right," she said. "There's nothing new. I am looking forward to your homecoming, though. It takes a lot to run a big house like this one!"

"I know," Vidalia said, biting her lip and feeling that familiar dread in her chest. She should tell her mother about the trip to Italy now. She'd be gone for two weeks longer than planned, and it would be better to give some warning. But she just didn't want to upset her mother. She couldn't handle it, not tonight. "I should go," she said. "I have to meet Marco soon."

"All right," said her mother. "Have a wonderful time. I'll put on a record and take a few turns around the dance floor for you."

"Okay, Mom." Vidalia felt a twinge of guilt as she pictured her mother dancing alone. "I'll tell you all about it."

Marco was already there when she got to their meeting place, a corner not far from the party. He was wearing a dark suit and leaning against a streetlamp.

"Tu es belle," he whispered to her as she came up and kissed him lightly on each cheek.

"You don't look half bad yourself," she said with a shy smile.

"Merci," he said with a nod, and he looked shy, too. He took her hand, and they walked onto the bridge that would lead them across the river to the Cartier party. Vidalia could already see the cars and the lights.

"I'll just smoke before we go," Marco said, stopping by the railing at the middle of the bridge. Vidalia gazed down at the churning green water as Marco lit a cigarette. When she looked up, he was watching her closely.

"You are sure?" he asked.

She was surprised that there could be any question now that they'd come so far.

"Yes," she said. And she felt so good in this moment, where

Marco was looking at her and she was looking back, this moment with the water rushing beneath them, with all of Paris whirling around them, this moment where their eyes were the only still points in the flying universe. "I'm sure."

Marco smiled.

"Then we go," he said, and dropped his cigarette into the river. He took her arm and, together, they walked across the bridge in the warm Paris night. Vidalia felt people turning to look at them as they walked, and she thought that to them she was a part of the beautiful, mysterious background of this city. She felt like she was moving through the pages of a glossy magazine, a blur to the people around them, perfect and unknowable.

They walked down the sidewalk to a tall building made of white stone. Big windows faced out onto the street from three floors, and a semicircular set of stairs led up to a grand front door that was sunken into the building. Holding Marco's hand, Vidalia climbed to the top of the stairs, feeling her earrings brush against her neck as she looked into the sea of people all waving and smiling back and forth at one another. Marco gave their invitation to the man at the door and Vidalia held her breath as he looked closely at it, breathing again only when he handed the small card back and nodded for them to go inside. They moved along with the people around them through an open foyer and into what looked like a ballroom. They paused to take glasses of white wine from a tray that a waiter held out to them and went to stand by a window at the back of the room, just outside of the crowd. Summer air came in through the window, carrying the smell of green things and flowers in the dark.

"It's a garden," she said, turning to Marco and nodding out the window.

"Good escape route," he said, smiling at her.

"Think I could climb out in these heels?" she said, glancing at him to make sure he was kidding.

He laughed.

"We won't need to do that," he said. "Here, take this."

Marco took something from a tray that a waiter was holding out to them and passed it to Vidalia, then took one himself.

"What is it?" she asked, looking at the little cracker coated in butter and a tiny pile of black bubbles.

"Caviar," said Marco, eating his and looking pleased.

Vidalia ate hers, too.

"Yum," she said, raising her eyebrows back at him with pleasure. "Delish."

Marco laughed and sipped his glass of wine.

"It's a nice party, no?" he asked her.

"Oh, I've seen better," said Vidalia, looking around disdainfully.

"Really?" Marco looked surprised.

"Just kidding," she said, smiling at him. "This is pretty great."

They stood for a while, watching more and more people come in, all of them in elegant suits and beautiful dresses. Vidalia was starstruck, seeing so many gorgeous people, so much luxury. After a while, Marco nudged her.

"We walk around?" he said.

"Sure. Do you see the Cartiers?"

He took her arm and slowly they made their way around the perimeter of the ballroom. Marco spoke casually as they walked. "No," he said. "It's surprising. I would think they would be greeting people. Oh, there is the monsieur." He nodded quickly at a gray-haired man by the door. Vidalia recognized him from the picture in *Paris Match*.

"It is crowded enough now," he said. "When we reach the door, go upstairs. The staircase is there to the left. You see the hall?"

She looked across the room to an open doorway with a velvet rope strung across it.

"Yes," she said.

"Through there," he said, looking around the dance floor as if he were thinking of nothing but who he might bump into here and what a lovely night it was. "And go to the back. There's a staircase there and you go upstairs. The bedroom with the picture is the third door down."

Vidalia nodded and, following his cues, smiled easily back at him.

"How do you know that?" she asked. She'd imagined herself poking around the rooms, opening doors, searching for the right one.

"Research," he said.

Vidalia nodded and knowing that Marco had planned this, she felt safe, like nothing could go wrong.

"You're okay?" he asked.

"I'm fine," she said. "I'm great."

"Good," he said. "So when we stop walking, I will get us more drinks and you act like you're going off to the toilets. Smile at me, you're having fun, okay? Then you go."

"Okay," she said. She could see it already, the two of them moving fluidly through the crowd of partygoers, everything smooth, everything exactly right, just like it always was with Marco. They had decided that she should be the one to go looking for the painting, because Marco said a young girl would arouse less suspicion, that if anyone found her upstairs, she could just pretend to be lost, looking for the bathroom or something, and people would believe her. Vidalia had been fine with that. This whole thing was her idea, after all. She figured she might as well be the one to do the dirty work.

"Allez," Marco said softly, and let go of her hand.

Vidalia turned to Marco and smiled sweetly, apologetically.

"I'll be right back," she said.

He gestured with his chin to the other side of the room.

"Another drink?" he asked, the perfect gentleman.

"Yes," she said.

"I meet you here," he said, and they drifted apart.

She turned to walk through the crowd, murmuring *pardon, pardon*, all the way to the doorway, where she didn't pause before lifting the velvet rope by its little hook and slipping into the hallway. She pictured herself as anyone else might see her, the shimmery violet of her dress disappearing into the darkness.

The party sounds faded as she walked quickly down the hall, her heels sinking into the soft carpet. There was a staircase at the end, just like Marco had said. She climbed the stairs and paused for a moment at the top. The party was almost inaudible here in the semidark of the hallway, and Vidalia had an incongruous feeling of being perfectly protected and safe. She was tucked away in a corner of the world where no one could find her. It was the same sensation she'd had on the balcony in Cannes.

The feeling stayed with her as she walked down the hallway, past the first door, but before she reached the second, she paused. She thought she heard something. Yes, it was a woman's voice rising and falling. Then, there was another female voice, murmuring in a soothing tone between breaks in the first. The voices weren't coming toward her or moving away. They were somewhere along this hallway, behind one of these doors. Vidalia followed the sound of the voices down the hall until she reached the door they were behind. It was slightly open.

"I know, I know," the first voice said and laughed unhappily. "My makeup." There were a few seconds of silence. "It's so stupid," the voice went on. "I keep thinking what a romantic he was. I get angry at him for that, for letting himself be so disappointed."

Vidalia listened hard to understand the French from behind the door. She was pleased to find that she was getting everything they were saying.

"Marie," said the other voice soothingly. "Your father would be happy to see what you've done here."

This must be Marie Cartier herself, Vidalia thought, leaning in closer to the door.

"Do you really think so?" Marie's voice was incredulous. "I don't know. It's all so stupidly symbolic, this house, this party, that article in *Match*. I'm not doing it for him anyway; it's for me and for Marius. My father didn't care about this kind of thing."

Vidalia thought of the photograph of the little girl and the windblown man on the water, and she felt a thrill of excitement. She was hearing the secrets that photograph held.

"No," said the other voice ruefully. "That's true."

There was a long pause and then Marie's voice, calmer now but incredibly sad.

"My father loved this view," she said. "He used to point to the tourist boats and tell me that Paris was romantic and beautiful, like a dream, even if it seemed just day-to-day sometimes. He always made me see the beautiful things. Whatever else he did, there was that."

The other voice murmured something. Marie laughed again.

"My God, I have to stop," she said. "We have to go back to the party. Marius will wonder where I am."

Vidalia stepped back from the door. There was silence. The two women evidently weren't jumping up to leave. She moved silently down the hall, and when she reached the door that Marco had told her to go through, she turned the knob, stepped inside, and shut it behind her.

The room was illuminated by the lights from the Seine, which poured in through the big window. There was the four-poster bed, the window seat where Marie Cartier had posed for the photograph in the magazine, and, next to it, the painting. Vidalia felt like she was dreaming as she walked across the room. The familiar figures danced through slivered half moons and colorful stars. She lifted the small frame from the wall. It was lighter than she'd expected. She sat down on the bed. The plan was that she would take the canvas out of the frame, roll it up, and put it in her purse. But instead of turning it over and prying it open, Vidalia looked out the window to see one of the big tourist boats floating by, the bright lights illuminating the banks of the river and the stone steps leading down to the water. And suddenly she felt something break inside her.

"Shit," she whispered, and looked down at the painting in her hand. There were hot tears behind her eyes.

My father loved this view.

Marie Cartier had sounded so sad when she'd said that.

He always made me see the beautiful things.

Vidalia felt something swell inside her chest. She was jealous of Marie Cartier, she realized, not for the same reasons as before, not because she was rich, but because of this father she'd had. What would it have been like to have a father who showed her all the things he loved? And what was it like to lose one? She looked at the painting in her hand and frowned. Had this belonged to Marie Cartier's father, too?

Suddenly, all the energy drained out of her, and she had the dull realization that she couldn't steal this painting after all. It didn't matter that the artist wasn't around. It didn't matter that it wasn't Ruby this time. Marie Cartier was a real person, too, and Vidalia didn't want to steal from her. Gently, she placed the small painting back on its hook and stepped away from the wall.

I have to get out of here, she thought.

She went to the door and walked carefully down the back hallway to the stairs, fighting the urge to run and choking back a frightened sob. When she got to the rope at the door that led back into the party, she stepped out into the room and moved away from it, afraid to look up and see who was watching her.

"Hey." Marco was next to her, his hand firm on her elbow.

"Hey," she said, still looking down.

"Come this way, we walk around again," he said in that same casual voice from before.

He thinks I did it, Vidalia thought. She didn't want to tell him that she'd failed to follow through on their plan. When Vidalia met his eyes, Marco smiled at her, a concerned expression on his face. She shook her head, trying to tell him that the painting wasn't rolled up inside her bag as they'd planned it would be.

"What happened?" he asked, smiling gently, casually.

"Uh . . . I didn't . . . Someone came in. I couldn't get . . ." She found herself lying to him without even planning to.

Vidalia turned to look around the room for Marie Cartier. What she saw made her gasp out loud and turn quickly back to Marco.

"Look behind me," said Vidalia, her eyes wide. "Is that Monsieur Dubois?"

She had seen the balding head, and then the sparkling, smiling eyes as he'd turned in her direction.

Marco looked behind her and then he turned away, too.

"Ah, oui," he said.

Vidalia felt like someone had punched her in the stomach.

"What is he doing here?" she asked in a shaky whisper. "He's supposed to be in the country."

"Don't look," Marco said in a forced casual voice. "I think he is with a girl."

"He's with a *girl?*" Vidalia was stunned by this whole turn of events.

Marco took her arm and led her in the opposite direction from Monsieur Dubois.

"Tout va bien," he said. *Everything's okay.*

"Let's get *out* of here," Vidalia said.

"Yes," Marco agreed. "We go."

As they walked, Vidalia saw Marie Cartier standing next to the older man from the cover of *Match*, her husband, Marius. They were both smiling and talking to the people around them. Vidalia looked quickly away. Margie had been right—nobody was as perfect and happy as they looked on the cover of a magazine. Why hadn't she believed it?

CHAPTER

20

VIDALIA STILL FELT SHAKEN on Monday morning, but when she sat down in front of her painting at the museum, she relaxed for the first time in days. She'd started to find her way into the picture recently. That straitjacket feeling had disappeared, and she was starting to feel like it was hers. Today she got so lost in her work that she forgot about Marie Cartier, Monsieur Dubois, and even Marco. She just painted.

That afternoon she took the train back to the institute and sat through Madame Zafar's class in a daze, hardly noticing the slides on the screen. Unlike at the museum, she couldn't stop thinking about Marco. After the party Friday night, he'd crept up her back stairs with her, and they'd both slept in her little bed. Saturday morning he'd had to go away again, though, and he wouldn't be back until late tonight. He hadn't called since he'd left her on Saturday, and Vidalia was afraid that she might be losing him.

After class, Madame Zafar came toward her across the courtyard.

"Vidalia," she said, "can I talk to you?"

"Sure," Vidalia said, startled.

"Please come up to my office for a moment," Madame Zafar

said. "I have to drop this off with Madame Geen, so I'll meet you up there."

"Okay, sure," said Vidalia.

Vidalia climbed the narrow stairs to the window at the top, and she stopped to look out at the courtyard. She could see people seated at the tables, laughing and talking. A group of girls came in through the glass doors. Vidalia looked around for Heather but didn't see her, and she realized that had to be what this was about. She heard Madame Zafar's quick footsteps on the creaking stairs behind her.

"Come inside," Madame Zafar said, pushing her office door open and stepping in. Vidalia followed her into the packed and tiny space. She saw the wide spines of art books stacked and tilted on shelves, a couple of small paintings hanging crookedly on the walls, postcards all around. It was the kind of place Vidalia felt most comfortable—in the middle of an interesting mess.

Madame Zafar gestured for her to sit in a big chair in the corner as she went to the opposite side of her desk. She moved some books from the chair to the floor and sat. Then she crossed her hands and looked at Vidalia.

"Is Heather okay?" Vidalia asked after several seconds of silence.

Madame Zafar looked at her for a moment longer.

"Not exactly," she said finally. "Did you speak with her last week?"

"I saw her Friday," Vidalia said. "What's going on?"

"She seems to be having some sort of a breakdown," said Madame Zafar.

"A *break*down?" Vidalia didn't know people had those anymore. Major depressions, manic episodes, psychotic breaks, okay, but a breakdown? It sounded so 1950s.

"Her host parents called me during the weekend, quite worried. She did not come in on Friday night."

"Friday?" Vidalia repeated. That was the night she'd seen her. Hadn't Heather been on her way home when they'd left the café?

"The Ostiers waited up for her and then called me very early Saturday morning. We were about to go to the police when she came back. And she has had a . . . difficult weekend since then. She would like to see you."

Vidalia was stunned. She should have called her. She'd completely spaced it in the aftermath of the party.

"Okay," said Vidalia quickly. "Okay, I'll go see her."

"She is in a medical clinic not far from here."

"Oh my God," Vidalia said. "Is she hurt?"

"Not badly. Her parents are on their way to pick her up."

"They're coming from East Hampton?" asked Vidalia.

"Yes," said Madame Zafar. "They should be here by tomorrow morning."

When Vidalia got to the clinic, a receptionist directed her to Heather's room. She took the elevator with two female doctors who spoke quickly to each other about charts and medications. When she got to the room, Vidalia found Heather curled up underneath a sheet in bed. Vidalia approached slowly, not sure if she was sleeping. But as she reached the edge of the bed, Heather turned to her. She looked pale and strange with no makeup on, her hair flat and dull.

"Hey," she said. "They told me you were coming."

Her voice was a little weak but not too unlike how she normally sounded.

"Hey," Vidalia said.

"Sorry to make you . . ." Heather pulled herself up onto her elbow, and Vidalia saw that she was wearing a white hospital gown. "They kept asking me who my . . ." She stopped again. "They really wanted to bring someone from school over to hang out with me. Since we talked the other day, I figured maybe you wouldn't mind." She looked down at the sheets and pulled them so they covered her upper body.

"I don't mind," Vidalia said quickly.

"Well, thanks," Heather said, leaning back again and letting one arm out from under the sheet in the process. "I didn't think Becky . . . It would've been weird."

Vidalia nodded. The inside of Heather's forearm was bandaged. Heather looked embarrassed again, and crossed her arms. Vidalia saw bandages on the other wrist, too.

"Did they tell you I tried to kill myself?" Heather asked, following Vidalia's gaze.

Vidalia shook her head. She felt hollow and shocked.

"Well, I didn't." Heather laughed bitterly. "My host parents just saw these scratches." She pulled one of the bandages aside and reached her arm out to Vidalia. There were uneven scratches lining the inside of her wrist up to her elbow. They were pink but they weren't deep.

"What are those from?" Vidalia asked, sitting down in the chair that was next to the bed.

"A safety pin." Heather sighed and closed her eyes, dropping her arm back to her side. "It's stupid. It wasn't a suicide attempt. The Ostiers just flipped out and called the school when they saw them."

Vidalia nodded. She was relieved that Heather hadn't really tried to kill herself, but she still felt like something strange and awful had happened, and that maybe she could have stopped it.

"Madame Zafar said your parents are coming," Vidalia said.

"Yeah, I guess. I bet they're freaking out. We haven't talked yet." She groaned.

"They must know you're okay," Vidalia said.

"Yeah, well, I'm sure my mom is having transatlantic hysterics as we speak," said Heather.

"Your parents are pretty cool," Vidalia said. "They'll probably handle it."

Vidalia had always loved the Warrens, who seemed just about as calm and stable as parents could get. In fact, one of the worst things about Heather ditching her had been not getting to see her parents anymore.

"That's what you think." Heather sighed.

They sat in silence for a minute, and then Vidalia spoke again.

"Madame Zafar said you didn't go home on Friday night . . . ?"

"Yeah," said Heather. "After I saw you, I just hung out at the park for a while, and then I was walking around. I ended up missing the last Métro—I can never remember if it's at twelve or one—and then, I don't know, I figured I'd just stay out. The city's really nice at night, really quiet. I didn't think anyone would notice. It's not like I always eat at home or anything." She smiled weakly and Vidalia saw that her eyes had filled with tears.

"Yeah," said Vidalia. "The city's nice at night." She thought of Heather sitting in the park while she was at the Cartiers' party, while she was out with Marco, while she and Marco were asleep in her bed.

"Anyway, obviously the Ostiers *did* notice," said Heather. "They were waiting for me when I got there in the morning. They were kind of upset."

"I assume that's an understatement?" said Vidalia, remembering how wry and funny Heather had always been. It didn't surprise her that she was making jokes now.

"Ya think?" asked Heather with a smile.

There was another pause.

"Is that when you cut yourself?" Vidalia asked.

"That was last night. It's not that big a deal, but my host mom saw, like, a drop of blood on my sheets and they made me show them my arms. Major drama." She sighed shakily and closed her eyes. "Pretty screwed up, I know," she said. "But I really wasn't trying to kill myself."

"Okay," said Vidalia. "I'm glad you're all right."

She sat there for a while, feeling shaky and protective of the frail figure in the bed, until she realized that Heather had fallen asleep.

⚜   ⚜   ⚜

When she left the clinic, Vidalia considered calling Julien. It had been over a week since she'd last seen him, and she never had called him after blowing him off that last Thursday when Marco took her shopping. She didn't have the energy to face all that, though. She walked slowly back to the Dubois', thinking about Heather and feeling surprised, still, that under that perfect exterior, she could be so unhappy. The memory of the thicket of uneven scratches on Heather's arm made Vidalia feel a little nauseated. She was wistful for their old friendship, when they'd played in the bushes out in back of her house, climbed trees, and built homes for elves and gnomes in the garden. The world had seemed so limitless then. Now everything had a horrible finality. Heather was cutting up her arms and getting sent home. Vidalia was doing things she'd never have expected, stealing things from people like Ruby. Where had all their happy childhood places gone?

The Dubois had returned from the country that day. When Vidalia walked in to the apartment, Clara looked dumbfounded, but Madame Dubois gave her new haircut an appraising gaze and said, "It looks quite good on you, actually."

Clara turned to her mother and then back to Vidalia and nodded. They approved. Marco hadn't called by the time they all sat down to eat. Vidalia was glad when Madame Dubois said that her husband wasn't getting back from his supposed trip until late that night. She was still terrified that he'd seen her at the party. Maybe he hadn't recognized her with her short hair, but would he remember when he saw her again?

Would he realize? How could she ever explain her presence there? And who had he been with? Vidalia couldn't meet Madame Dubois' eyes when she thought about it.

Clara, though, felt differently about her father's return.

"What time is Papa getting home?" she asked as they started to eat.

"Late," said her mother, "after you are asleep. You will see him in the morning."

"What time does his airplane get here?" asked Clara.

"At eleven o'clock if it's on time," said her mother.

"To Charles de Gaulle or to Orly?" asked Clara.

"Orly," said her mother.

"It takes thirty minutes to drive here from Orly," said Clara, her forehead wrinkling. Vidalia could practically see her counting in her head. "He will be back at eleven thirty."

"His plane could be late and he'll have to wait for luggage," said her mother. "So, midnight," Clara said. "I've stayed up to midnight before. Can't I wait for him?" Her voice stretched into a whine.

"*Non!*" said her mother. "It's too late."

Clara sullenly ate her soup. Vidalia figured Marco would be back around eleven or twelve, too, but no one was telling her she couldn't wait up for him.

When she called after dinner, Marco's voice on his outgoing message sent chills down her spine—What if it was over? What if that voice never spoke directly to her again?—and she knew she sounded nervous when she left her message. She hung up wishing she could go back to that night and just take the painting like she was supposed to. But she still knew that she couldn't have, no matter what. After hearing Marie Cartier talk, she wouldn't have been able to steal from her.

By midnight he still hadn't called. She dialed his number again.

"*Allo.*"

She didn't say anything for a second, she was so surprised to hear him answer.

"Vidalia?" he asked. Of course he knew it was her from the number.

"Hi," she said. "You're back."

She waited, wanting to hear how he'd sound.

"I just arrived," he said.

He didn't sound strange or distant, just like himself. Still, she was tentative.

"How was the weekend?" she asked.

"It was good," he said. "How are you?"

"I'm okay."

"I want to see you," he said. "Are you free tomorrow in the afternoon?"

"After class," she said, half-relieved, half wondering if he was making a date to break up with her.

"Okay," he said. "I'll meet you, we'll have dinner, a nice evening. To make up for Friday."

"I'm sorry," she said in a rush now that he'd mentioned it. "I didn't mean to . . ."

"Shhh," he said. "We talk tomorrow, okay? It wasn't your fault."

"Okay," she said, and now she did feel like he meant it, and something grew lighter inside her. "I'll see you tomorrow then."

"Yes." His voice was warm. "Tomorrow."

The next morning, Vidalia came down early before leaving for art class. Clara and her father were sitting at the dining-room table eating breakfast. Vidalia joined them and poured herself a cup of coffee, greeting Monsieur Dubois self-consciously.

"Good morning," he answered, giving her an especially twinkly smile.

"You have changed," he said cheerfully.

"I've . . . Oh, right, my hair," she said.

"I would not have recognized you if I didn't see you in my own home," he said.

Vidalia looked nervously at him, but his face revealed nothing as he poured more coffee.

"How was your trip?" she asked. *The one that started* after *Friday night,* she added in her head.

"Very nice, I got work done," he said. "That is what is important."

Vidalia took a sip of coffee and noticed Clara sulking at the other end of the table.

"Unfortunately, I have another trip right away, an unexpected one," he said. "Clara is upset with me." Vidalia saw his leather briefcase and a packed bag sitting by the doorway. He walked to the end of the table and leaned down to Clara.

"Give Papa a hug before he goes," he said to her. She sulked at him, her arms crossed over her chest. "There is nothing to do, my *chérie*," he said. "We will go to the country when I get back." He kissed her quickly and walked to the door. When he was gone, Clara looked up at Vidalia, her arms still crossed.

"Your father works a lot, huh?" Vidalia said, sipping her coffee.

"Yes," Clara said haughtily. "It is what all fathers do if they have a good job."

"Well, I don't have a father, so I wouldn't know," Vidalia said.

Clara looked sincerely shocked.

"Everyone has a father," she protested.

"Not me," Vidalia said. "At least, I never met him."

"That is very strange," said Clara, recovering from the news and shifting into her standard disapproval of all things Vidalia.

"I guess," Vidalia said, "it always seemed normal to me."

"You didn't miss him?"

"I didn't even know him." Vidalia shrugged. "How could I?"

Clara looked puzzled.

"But you miss your dad when he's away, I bet," Vidalia said, sensing a chink in Clara's arrogant armor.

"I do miss my father," said Clara, her voice shaking just a little. "But his work is very important."

Vidalia nodded, watching as Clara drank her hot chocolate and struggled to keep her cool.

"He's really proud of you," Vidalia said. "When you're not around he talks about how smart you are."

"Really?" Clara looked up, half-eager and half-suspicious. "What did he say exactly?"

"Well, one night when a guy named Marco was here, he

was talking about how well you do in school. He said you had the best grades in history."

"Yes, it's true," Clara said, puffing up a little. She paused before asking, "Marco was here?"

"Yeah," Vidalia said. "A couple of weeks ago. You know him?"

"Oh, yes," Clara said. "I have always known him, my whole life. He is very nice, don't you think?"

She looked up almost shyly at Vidalia. *"Et il est très, très beau aussi."* Clara blushed and covered her mouth as she started to giggle. Vidalia couldn't help laughing, too.

"You're right," she agreed. "He is very handsome."

Clara met Vidalia's eyes with a warm, conspiratorial look, and Vidalia smiled back at her. Maybe little Clara was human after all.

Madame Zafar called after breakfast to ask Vidalia to meet the Warrens at the clinic that afternoon. It seemed weird to her that they'd want her around, but Madame Zafar said that Heather had specifically asked if she could be there. She'd be excused from art history for the day.

That afternoon, as she walked to the clinic, her phone rang. It was her mother.

"Hello," Vidalia said. She still felt good from the last time they'd talked, when her mother had sounded so okay.

"Vidalia," she said, and Vidalia could hear that she was already crying.

"Mom, are you all right?"

Silence. Vidalia stopped and leaned her big folder filled with sketches against her leg.

"Mom?"

"I . . . I cut my hand," she said. "Yesterday, on a pane of glass."

"You did? How badly?"

"I thought it was all right. I put a Band-Aid on it, but then last night, I could feel that there was a piece of glass still in the cut and I thought, *It's going to get into my blood flow and go straight to my heart.* I couldn't sleep all night. A tiny sliver of glass will kill you if it gets to your heart!"

Her mother's voice was panicked, close to hysterical.

Vidalia forced herself to speak calmly. That was how it worked, after all—when her mother fell apart, she had to keep it together.

"But you're okay, right, Mom?" she said. "No glass got to your heart. You're fine."

"I don't know," she sobbed. "It could still be in there. The glass was very jagged. It was one of those old windows. It broke and I tried to pull it out of the frame, but it caught my palm right next to the thumb. It's a deep cut. I think I can see the muscle."

"You can see the muscle in your hand?" Vidalia asked, still speaking slowly even though her heart was racing. Was this glass-to-the-heart thing a real possibility or just one of her mother's paranoid fantasies? Vidalia didn't want to think about what would happen if something bad really happened to her mother while she was gone. "If that's true, then you need to go to the hospital, Mom. You need to go to the emergency room."

Her mother started crying harder.

"Can you do that, Mom? Can you drive yourself to South-ampton Hospital?"

It had been a while since anyone had used the car, but Mr. Nichols started it whenever he was over just to make sure it was running.

"No," her mother sobbed. "No, Vidalia, I can't."

Vidalia stood perfectly still in the middle of the sidewalk on Montparnasse, people rushing all around her.

"Mom," she said finally. "Mom, I'm calling Aunt Pat."

This was an emergency, and it was too much to ask Mr. Nichols to come over. Aunt Pat was the only possibility.

"Vidalia, no!" her mother sobbed. "You promised! You can't!"

Vidalia stood and listened to the ragged sobs. Her own breathing was shallow and her head felt light.

"I have to, Mom. I'm sorry."

She hung up the phone and searched her bag for her note-book. There was Aunt Pat's number, on one of the first pages. She got out her phone card and dialed.

"Oh, hey," Heather said, when Vidalia walked into her room just a little while later. "How's it going?"

"All right," said Vidalia, catching her breath. Aunt Pat was on the way to her mother right now. She'd promised to call Vi-dalia when she knew anything. Her voice had been tight and controlled on the phone. Vidalia couldn't tell if she was scared of what might have happened to her sister or just angry that she had to deal with her. She'd had to call, though; this was a real emergency. At least she thought it was. "You?"

"Good." And Heather looked better, actually, more like herself. It must be the prospect of going home. They were on such opposite ends of the spectrum here. The last thing Vidalia wanted was to go back to her mother and the mess that was waiting for her. And all Heather wanted was to get back to East Hampton, to her friends, to the beach, to her pretty pink bedroom.

"My parents should be here pretty soon," Heather said.

"Madame Zafar said around one, right?" Vidalia asked.

"Yeah," Heather said.

"You seem better," Vidalia said, and the nervousness was back. Somehow sad Heather had been easier to deal with. Now that she seemed okay, it was hard not to think about how they weren't friends anymore, and why.

"Yeah," Heather said again, and Vidalia wondered if she was thinking the same thing. She didn't seem to know where to look. Vidalia stood awkwardly halfway between the door and Heather's bed.

Just then, they heard the Warrens coming from down the hall and both turned to the doorway as they entered. They looked frantic and exhausted. Mrs. Warren, just as thin and fashionable as she'd always been, dropped her bag by the door, rushed across the room to the bed, and threw her arms around Heather.

"Honey," she said, holding her tight.

Mr. Warren patted Vidalia on the arm and then moved toward the bed. He reached out to stroke Heather's head as she and her mother hugged. Vidalia watched, wondering if she should leave. But after a while, Mrs. Warren looked up at her.

"Vidalia," she said, smiling and wiping her eyes. "Thank you for being here. And you look incredible. Your hair!"

"Thanks," said Vidalia, and turning to Heather, she added, "I didn't really do anything. I just came to visit."

"You did so," said Mrs. Warren, reaching her arm out to her. "It's important to have someone who really knows you nearby when something like this happens. I felt so much better when Françoise Zafar told me you were here."

Vidalia walked over and let Mrs. Warren hug her. It was a long, loving hug, and Vidalia gave in to it, resting her forehead against Mrs. Warren's shoulder. She was glad the Warrens were here to take care of Heather. She wished they could take care of her, too.

Heather was looking at Vidalia from her bed when Mrs. Warren finally let go.

"Yeah," Heather said. "Thanks."

Their eyes met and Vidalia saw that she meant it. She nodded quickly.

"No problem," she said.

"Well," Mrs. Warren said to Heather. "Let's get you up and out of here. We're going to get your things this afternoon and head straight home tomorrow morning. We've already canceled the rental down south."

"Really?" Heather looked relieved.

"Yes, really," said Mr. Warren. "First, we'll get some lunch and then head over to the Ostiers' to pick up your things, all right?"

Heather nodded and everybody started moving to get ready.

"Vidalia," said Mrs. Warren, "you'll come to lunch with us, won't you?"

"Oh, uh . . ." She glanced at Heather.

"You should come," Heather said.

"Okay, sure," Vidalia said, glad to have something to do so that she didn't have to think too much about her mother.

Mr. and Mrs. Warren talked to one of the doctors Vidalia had seen in the elevator the day before, a woman with a stethoscope around her neck, who assured them that, physically, Heather was fine.

"But," she told them in strongly accented English, "I think a psychiatrist is a good idea." She gave a warning shake of her head. "These things can become more serious if not treated."

The Warrens exchanged worried looks and thanked the doctor. When Heather came out of the bathroom, dressed and ready to go, they all gathered her things and left the clinic.

They ate lunch at a café not far from where Vidalia had met Heather last Friday, when she'd been crying. Mrs. Warren was concerned and kept asking Heather how she was, which, soon enough, had Heather annoyed.

"Mom, I'm fine," she snapped, when her mother leaned over to look at the bandages on her arms again. "I told you, it's nothing. They were just freaking out for no reason."

"Oh, I know," said Mrs. Warren with a forced cheerfulness that made Heather roll her eyes.

"Heather," said Mr. Warren in a warning tone. "Your mother's been very worried about you."

"It's okay, Bob," said Mrs. Warren.

Vidalia watched as the family quickly slipped back into the ways in which they'd always behaved together.

"So, Vidalia, why don't you tell us about your summer here," Mrs. Warren said, changing the subject. "How has the art class been?"

Vidalia entertained them all with stories about the ferocious Monsieur Benoît, and they responded with laughter and cries of, "How French!"

"Oh, you poor thing," said Mrs. Warren, shaking her head, when Vidalia had finished.

"It's been great, though," said Vidalia, surprised to realize how fully she'd come around to Monsieur Benoît. Caroline had been right that first day. "I mean, he's kind of harsh, but I've learned a lot from him."

Aunt Pat called as the Warrens were paying for lunch, and Vidalia stepped outside to talk to her. Her mother had needed a few stitches, but she was okay.

"At least her *hand* is fine," Aunt Pat said. "Vidalia, what's been going on? Your mother is worse than I've ever seen her."

The way Aunt Pat sounded—really scared and upset—made Vidalia feel a little sick. What did that mean, worse than she'd ever seen her?

"I don't know," she said. "She's been okay until now."

"Well, you should have called me before," Aunt Pat said, sounding close to tears. "Anyway, I've already made an appointment for a psychiatric evaluation. Don't worry about anything else. Just enjoy the rest of your trip, and we'll see you when you get home in a week and a half."

The evaluation sounded scary, and she didn't want to think about how mad her mother was going to be at her for setting all this in motion, but Vidalia was relieved that someone else was taking care of her mother for once.

"Thanks, Aunt Pat," Vidalia said. She hadn't changed her ticket yet, or mentioned to her mother that she planned to, but she could do that when this crisis was resolved.

Vidalia helped get the Warrens set up in the hotel on Montparnasse where they were staying that night, speaking French to the person at the desk and helping them carry their bags upstairs. She almost managed to forget about her mother and her hysteria that morning as she took part in the Warrens' affectionate busyness. She was sorry to say good-bye to them once it was all taken care of. She was even sorry to say good-bye to Heather.

CHAPTER
21

AFTER THE WARRENS WERE taken care of, Vidalia went to the institute to meet Marco. She hadn't had time to let him know she wouldn't be in class. She saw him at the table at the back of the courtyard when she walked through the door, but Madame Zafar intercepted her on her way over.

"Vidalia," she said. "How is Heather?"

"She's a lot better," Vidalia said. "I think she just wants to get home."

Madame Zafar shook her head.

"There is always one . . ." she said, apparently to herself. Then she met Vidalia's eyes again. "Thank you, Vidalia. You've been a great help with this."

Vidalia shrugged like she had when Mrs. Warren had said the same thing.

"It was fine," she said. "I didn't do that much."

Madame Zafar nodded sharply.

"We will talk more later," she said. "I want to hear about your experience with the Beaux-Arts as well. We need feedback on this program."

"Okay," Vidalia said as Madame Zafar headed back across the courtyard.

Vidalia turned to where Marco had been sitting, but he was already walking toward her.

"Hi," he said, kissing her on each cheek. "What's happening?" He looked after Madame Zafar.

"Oh," Vidalia said. "A friend of mine got sent home. . . ." But there was so much that she needed to figure out with Marco that she didn't want to get into Heather's whole story. They were going to have to talk about the party.

"How about a coffee?" he asked her.

"*Allez,*" she said, and he laughed.

What was it with him that she felt so uncertain when they were apart, and then, the second they were together, it all felt easy and okay again? He took the big portfolio she'd been carrying around all day and they walked to the Luxembourg Gardens. It was warm and breezy where they sat at one of the tables at the café in the garden. It was almost like the other night had never happened. But it had.

"I'm sorry about Friday," she said. "You know, I just couldn't . . ."

"No, no," he said, leaning across the table to her. "You did nothing to be sorry. It was bad luck that she came to the room. You did well. You got out, you didn't get caught."

"Yeah, but I also . . ."

Vidalia wanted to tell him the truth, that no one had walked into the room, that she had changed her mind. But Marco looked at her so warmly and her desire to go to Italy with him was so strong. She didn't want to tell him that she'd changed her mind about any of it, for fear that it would slip out of her grasp.

"I don't know." She shrugged as the waiter put her cup of espresso in front of her. "It's just too bad," she said. "I mean, we'd prepared so much and everything."

"We do it another time," he said, smiling at her. "And we succeed."

Vidalia swallowed hard but didn't say anything.

He nodded at her portfolio, which he'd set down against the table.

"What's inside?" he asked.

"Sketches," she said. "For the painting I'm working on. You want to see them?"

"Yes," he said.

Vidalia picked up the folder and opened it. Sliding over to sit closer to him, she pulled out the series of sketches and spread them on the table.

"See, this is the whole thing," she said, "and these are a bunch where I was trying to get the girl's face right. It's hard. It's like her face changes. It has all these different expressions in it."

Marco was looking at the faces.

"Different?" he asked.

"Yeah, it's like a real person's face, like it has the potential for all different kinds of thoughts or feelings."

"Here she looks sad," said Marco, pointing to one of the faces.

"I know," sighed Vidalia. "That's the problem. When I draw her she looks only one way."

She looked down at the sketches.

"I wish I knew how to make her face look really alive. There's just something I'm missing."

Marco pulled one of the more recent sketches from the pile and leaned back to look at it.

Vidalia chewed the inside of her cheek as he gazed at the sketch.

"What is the date of this painting?" Marco asked.

"It's Renaissance," said Vidalia. "Fifteen eighty, something like that."

"This one is really good," he said.

"You think?" She looked down at the sketch. It was one of the last ones she'd done and so it was one of the most complete. "I've been staring at them for so long I can't even tell anymore."

"No," he said. "This one is beautiful."

Vidalia felt flattered and she tried to see it through his eyes. But it was still so far from the original. Marco looked at her.

"Could I . . ." He looked into her eyes. "Could I have this one?"

"Oh," she said. "I mean, it's just a sketch. . . ."

"Not if you need it," he said. "But I would like it on my wall."

"Okay, sure." She was flattered. "If you really want it."

"I do," he said, smiling at her, taking the paper in his hands and looking at it. "I like it very much."

Vidalia leaned back and sipped her coffee. She could hardly remember what she'd been so worried about. The party was a distant memory. Everything was going to be all right.

❧   ❧   ❧

The rest of the week went by quickly. Every morning, Vidalia painted. Only a week and a half of classes remained, and there was still so much left to do. After class on Friday, she decided to go see Julien at the bookstore. It had been almost two weeks since they'd gotten back from their trip to his parents' house, and she hadn't seen or talked to him since. Julien would still be glad to see her, though. It was Julien, after all. He took things in stride.

But when she walked into the store, she saw Margie, not Julien, at the register.

"Hey, Vidalia," Margie said. "Haven't seen you around in a while."

"Hi, Margie, I know—I've been busy with school and everything." She shrugged to make it seem like not a big deal. "How's everything here?"

"Not bad," said Margie. "Though I'm a little bored right now." She stuck her tongue out of one side of her mouth and rolled her eyes back. "Been sitting here all day."

"Sucks," said Vidalia, realizing she must be working for Julien.

"You looking for Julien?" Margie asked.

"Yeah, I thought I'd come in and say hi," said Vidalia, making sure to sound casual.

"Well, he's not here," said Margie, looking bluntly at her, like she was watching for a reaction. Vidalia didn't give one.

"Oh, okay," she said, shrugging.

"He's with Katarina," said Margie, still looking at her.

Vidalia could tell Margie was wondering if this was going

to get a reaction, and she struggled not to show one.

"Okay, well can you tell him I stopped by?" said Vidalia.

"Sure I can," Margie said, and snapped her gum. "He and Katarina are a real item now."

"Really?"

"Yeah," said Margie slowly. "It's awful."

"How come?" asked Vidalia.

Margie sighed dramatically and leaned back in her seat.

"Such a princess, that girl," she said. "She's got him running around picking up her hankies." She shook her head ruefully before looking back up at Vidalia. "What ever happened with you two, anyway? I thought you were getting together for a while there."

Vidalia tried to look surprised. "We're just friends," she said.

"Right," said Margie, like she didn't believe her. "Well, don't forget to be nice to him." She was eyeing Vidalia in that intent way again. "Because you know Julien's always nice to everyone."

Vidalia looked away. She'd been avoiding Julien since their trip down south, and Margie seemed to know it. It was probably too late to take Margie's advice and be nice. She'd apparently already hurt Julien's feelings.

"Yeah," she said uncomfortably. "He's great."

A man with glasses approached Margie and handed her a book. Two more people came to wait behind him. Margie was busy all of a sudden. Vidalia stepped back.

"Well, bye," she said. "I'm gonna take off."

"Bye, Vidalia," said Margie. "Come by and see us some-time."

"I will," Vidalia said as she turned to the door.

Stepping back outside, her mood was heavier than it had been going in. Not that she wasn't happy for Julien, but she just felt a little lonely all of a sudden.

CHAPTER

❧ 22 ☙

ON MONDAY OF HER last week of the semester, Vidalia stayed after art class to talk to Monsieur Benoît about the colors she was using for the forest. He thought she should go darker, and he showed her how she could do it without making the whole midsection of the picture look muddy. *Le Maître* had started taking her seriously, Vidalia thought. Caroline had been right—he just started things out harshly. Thinking about this as she walked to the Métro station, she looked up and saw Marco.

"Marco?"

His eyes widened, then lit up as he saw her.

"Vidalia," he said, putting his arm out to her. "I was afraid to miss you!"

"What are you doing here?" she asked.

"I . . ." He paused and slowly smiled. "I came to see if you want to have lunch."

"That's a surprise," she said.

"Well, it's a beautiful day," he said, and he took her hand. "And you have two hours until your afternoon class, no?"

"Yeah," Vidalia said, pleased. "I have time."

"Besides, I want to see this painting you've been telling me about," Marco said.

"Really?" she said. She'd been wanting to show him, too, but so far hadn't asked him to make the trip to the museum. It was so nice that he'd done it on his own.

They walked up the street and went inside, Vidalia waving to the guard as they passed him. He nodded to her with a smile, and Marco followed her in. She led him through the gallery, past the portraits she'd considered on the first day, and to her painting.

"This is it," she said, glancing at him, nervous suddenly that he wouldn't like it. But he gazed up at it with an absorbed expression.

"See," she said, "the girl and the unicorn are so close, and the real world is far away from them. They're safe but they're also alone, like they're cut off from the rest of the world."

Marco nodded, gazing up at the painting.

"It feels really sad to me lately," Vidalia continued. "Like she's holding on to this animal and they love each other so much, but who knows how long they'll be together?"

"I didn't see that," said Marco.

"I didn't either until recently," said Vidalia. "I'm always seeing new things in it."

Vidalia turned and saw Jacques walking toward them. She smiled at him.

"Do you want your easel?" he asked from across the room. "To show your friend?" He gestured toward the locked door with the easels in it.

Vidalia looked at Marco. "Do you want to see my painting?" she asked.

"Yes," he said, looking back at the guard. "Of course, can I?"

"Sure," she said, trying to be nonchalant about it.

"*Merci, oui,*" she said to the guard.

The guard let them into the storage room. Vidalia switched on the light and led Marco to her easel, crowded in among the others. She saw him glance up at the small window that was propped open above them. A breeze blew in from outside.

"*Voilà,*" said Vidalia. "It's not quite done." She looked at him. He gazed at it and, after a few long moments, looked back at her.

"I already knew you are very good," he said. "But this is more than I expected."

"Really?" she asked, trying to be modest. "I mean, I haven't gotten the forest all the way in yet, and the city . . ."

"Yes, but you can see," he said, "it is very beautiful." He crouched in front of the easel so that he was looking right at the girl and the unicorn. "And I think you got her face." He smiled up at Vidalia.

"It's a little better, anyway," she said. Actually, she did think she'd gotten it.

"When does your class end?" he asked.

"Friday," she said. "So I still have a week to finish." She groaned. "I hope it's enough."

"Let's go for a walk," Marco said, taking her hand and smiling at her.

The guard locked the room behind them with his skeleton key, and she and Marco walked to the front of the museum, looking at the other paintings. She pointed out the portrait of the girl she'd almost picked.

"It's nice, but you are doing the best one," he said.

"I know."

After they left the museum, Vidalia let Marco convince her to have lunch with him instead of going to art history. They were just reviewing today, anyway, and when he smiled and said, *"S'il te plaît?"* she couldn't resist.

They bought sandwiches at a patisserie and went to the Parc Georges Brassens nearby to eat them. There were flower gardens in front of them, and kids were playing in a sandbox. The breeze was warm, and they leaned into each other on the grass.

"Vidalia," Marco said after they'd finished eating. "I also came because I want to talk to you."

"About what?" She was lying on her back now, with her head in his lap. Her eyes were closed.

"I have a plan," he said.

Vidalia's eyes snapped open, but she couldn't really see his face against the bright sunlight behind him. She squinted up at him and thought about their last plan, and how badly it had gone.

"This one is bigger than last time," said Marco. "But easy."

"What is it?" she asked, feeling that familiar quickening excitement in spite of all her fear and good intentions.

"I don't want to tell you," he said. "This time I plan it, I get the money, I take us to Italy. I take care of it. You don't have to do anything."

"Yeah?" said Vidalia. If she didn't have to steal anything, maybe it would be okay. The roll of bills Marco had given her that night on the bench was still in her backpack, untouched.

"Yes," he said. "Your classes end next week, so we have to plan this vacation if we're going to do it. I want to go to Italy, don't you?"

He drew his fingers over her forehead, and she closed her eyes again.

"Yeah," she said. "I really want to go, but . . ."

"I promise you, Vidalia," he said, "you don't have to do a thing."

Vidalia thought of walking along the streets of Rome with Marco. She thought of going home to her mother. Aunt Pat was there with her now. She could still go away with Marco, she told herself. She could.

"Okay," she said. "I don't have to do anything?"

"Just change your airplane ticket," he said, and she could hear the smile in his voice. She reached up and caught his hand in hers and smiled back at him, the sun warm on her face.

CHAPTER
23

ON FRIDAY, VIDALIA FINISHED her painting. Lovingly, she went over the girl's face and the unicorn's sad eyes. She made the forest behind them even darker and thicker than she'd had it, and then she moved to the cathedral on the hill behind them, the gleaming blue of it so far away that it was hard to tell if it was real or just something the girl had imagined.

At the end of class, when everyone was putting away their easels and cleaning their brushes in the back room, Vidalia looked up to see Monsieur Benoît walking over to her.

"Vidalia," he said, and she remembered how he'd refused to let her introduce herself on the first day. "You have done well, better than I expected."

"Thank you," she said. Was he warming her up for some final critique?

"Keep working," he said. "What you have done here is promising."

"Okay," Vidalia said, nodding, meeting his eye. "I will."

"You must not be distracted by—" he waved his hand dismissively—"other things." He looked at her for a second longer and nodded sharply before turning and walking away.

Vidalia, realizing that he'd just given her some kind of

serious French art blessing, tried to hide her smile. She'd done it. She'd proved herself to *le Maître*.

"We're all going out for lunch," said Caroline, walking up to her. "Will you come?"

"*Oui*," said Vidalia. She had time before her last art history class.

They walked to a pizza place near the Métro in a talking, laughing group. After ordering their pizzas at the counter, they pulled several tables together, taking over one corner of the place. There was feeling of excitement and release, now that class was over. Everyone talked about Monsieur Benoît and their paintings and the vacations they were all about to take with friends and family.

"*Et notre américaine*," said Bruno, once they were eating their pizzas. *Our American.* "Did you finally learn the European ways?"

"I think so," said Vidalia.

The others all laughed and smiled at Vidalia, everyone remembering that first introduction six weeks ago.

"We didn't think you'd come back after that first day," Jeanne said. The others nodded.

"Really?" said Vidalia. "You thought I'd let *le Maître* drive me away? That wouldn't have been very American of me."

The others laughed and Caroline said, "Ah, *le Maître*, he'd like it if he knew you were calling him that!"

She exchanged fond good-byes with all of them as they went their different ways after lunch.

"Good luck at the Beaux-Arts!" she said, waving to them.

"And don't forget your French style when you're back in

the U.S.," said Bruno. "I imagine they need some help back there!"

Vidalia laughed and went down the stairs to catch her train.

Taking the Métro back to the institute, she had a strange feeling of roiling excitement. It was Marco and his promise to her, Marco and his plans. She still hadn't changed her ticket. She'd do it first thing tomorrow morning, using the money from Ruby's painting to pay the change fee. Her time in Paris might be ending, but there was so much more in store for her before she had to go home.

After art history that afternoon, Madame Zafar called Vidalia up to her office to have their talk about the Beaux-Arts.

"And how about Laurent Benoît?" the teacher asked, after Vidalia had told her about her painting. "Was he very difficult?"

"Oh, well," Vidalia started. It hadn't occurred to her that Madame Zafar would question *le Maître*'s teaching methods. "He didn't seem exactly thrilled to have me in the class at first, but it got better. He told me that I'd made a lot of progress."

"Yes," said Madame Zafar. "He phoned me before class today. He was very impressed with you, Vidalia. You should be proud. He is not easily pleased."

Madame Zafar looked Vidalia in the eye as she spoke, and Vidalia felt even better about Monsieur Benoît's praise than she had this morning.

Back at the Dubois' apartment, she remembered that Madame Dubois and Clara had gone to the country for the day.

Madame Dubois had said several times that Vidalia should go with them at some point, but it had never happened. On her way up to her *chambre de bonne*, she passed the Dubois' bedroom. The shades were drawn and the light was dim, but she saw Monsieur Dubois' briefcase on the bed. It was the briefcase she'd seen so many times waiting for him by the door as he was on his way off on another business trip, the same one that had signaled to her that he was home from these trips when it appeared back in the hall. Clara's face always lit up when she saw it. It was the mystery of Monsieur Dubois, the mystery of what a father did when he left the house. It felt completely foreign and, as Vidalia looked at it, she suddenly really wanted to know what was inside.

She crossed the bedroom and ran her hand over the smooth brown leather. Her heart sped up, and she reassured herself that the house was empty. Anyway, she'd hear anyone come in downstairs long before they could get up here. This was what it would have been like to have a father, she thought. There would have been a briefcase filled with his work and his connection to the world outside the house. Sitting on the edge of the bed, she picked up the briefcase and laid it across her lap. It felt cool and heavy on her thighs. The light that came in the window was dim, but she could see clearly enough. The clasp opened with a luxurious click. Vidalia raised the lid and looked inside.

There were papers marked with numbers and handwritten notes, sheaves of paper clipped neatly together and labeled. One said "*Genève*," with a list of what looked like titles underneath, each with a price in euros next to it. Her heart still racing and listening for the door downstairs in case he should come in and find her here, Vidalia scanned the list.

"*Hayfields, Mother and Child, A Boat at Sea.*" Five hundred euros next to one, a thousand next to another. And after many of them was the word "Sold" and then, in parentheses, "Marco."

What did this have to do with Marco? And suddenly she remembered something: Marco saying to her, "Not so exciting, but people will pay a lot for this." He'd said it about the painting that she'd kept under her bed, the painting he'd bought at an estate sale in Geneva. Vidalia flipped quickly to the next page and the next. She saw more lists, more numbers, and, again and again, Marco's name next to them.

And then there was something else: a sketch, *her* sketch. At first, all that came to mind was that she'd done it several weeks ago, before she'd figured out the postures, before she'd understood what was passing between the girl and the unicorn.

The second thing she knew was that it was the one she'd given to Marco. She'd been so flattered that he wanted it in the Luxembourg café last week.

She lifted it up. Another piece of paper was clipped to it. She looked and saw that there was a date written, "*le 8 août,*" August eighth, which was, she realized, today.

Today was the day Marco was carrying out his final, secret plan, the one that would take them to Italy. Today, she suddenly knew, was the day that Marco was going to steal *La jeune fille à la licorne* from the Musée Apollinaire.

Vidalia thought of Marco glancing up at the open window

in the storage room at the museum; she thought of Monsieur Dubois meeting her eyes at the Cartiers' party; she thought of Marco walking down the stairs into the Dubois' living room that first night.

She flipped frantically through the rest of the papers in the briefcase, glancing over them, and there at the bottom she saw a name she recognized.

Ruby Priata, €2,000, was written neatly on one of the sheets of paper.

Slowly, Vidalia closed the briefcase. She didn't want to know. Whatever it was, she really didn't want to know.

She put the briefcase back on the floor next to the bed and let herself out of the Dubois' apartment. In her room, she called Marco.

He answered right away, sounding rushed.

"Vidalia," he said.

"Hi, Marco," she said.

"I don't have much time—you know I'm busy tonight." She could hear the excitement in his voice, and she remembered when she'd been a part of that excitement, in Cannes, at the Cartiers' party, earlier today.

"I just wanted to ask you something," she said, and she paused.

"What is it?" asked Marco.

"I finished my painting today," she said, feeling her way through the question. "And I was wondering what you did . . ." Her voice felt stiff. "If you still have the sketch I gave you, a couple of weeks ago, the one of the girl and the . . ."

"Yes," he said. "I have it at home, on my wall. Why, you want it back?"

"No," she said slowly. "No, I just wondered because I was working . . . and I thought I'd like to look at the earlier . . ." She trailed off. "Never mind."

"Okay, let me call you tonight, maybe at ten I will be done. This is really the big thing tonight, you know? I'll call to tell you how it goes."

"Yeah," she said. "Call me. Marco?"

"Yes?" he asked.

"What is it?" She was giving him one more chance. "What are you doing tonight?"

"Something from a rich family; they hardly know it's gone," he said. "Like the Cartiers, but this time nobody walks in."

"Okay," she said. "So, I'll talk to you soon."

She hung up her phone and sat perfectly still on her little bed. Marco was lying to her. He'd been lying to her all along. Marco and Monsieur Dubois had caught her in some kind of web where she was stealing or, now, leading them to things that they would steal. Marco had been using her, for what, money? Had anything he'd said to her been true?

Anger rose up in her chest. She thought of Jacques, the guard who loved that painting just like she did, and she thought of how untrue it was, all the things that Marco said about how stealing things didn't hurt anyone. It would hurt the guard, and it was hurting her now. She had to stop him, but what could she do?

Vidalia wished suddenly, painfully that Heather and her

parents were still in Paris, and as she thought of them, gathered together, smiling and concerned, she started to cry. Why did she have to be so alone? And why did Marco, who was supposed to be the one who cared, have to lie to her?

She let herself cry for a while, thinking despairingly of her mother, of Heather and her parents, of herself. Where would she go tonight? She couldn't stay here knowing that the Dubois had been using her this way. And she thought of Julien. Julien was the only one who had really been a friend to her here. Maybe he'd let her stay at his place. Maybe they could sit together on his roof and eat chocolate. She could tell him everything, and he'd say again that it was all going to be okay.

She dialed his number.

"Allo?"

"Julien, hi," she said, her tears starting up again when she heard his voice.

"Vidalia?"

"Yeah, it's me," she sniffed. "Julien . . ."

"Oh, it's nice to hear from you!"

Vidalia paused. She'd never heard Julien sound so hearty and insincere.

"How are you?" he asked in the same too-cheerful voice.

"Um," she said. "I'm not that great." Another pause. "How are you?"

"Good, good," he said. "I am with my girlfriend, Katarina. You met her, I think?"

"Oh, yeah, I did. At the bookstore," Vidalia said slowly,

realizing that maybe it was too late, that maybe Julien didn't want to help her—or even talk to her—now.

"So," he said. "Are you going home soon?"

"Yeah, my classes end this week," she said, feeling panic rise in her chest. This wasn't the conversation she wanted to have with him. "I'm leaving in a couple of days."

"Well, it's nice of you to say good-bye," said Julien. "Too bad I can't see you before that, but I think you must be busy."

Vidalia got it. She'd blown him off for too long. Funny how it hadn't even occurred to her that he might not be there when she needed him.

"Julien," she said quickly. "I know you're busy, but I just want to tell you that I'm going to the Musée Apollinaire, you know, where I've been painting with my class."

"Now?" asked Julien.

Vidalia didn't know why she was telling him this except that she wanted one person in the whole world to know where she was.

"Yes, tonight. I think something's going to happen. I don't know . . ."

"What's going on?" he asked slowly, and she felt like it was really him again, and that he was listening to her.

"It's too much to explain right now," she said. And it was true. How could she tell him everything that had led her to this moment? "I just wanted to say good-bye, I guess."

"Okay," said Julien. "Well, good-bye, and *bon voyage*."

"Bye, Julien."

And she was alone in her room again.

Her tears were gone. Nobody was going to save her—not Julien, not anybody. She realized it had been silly to think that he could. After all, she was the one who had stolen Ruby's painting, who had come up with the plan to steal from the Cartiers' party, who had shown Marco *La jeune fille à la licorne* at the Musée Apollinaire. She was the one who had to stop whatever was about to happen.

Vidalia shoved all of her belongings in her backpack, leaving the cell phone that Clara had given her on the bed. Then, without knowing what would happen when she got to the museum or where she'd sleep tonight, she left the Dubois'.

CHAPTER 24

THE MUSEUM LOOKED SILENT and still when Vidalia got there. Maybe, she thought, just maybe, she'd been wrong. Maybe Marco hadn't really planned to come here tonight. But walking up to the metal gate, and into the earthy, green-smelling garden, she heard a metal clang from behind the building. She walked across the grass and around to the back.

Marco was standing on a ladder, forcing the small window that led into the storage room, the one where she'd shown him her painting where they stored the easels. She saw him moving, catlike and strong, and she felt the same fascination as always, the same lurch of what she thought was love but that also sometimes felt like fear.

She stepped closer. He turned quickly to her, like he was going to jump or throw something. She recoiled. And then he saw that it was her.

"Vidalia." He looked shocked to see her. "How did you know I was here?"

She shook her head and stayed where she was, too confused to tell him anything, true or made up.

"Marco," she said, shaking her head. "This isn't a good idea. You're going to set off an alarm."

"There is no alarm in this old place," he whispered hurriedly. "Vidalia, I know you love this painting, but it will take us to Italy. We can have our two weeks together. And more than that, I will come to New York to see you; we will do so many things." He looked at her, and his eyes had that energy that she'd always loved so much. "And you've finished your painting, no?"

"Yeah, but . . ." So that was why he'd wanted to know what day she'd be done.

"Come," he said, and he took a step down the ladder and reached his arm out to her. "Come inside with me."

"No," she said.

He looked at her for a second, then lifted himself up and through the window. She heard him drop to the floor inside. She kept waiting for an alarm to go off, but nothing happened. She had to go in and stop him. Dropping her backpack on the ground, Vidalia climbed the ladder, pulled herself through the window, and jumped to the floor next to him. He was fiddling with the lock on the storage-room door. The students' paintings were gone—Monsieur Benoît had brought a truck to take them to the atelier—and the room was empty except for a stack of easels leaning against the wall. Marco snapped the lock and pushed the door open.

Inside, the gallery was dim, lit only by the moonlight that fell through the stained-glass windows and the green light cast by the SORTIE sign over the door.

"Marco." She tried to stop him, but her voice was too quiet and he was too caught up in his thoughts and his plan.

She followed him across the room, catching up to him so that they arrived in front of the painting at the same moment. Vidalia looked up at the girl and the unicorn and, tonight, in this light, it was like the girl was looking out at her, like she'd raised her eyes from the unicorn's gaze to meet Vidalia's.

Vidalia turned to Marco. His expression was gleeful and hungry. His eyes fixed on the painting, he raised his arms to it, putting his hands to each side of the frame. Vidalia watched his sure, quick movement and then she stopped him.

"Marco," she said, putting her hand on his arm to pull him back. He turned to her, his expression startled.

"What's wrong?" he asked.

"You can't take this one," she said.

"But Vidalia," he said, and his voice was persuasive, encouraging, like it had been at the Moroccan restaurant, and in Cannes, and every other time he'd led her past her own qualms. "It's the last time. We will go to Italy with this. You don't have to go home yet. This is what you want."

Vidalia felt like she'd abandoned him inside a game they used to play together.

"No," she said. "It's not what I want."

Marco dropped his hand to his side now and just looked at her.

"What do you mean?" he asked.

"You *lied* to me," she cried, and she felt her anger return. "I found my sketch today. In Monsieur Dubois' briefcase. What was it doing there? Why did he have Ruby's painting written down? Why was he at the Cartiers' party?"

Realization broke across his face, and he nodded.

"That is how you knew to come here," he said. He wandered across the room and dropped onto a wooden bench by the wall.

Vidalia stood where she was, watching him. She waited, hoping for some explanation that would make everything okay, and knowing there wasn't one.

"I showed Roger your sketch and he say he can sell this painting for a lot of money. He'll pay me more than he ever has before. We can go to Rome." He looked pleadingly at her. "I didn't want to lie, but it was better for you."

"What was better?" she asked angrily. "That you made lots of money off me? I saw how much Ruby's painting really sold for. It was a lot more than you told me."

"Yes, but it was not for me," he said. "I just bring these things to Roger. He sold them and he paid me. I . . ." He paused and Vidalia could see the rebellious, independent image of himself that he'd built for her crumbling. "I just sell to him." He shrugged. "I just do what he tell me."

"He's . . . he's an art thief?" Vidalia asked.

Marco just looked up at her.

"But what about his job? The one he travels for? Is that even real?"

"He has another job," said Marco, sounding tired. "He just do this a little on the side, to make extra. To pay for the nice apartment, all of Clara's things."

Vidalia thought of how harried Madame Dubois always looked. Did she know about this, too? Everybody had so many secrets.

"So, what?" she asked. "He told you to bring me to that gallery? He told you to get me to steal something?" She felt so stupid.

"No," he said. "I took you because I wanted to know you." He shook his head and put it in his hands. "I know you don't believe me now, but Roger, he told me your mother had a gallery, that he invited you to his home to try to make another little connection, maybe to sell work to her. You know, he is always looking for a contact somewhere. But he didn't know that I saw you after."

Vidalia drew in her breath. "That's why I'm staying with them?"

"I think first they do this for the money, too," said Marco, confirming what Heather had told her at the café that day. "But they maybe choose you instead of someone else for this reason."

Vidalia just stared at him, trying to take it all in.

"But that is not why I wanted to see you, Vidalia." His voice was insistent and he was looking up at her, trying to make her believe him. "Roger, he never suggested that you steal. You and me, we were having fun. I sold him Ruby's painting, but he never knew it was you."

"So, they don't know I'm even involved in this?"

"No," he said, looking down. "They know. It was because of this painting I asked you to hold for me. Catherine saw it under your bed."

Vidalia remembered the brown package and Madame Dubois' expression when she'd first gotten back from Julien's.

"They were angry at me at first, but then I told them your

idea about the Cartiers' party. I told them you could help me."

"So, they knew about that," she said slowly.

"Yes," said Marco, looking pleadingly at her. "I had to tell them so they wouldn't stop us. I wanted to keep doing this with you. I wanted to go away with you."

Vidalia nodded. Of course it had been fun to plan and to imagine and to create a new self with Marco. She touched her hand to her short hair. It had been wonderful, but it was over now.

"It doesn't work, though, and Roger was angry because he got us this invitation and you had been seen there. He was afraid that because someone walked in and almost saw you taking the painting, that we might all be caught."

"I didn't," she said. "I mean, they didn't catch me. I could have taken the painting. I didn't want to."

He looked puzzled. "Why?" he asked.

"I heard them, her—Marie Cartier—talking and I realized that even if all the stuff you said was true about rich people and us just taking a little of what's out there and them not deserving to have it all—even if all that was true—that Marie Cartier was a person, you know? With feelings and a complicated life and everything and . . . and I didn't want to steal from her."

She could see that he didn't understand.

"What about the other people who love this painting?" she asked, looking up at it. "What gives you the right to take it away from them?"

Marco just looked at her.

"It's not ours to take even if we want to go to Italy or what-ever. And I can't go to Italy anyway," she said miserably. "I have to go home. My mother's sick."

Marco looked up at her.

"There is no gallery," he said flatly.

Vidalia looked at him and shook her head slowly.

"Roger found it out a couple of weeks ago."

She nodded, warily, slowly. Marco stood and ran his hand through his hair a little manically then turned to face her again with a decisive motion.

"So, you lied to me, too," he said.

She nodded again. "Yeah," she said. "I lied."

"Okay." He turned to the painting and raised his arms. "Then I take this. It is too late not to." He raised his arms and put both hands on either side of the frame and lifted it from the wall in one jerking motion.

Vidalia reached for him and she must have said no, or said his name. She hardly knew, though, because Marco—thrill-ing, beautiful Marco—was pulling hard away from her and, just then, the sound of a screaming alarm filled the air. The painting had been alarmed even if the museum was not, she thought as she raised her hands to her ears. Marco had been wrong. His plans hadn't been foolproof after all. Their eyes met in surprise and then the painting flew from Marco's hands. She watched it crash to the ground. Marco ran toward the storage room and the window. Then uniformed men came in through the side doors and the front doors and there were lights everywhere. Vidalia felt hands on her arms and saw two men grab Marco by the waist as he tried to get back up to the window. They pulled him down and dragged him over to the side as other hands pulled her to the opposite side of the room. Vidalia called his name, and he looked up at her and said something. She shook her head. She hadn't heard.

"*Je suis désolé,*" he said again. *I'm sorry.*

CHAPTER
❧ 25 ☙

VIDALIA WAS SITTING IN front of a desk in a tiny office with Jacques across from her. She was crying, looking down at her lap, too ashamed to raise her head and meet his eyes. She didn't know where Marco was. The uniformed men had led her in. They'd shut the door behind them and now here she was, alone with Jacques.

"Vidalia," he said. She kept on crying, huge sobs shaking her. This had all turned out so horribly. All she'd wanted was . . . What? To be in love with Marco, to run away with him, to be happy and free for a little while. But nobody would understand that.

"*Vidalia, arrête de pleurer maintenant.*" *Stop crying,* he was telling her.

And she tried. She slowed her sobs and wiped her nose with the tissue Jacques handed her, then she raised her head. Jacques looked across the desk at her with a serious expression for a long moment.

"Where's Marco?" She knew it was the wrong question, but she couldn't help it.

"You won't see your friend again tonight," Jacques said

slowly, watching her carefully. "You need to tell me what happened here, so we can sort this out."

Vidalia nodded.

"But first," Jacques went on, "who can I call to pick you up?"

Vidalia was swept with panic, her mind blank for a long moment.

"Madame Zafar," she said finally. "Françoise Zafar from the American Institute."

The next morning, Vidalia woke up cramped on Madame Zafar's couch. She'd told her teacher everything the night before, from her lie about her mother's supposed art gallery back in East Hampton, to Ruby and her painting, to Cannes, and all the way up to that night.

Now Madame Zafar sat at a wooden table by a window, drinking coffee and reading the paper, her rectangular glasses low on her nose. When she'd arrived at the museum, she'd looked frantic and messy, but she was back to her usual composed self this morning.

"You will come to the institute with me today, Vidalia," the teacher said. "There is a towel in the bathroom if you would like to shower." And she turned back to her newspaper.

Meekly, Vidalia went into the bathroom to get ready for the day.

The institute was silent when they got there, with everyone off on their European vacations. When Madame Zafar led Vidalia into Madame Geen's office, the older woman looked up with a surprised expression that was quickly replaced by consternation.

"Vidalia?" Madame Geen asked. "What's happened?"

"We have a problem," said Madame Zafar, and they all sat down and Vidalia had the pleasure of telling her whole story again. When she was done, Madame Geen turned to Madame Zafar with wide eyes, and they looked at each other for a moment before Madame Zafar spoke.

"What we must think about is how we will respond to this very serious situation, Vidalia," she said, turning to her. "From what the guard told me last night, the director of the museum is very unlikely to get the police involved, at least as far as you are concerned."

"Oh, thank God," breathed Madame Geen.

"It seems," said Madame Zafar, "that it is not in the interest of the museum to publicize the poor quality of their security and the fact that two teenagers nearly made off with their most valuable painting. The boy has taken full responsibility. He says Vidalia didn't know what was happening, that she was tricked into this." Madame Zafar looked sharply at Vidalia. "He also says that he took another painting from a gallery, by an artist named Ruby Priata." Vidalia's eyes widened as she understood.

"But the police were there last night," she said. "They took Marco. . . ."

"No," said Madame Zafar. "That was a private security company that works with the museum. You are very lucky that it was not the police, Vidalia."

"Et nous aussi"—And so are we—said Madame Geen, looking in horror at Madame Zafar.

"Yes," agreed Madame Zafar. "The reputation of the American Institute, the functioning of our programs, the scholarship funding from which you yourself have benefited—you put all of this in danger, Vidalia. Do you realize that?"

Vidalia felt her face burning and her eyes tearing up again as she nodded.

"We will have to discuss what the appropriate response will be. I am fairly certain that the scholarship we awarded you will have to be rescinded."

Vidalia nodded. She'd have to pay the institute back then for this summer. How would she ever do it? It was eight thousand dollars or something. Her mother didn't have that, and of course, she didn't, either. She swallowed the sob that welled up in her throat.

"And these people? The Dubois?" asked Madame Geen. "How did they . . . ?"

Madame Zafar shook her head. "When I met with the woman, Catherine Dubois, in the spring when we were looking for host families, she asked for details about the students. She asked me about professions of the parents. I had just received Vidalia's information and I mentioned her mother's art gallery." She looked sternly at Vidalia, who cringed. "They've taken advantage of the program and of Vidalia in a scandalous way."

Vidalia looked down at her hands.

"Ah, oui!" agreed Madame Geen.

Vidalia thought of Clara smiling and saying that Marco was *très beau*. Poor, poor Clara. She'd have a lot more to deal with than missing her dad now.

"Your flight is on Monday, correct?" Madame Zafar asked.

"Yes," Vidalia said, glad that she'd never changed the ticket after all. Had she known, somehow, that the trip to Rome was never going to happen? That it really was too good to be true?

"You will stay at the institute today and tomorrow then," said Madame Zafar. "Madame Geen and I have quite a bit of work to do to close things up for the summer, and you will fly back with her group on Monday as planned."

"Now we have to call your mother, to tell her what's happened and what's to be done," said Madame Geen.

Reluctantly, Vidalia nodded. It had always been Vidalia's job to clean up her mother's messes. What would happen now that their roles were reversed?

"You can call and speak to her," said Madame Geen. "And then you'll put me on afterward." She moved the phone on her desk toward Vidalia. "Tell me when you're ready to put me on the line. I'll be just down the hall."

Madame Geen and Madame Zafar bustled out of the office, leaving Vidalia to pick up the phone and call home.

"Hello-oo!"

Her mother sounded unusually cheerful.

"Hi, Mom," Vidalia said glumly. "I have something to tell you."

Within a minute or two, her mother was in hysterics and the phone had been passed to Aunt Pat, who sounded stunned at first and then just angry.

"All right, Vidalia, let me talk to your teacher," Aunt Pat said in a grim voice.

Vidalia pictured her in their kitchen wearing her tennis outfit, her blonde hair pulled back in a ponytail, the way she usually was when she'd picked up Vidalia to bring her somewhere. Vidalia's mother liked to say in a contemptuous voice that Aunt Pat had "married money" and that it made her think she was better than everyone else. Vidalia knew Aunt Pat's husband was a lawyer and they did all right, but she always thought her mother was kind of exaggerating.

Once she'd given the phone to Madame Geen, Vidalia went down to the courtyard. She felt exhausted. It had been easy to get into all this with Marco, but it was proving a lot harder to get out.

CHAPTER

⌐ **26** ⌐

THE NEXT DAY, THE day before her flight, Vidalia spent the morning sketching alone in the courtyard, but at lunchtime, Madame Geen and Madame Zafar came to tell her that they would be going out to meet with some supporters of the institute.

"We will be back within two hours," Madame Zafar said. "You may go get yourself some lunch but, Vidalia, under no circumstances are you to contact this boy, Marco, and you must be here when we get back."

Vidalia agreed, and they left her in the courtyard. Even if she wanted to get in touch with Marco, she didn't have her phone with his number in it. She still felt that desperate desire to see him and to find out what had happened to him on Friday night, but there was something else that she really had to do. She had to say a proper good-bye to Julien.

When she got to the bookstore, it looked just like it had the first time she'd seen it, as if nothing had changed since. People stood reading and talking and laughing in the small courtyard in front. The glass storefront reflected the clouds overhead and Notre-Dame across the river, and then she saw herself reflected as she walked through the people toward the door. As she got closer, she saw Julien through the window. He was smiling, as usual, and talking with someone.

Vidalia slipped inside with some other people, and Julien didn't see her until she was right by the register. When he did look up, though, he smiled. Vidalia smiled back, relieved. He looked like he was glad to see her, in spite of everything.

He excused himself to the man he was talking to, and said to her, "I have a break soon, you want to get a sandwich?"

She nodded and turned to look at the books on the shelves while she waited.

Fifteen or twenty minutes later, they'd bought their sandwiches and were walking down the stone steps from the street to the Seine to sit by the water.

"So, I'm going to my parents' house this weekend," Julien said. "I know they'll ask about you. How should I tell them you're doing?"

He looked sideways at her as he asked. Vidalia met his eyes for a moment, and then squinted out at the glittering water of the Seine, holding back tears. She felt like she'd been crying for a week.

"I'm not so good," she said, and shook her head. "But you don't have to tell them that."

"How did things turn out at the museum last night?" he asked casually, and took a bite of his sandwich.

Vidalia crossed her arms over her knees and wondered if she should tell him the whole story and whether he even wanted to hear it.

She sighed. "Not great," she said.

Julien nodded, like that was the answer he expected. "You worried me," he said.

"Well, thanks," she said. "I was there. I was trying to stop something from happening. . . . It's a long story." She looked at Julien and shrugged. "It's been a crazy summer."

A tourist boat glided through the water past them, and they watched the people with their cameras and binoculars looking out at Notre-Dame.

"I saw you with this guy once," Julien said. "What was his name?"

Vidalia looked at him, surprised. "Marco," she said.

"It was before we went to my parents. You were walking in the Jardin du Luxembourg together." He shook his head. "It was obvious what was happening."

She just looked at him.

"Was it because of him you were at the museum?" he asked.

"Yeah," said Vidalia. "He . . . he wanted to steal something. I was trying to stop him. I guess it worked out." She shrugged again.

"You were in love with him?" Julien asked.

She turned to see him looking at her with his warm brown eyes, so different from Marco's pale blue ones. She nodded, and there was a pause.

"I didn't mean to hurt your feelings," she said hesitantly.

"Well, you don't decide who you fall in love with," Julien said with a shrug. "But it wasn't very nice to disappear like this." He turned to look right at her.

She squirmed, but she met his gaze. "You're right," she said. "It wasn't nice. I'm sorry."

"But what do you Americans say? Shit happens!" Julien laughed and Vidalia couldn't help laughing, too.

"Yeah, I guess we say that," she said.

They sat there in companionable silence for a while.

"I have to go back to work," Julien said finally. "When are you leaving?"

"Tomorrow," she said, standing with him.

She thought he'd ask again what had happened at the museum, but he just looked at her for a long moment.

"So, good-bye," he said. He opened his arms. "It was nice to know you, Vidalia Sloane."

She hugged him, and he wrapped his arms around her. They stood there briefly, and Vidalia closed her eyes and felt Julien's warmth all around her.

"Say good-bye to Margie for me," she said as they stepped apart. "And your parents." He nodded. "And Katarina," she added with a smile.

"Okay," he laughed. "Good-bye is maybe the one thing she'd be glad to hear from you."

Vidalia smiled. She'd been right then. Katarina was jealous. It gave her a tiny bit of satisfaction to hear it. Julien raised his hand one last time to her, and then he jogged off toward the stone stairs leading up to the street, leaving her by the green water of the Seine. She watched him climb the steps to disappear into his bookstore, into his life, into his Paris, which she'd so briefly been a part of.

Vidalia turned to walk back to the institute, feeling heavy and sad, sorry to have said good-bye to Julien and sorry that she hadn't been a better friend.

Before going back to the institute, Vidalia did something she'd been meaning to do. She got on the Métro and went to the gallery near the Luxembourg Gardens, where she and Marco had gone to Ruby's show. When she got there, she approached the doorway quickly and droppped an envelope in the mail slot. Inside of it was five hundred euros, and on the outside was written RUBY PRIATA.

She was back in the courtyard when her teachers returned from their lunch. They checked in on her briefly and then went upstairs again to their offices. Vidalia was sketching and wondering over and over what had happened to Marco the night before and where he was now, when she looked up to see the front door that separated the courtyard from the street swing open.

It was Marco. Her eyes widened and she glanced quickly up at the windows of the offices above, praying that neither of her teachers was looking down. Marco saw her and his eyes lit up. He started to walk into the courtyard toward her. Quickly, Vidalia raised her hand to stop him and gave him a warning look.

"Stay there," she whispered, and he stepped back into the entryway, where he couldn't be seen from above. Vidalia stood, as casually as she was able, set down her sketchbook on the table, and walked toward Marco.

"What are you doing here?" she asked him as she stepped into the darkened entryway. Since no one was really around, the lights hadn't been turned on.

"I called your phone," he said, rushed. "And Catherine answer. She said you are leaving and aren't there anymore and maybe you are with the institute. I came to see if I can find you. Vidalia, I am so sorry."

Marco looked like he was about to start crying.

"I don't mean for it to happen like this, you know?" he looked pleadingly at her.

"Shhh," Vidalia said. His voice had risen, and she was afraid he could be heard from the upstairs offices where Madames Zafar and Geen were still working. "Come here." After leading him by the hand down the hall and into a classroom, she shut the door behind them. It was so good to see him. She looked at his face, miserable with guilt and regret. All of Marco's bravado, all his cool, all his arrogance were gone. He looked desperate.

"I know you say I lied to you when we were at the museum the other night, but I just want to say to you that I didn't mean to hurt you or to get you in trouble. Really, Vidalia, all I wanted was to have this time with you. And I told them, you know, that it was all me, that you have done nothing."

"I know," Vidalia said. "But what happened to you? Where did they take you the other night? Are you okay?"

"I am okay," Marco said. "They take me to the police and ask me about the Dubois. I have a date for court in a few weeks." He teared up again. "I don't know what will happen now."

Vidalia just shook her head.

"But how are you?" Marco asked. "Are you in very much trouble?"

"Well, not as bad as you, but yeah," said Vidalia. "I've been here all weekend and I'm going home tomorrow, but I think they're going to make me pay them back for the program or something. I have no idea how I'm going to do that." She shook her head. "They're pretty mad at me here, obviously."

Marco nodded and he was still looking at her, his blue eyes pleading.

"Vidalia, I am sorry," he said. "I didn't want to get you in this." He shook his head and put his hand to his forehead. "This isn't what I planned."

All this time she'd been looking to him to tell her what was possible, to make the plans that she would help to carry out. But now Marco looked so vulnerable and sad. Vidalia put her arms around him.

"And the Dubois, of course, they are done now," Marco said, looking alarmed. "This was pretty big, Vidalia, pretty serious."

"It was both of them?" Vidalia asked. "Madame Dubois, too?"

"Yes," said Marco. "It is Roger who runs things, but Catherine, she helps."

He relaxed against Vidalia and put his arms around her, too.

"You'll be okay, Marco," she said in his ear. "I know you will."

He put his hands on the back of her head and she remembered the first time he kissed her, on the bridge over the canal. He'd held her head this way then, too. He pulled away from her, and their eyes locked as they had so many times. Vidalia leaned in and so did Marco, and they kissed. She felt all of the excitement and all of the love of the past six weeks in that kiss, and alongside it, the sadness of knowing they were about to be apart.

"I don't want you to go," Marco said, kissing her again.

"I know," she said, savoring the feeling of his warm lips, his tongue on her neck, her ear.

Just then Vidalia heard footsteps in the hall. She pulled back sharply. They couldn't be caught here, not now. The footsteps drew away, though, and she heard a door shut somewhere in the building. But that meant that whoever it was had walked past the courtyard and seen that she wasn't outside.

"I have to get back," she whispered. "Marco, you have to go."

He looked at her again with those sorrowful eyes. She kissed him one more time.

"Vidalia," he whispered, holding her face in his hands. *"Je t'aime."*

Why did it have to happen this way? Why did they have to be separated now?

"I love you, too," she whispered, and Marco kissed her again, a long, deep kiss, before looking into her eyes and saying, *"Au revoir."*

CHAPTER

27

AUNT PAT WAS AT the airport to meet her in New York. Vidalia could see her worried expression from across the lobby.

"Hi, Aunt Pat," she said, tentatively touching her arm.

"Oh, God, Vidalia. Are you all right?" Aunt Pat hugged her tightly then stood back and looked at her. Tears came into her eyes as she said, "I can't believe how long it's been since I've seen you."

Vidalia smiled weakly.

"Come on," said Aunt Pat. "The traffic's going to be awful going back out, and I just have to get a game of tennis in before picking the kids up from drama camp or I swear I'll explode."

In the car, Vidalia explained again what had happened and saw her aunt's knuckles growing white around the steering wheel as she did.

"It'll be okay," Vidalia said, trying to calm her down. "I mean, everyone's upset, but I really do understand that it was all wrong and I definitely won't do anything like that again."

Far from reassuring her aunt, these words seemed to make her even more upset.

"I guess I was just hoping I could live my life and that things would be all right, but that's never been the case with our family," Aunt Pat said as she stared at the road ahead. "I just should have been there a whole lot more."

Vidalia wasn't sure how to respond to that. Eventually, she turned to look out the window at Long Island rolling by.

"Baby!"

To Vidalia's amazement, her mother had swung the front door wide open and stepped outside, her arms spread as she watched her daughter walk up the path through the overgrown grass. It had been ages since Vidalia had seen her mother go through the front door. Something had changed.

The next couple of days involved the long series of explanations that Vidalia had expected. Aunt Pat was stopping by, making lists and phone calls and generally keeping both Vidalia and her mother a lot more on their toes than they usually were. At least she was on top of things, though. Vidalia had been home for only two days, but her aunt had already driven her mother to two doctor's appointments. It also turned out, weirdly, that even though her mother hadn't wanted Aunt Pat around all these years, she was willing to leave the house with her. She seemed to feel safe when her little sister was in charge.

Characteristically, Vidalia's mother had decided not to see Vidalia's misadventure as a bad thing.

"Childish foibles," she said airily when Aunt Pat tried to sit her down to talk to Vidalia about it. "She'll outgrow it." And she breezed out of the room, the four or five yellow scarves she'd wrapped around her neck and waist blowing out behind her.

"They've decided that you'll have to reimburse half of the scholarship you received, Vidalia," Aunt Pat told her after one of her long phone calls with Madame Geen. "Can you imagine a bigger waste? And how do you think you're going to do it? It comes out to thirty-five hundred dollars."

"I guess I'll work at the ice-cream store again," Vidalia said.

"Well, you'd better get started soon," said Aunt Pat. "Because it's going to take some time to earn that much scooping ice cream."

The painting arrived on Wednesday. Madame Zafar had sent it, along with a note, telling Vidalia that in spite of what had happened, she had done well at the institute that summer and she hoped she would do well in the future, too. Vidalia brought the package into the living room and opened it. There was the girl and the unicorn and the icy cathedral.

"Oh, Vidalia," her mother said. "It's beautiful."

They both gazed at it for a few minutes, and then her mother lifted it to a place on the wall, high up, overlooking the room. Vidalia sat on the couch watching her hang the painting, and thinking about the original, hanging where it belonged in the Musée Apollinaire.

Later that afternoon, she heard the phone ring from upstairs.

"Vidalia!" called Aunt Pat. "It's for you!"

Vidalia grabbed the extension in the hallway outside her room.

"Hello?"

"Hey, Vidalia," she heard. "It's Heather."

"Oh, hey," she said. "How are you doing?"

"I'm pretty good," Heather said, and sighed. "Spending a little too much time with the shrink, but what can you do?"

"I hear you."

"So what happened?" Heather asked. "Becky said you didn't go away with Marco, and you were staying with Madame Zafar at the end?"

"Oh, I got into a little bit of . . . trouble, I guess you could say."

Heather laughed.

"I guess we really represented for East Hampton over there."

"I guess so," Vidalia said.

Heather laughed. "So, I was wondering if you'd want to maybe hang out?"

"Yeah," Vidalia said. She remembered how angry she'd been at Heather for so long. It was weird—it felt like that had been a million years ago and at the same time it felt like no time at all had passed since she and Heather had been best friends playing in the bushes out back. "Sure, why not?"

They made a plan to meet at the beach the next day. After hanging up, Vidalia got her sketchbook and her pencils.

"I'm going out," she said to her mother and Aunt Pat, and without worrying about what her mother would do without her, she climbed on her bike and rode all the way down Swamp Road to a spot on the bay where she and her mother used to swim. Vidalia dropped her bike in the sand, climbed into a sheltered place in one of the dunes, and took out her sketchbook. She looked out at the blue water and started to draw.

ACKNOWLEDGMENTS

FIRST THANKS GO TO those who read and helped to guide Vidalia's story in the very beginning, especially Kristen Kemp and Jean-Christophe Castelli. The middle part of the process was the longest, and Kate Morgenroth and the Yayaya's—Olugbemi-sola Amusashonubi-Perkovich, Bridget Casey, Edith Cohn, Kristi Olson, and Hannah Trierweiler—kept me going with their close readings, thoughtful comments, and unwavering encouragement. Several people stepped in to offer invaluable precisions and corrections when the end was finally in sight—my friend and French consultant Isabelle Mullet, East Hampton expert Carissa Katz, and painter Brandon Soloff. Thanks also to Sara Press, photographer of my life and jacket photo, and to Jason Engdahl for doctoring said photo.

This story is illuminated by a number of artists' work. For ideas and inspiration, thanks to Little Edie Bouvier Beale, Candace Breitz, Jean-Luc Godard, Leonardo da Vinci, Pablo Picasso, Joan Miró, Sloane Tanen, Rogier van der Weyden, the medieval weavers of the *Dame à la licorne* tapestries, and Rita Ackermann, whom I especially thank for having a painting stolen in Paris, and for telling me about it. I also thank the institutions that, knowingly or not, supported the writing of this book: Mediabistro, NYU, Reid Hall, and Shakespeare & Company. (And my apologies to the poets; I was only kidding.)

A massive and multicolored bouquet of thanks goes to Joy Peskin, who was first a great reader and teacher and then the best editor I could have asked for—my appreciation knows no bounds. Thank you to everyone else at Penguin who helped this book come together, including—but, I'm sure, not limited to—Tim Ashton, Nancy Brennan, Theresa M. Evangelista, Kendra Levin, Nico Medina, and Janet Pascal. And a great big thank-you to my agent, Rosemary Stimola, for jumping in and working it all out.

I will be forever grateful to the Parisian friends who have taken me into their lives and homes over the years and who provided many of the details of Parisian life as described in this book—especially Emmanuel, Francis, Cécile, Bernard, and Hubert—as I will be to Alla Katsnelson, Bernadette McManus, Lucas K. Peterson, Anne Swan, Rory Watson, and Richard Watson, who were all there with me as I struggled to get this done. The very biggest thank-yous go to my sister, Siobhan Watson, for reading and loving this story from the first word to the last, and to Adam Mortimer, for being there throughout.